Best wishes
from the author
Dean Hughes

Ruth Trewartha
Markham
Ont

Briarwood Farm
October 1973

ALONG THE SIDEROAD

DEAN HUGHES

TORONTO
NELSON, FOSTER & SCOTT LTD.

© Dean Hughes 1973

ISBN 0-919324-14-2

Printed in Canada by
The Bryant Press Limited

Contents

1

The Ice Goes Out—
and a New Idea Comes In

Mr. Charles Brewster lay slouched on a bale of straw along the south side of the big main barn, with his head leaning back rather uncomfortably against the stonework of the foundation. But to off-set his stone pillow he had the paradisical solace of the warm mid-March sun. The barnyard was protected from the weather on three sides; the sheep-barn at the west, the horse-barn at the east and the main barn behind him along the north side. The three buildings formed a "U" and were joined together at the spot where their corners converged. Thus, Brewster, if you stood well back, seemed to be a sort of reclining Bangkok Buddha, cradled by the outside arms of the barns on each side of him. He had been spending an hour or so after lunch the past few days in this cocoon of pre-summer warmth, instead of having his nap in the house.

But Charles Brewster wasn't aware of anything relative to his present surroundings. He was sound asleep. And he was dreaming. He was struggling to write a piece of copy extolling the merits of kidney pills. But he was obviously having dream trouble because he began to squirm and to emit strange, spasmodic, stentorian snorts and gurgles. Finally he came up with an unusually loud snort and broke through to reality.

Leaning forward on the bale of straw he rubbed his eyes, squinted against the sun and muttered "Damn." Then he recalled the dream and a smile curled around his pudgy lips as he realized he wasn't working for Greene and Company any more. He had resigned on August 1st the year before and that was eight months ago. True, he was still consultant and adviser on the Hafney Feed and Fertilizer account but that only took up part of two days a week and he did almost all the work at home, right here on the farm.

Of course it wasn't a farm in the fullest sense of the word. Not any more. At the time he had resigned from Greene's he had sold 94 of the original hundred acres that he and Millie had bought a few years before. That had left him six acres. It had also left him with the old brick farmhouse, all the farm buildings, a section of the creek, the pond and the orchard. And it had left him Walter, the steady, hard-working former bachelor-owner of the farm when Brewster had first bought it and who had stayed on after the sale of the 94 acres.

Mr. Brewster yawned, slid unceremoniously off the bale of straw and then stretched himself up to his full rotund five-feet-eight. He slapped the straw off his olive-green coveralls and slipped on his windbreaker which he had discarded in favour of the sun's comfort. Then he stood looking to the south through the wide-lens focus between the barns and on across the meadow. It was a tangle of gray-green, last year's grass blotched with grimy snow where the March sun hadn't burned through the deeper drifts. Beyond was the creek and rising as a backdrop behind that, the steep bank where the snow still lay in unmelted patches in the cedar shadows facing toward the north.

He could see the very spot where he and Millie had stood and dickered with Mr. Henderson, the real-estate agent a dozen or so years before. It was getting to be so long ago that he couldn't clearly remember. But it was there on the edge of the creek beneath the boughs of a gnarled grandfather willow that Henderson had quoted them the price of $13,700 for the original hundred-acre farm. And he remembered how he and Millie had gone back to their apartment in the city and drooled at the thought of owning it. Then, the very next day, he had set the machinery in motion for buying it.

Well, it had been a good investment. He had sold 94 acres of it for $200,000 and still had a few acres left. Now he was virtually free of the Greene Advertising Agency and at the comparatively early age of half a century he could do as he wished for the rest of his life — if he and Millie managed to live on the interest. Mr. Brewster smiled, pulled up the zipper on his windbreaker and turned to go back through the cow-stable door and on to the house.

It was just as he reached the verandah that he saw Walter's tall, lean figure across the lawn from the cottage where he slept and spent his off-time hours. But was it Walter? This Walter was moving with a sort of heel-and-toe motion as if he were in a speed-walking race. It wasn't Walter's tortoise pace at all. In fact he was in such a state of propulsion that he went a few feet past Mr. Brewster before he got his legs stopped.

"She's goin' out, Mr. Brewster, she's ready to go out any minute."

"What's ready to go . . . ? You mean . . . the ice, Walter?" Mr. Brewster remembered other springs when the ice in the creek went out.

"Yeah, she's a-heavin' and crackin' like hell. She'll be bustin' up any minute."

"Okay, I'll get Millie, Walter. Be right over. I want to see that."
Mr. Brewster rushed into the house by way of the kitchen, where
Millie was getting a chicken casserole ready for supper that night.

"Okay Mill, drop the works, drop the works, drop the works."

"Drop what works, Charles? Sure, I'm willing to drop all the
works. What's the matter?"

"Ice breakin' up in the crik. Walter just told me. Get on your
old things."

"I can't go wrong — what else have I got?"

Three minutes later they were approaching the bank of the creek
near Walter's cottage.

"Shake a leg, she's a-goin'!" yelled Walter as they stumbled up
towards him. "Look at that king-pin slab of ice — all she needs is
to tip a little more and she's away."

At that moment there was a strange grinding sound a hundred
feet farther downstream. It was followed by a series of loud cracks
as the jagged chunks of freeing ice were split apart by the uplift of
the increased water volume underneath. The ice cakes ground
against one another, like teeth against teeth. Some of the chunks
slithered out on top of the ice that had not yet cracked apart. And
very quickly the scene resembled a sort of moonscape with ice piled
helter skelter across the width of the creek. The ice between this
point and where the Brewsters stood started cracking and straining
as if determined to wrest itself free from the shackles of winter.
Then, suddenly, as if someone had pressed a button, right in front
of the Brewsters, there was an incredible cracking sound at the bend
of the creek. Following the sound the ice heaved in the middle,
separated into fractured chunks and started piling up. The accu-
mulated weight pressed against and on top of the ice below it and
started a momentum which was soon extended down a considerable
length of the creek. As they watched during the minutes that followed the frozen creek was changed into a grating, grinding, crunching, turmoil of ice chunks. Propelled by the force of the powerful
spring run-off they were carried in groups of two or three or more
into the main current and started their way downstream.

"Ain't this somethin', eh, Mr. Brewster?" said Walter, as if he
were showing off a spectacle he had been especially preparing for
them for some time.

The Brewsters nodded. They had seen other ice break-ups in
previous years but had never seen it happen so suddenly and dramatically. Sometimes the ice had gone out when they were asleep at
night. Sometimes it had gone out more gradually and with less
theatrical demonstration. But this was the big one and they stood
speechless watching the silver chunks of ice tossing up and down,
pitching and rolling from side to side, twirling like corks with their

jagged edges caught on projecting ice on the bank, then floating serenely for a moment like big, white, gleaming sailing ships.

Suddenly Millie Brewster let out a scream and pointed.

"There! Look! On that chunk of ice up there!"

They looked and saw a muskrat riding downstream on an ice raft about four feet square. He was slithering from side to side but managing to keep himself from sliding into the water.

"Yeah, that old boy got caught in his hole with the water comin' up," explained Walter.

"He won't last long there, eh Walter?" commented Charles.

"Nah, he'll slide off and swim to shore. He'll be all right."

"Charles, why don't we walk down along the shore and see what's happening farther down through Geordie Watts' place and down in Martin Baldry's bush?"

"Quite a walk, Millie."

"And she ain't easy walkin', Mrs. Brewster. But she'll sure give you an appetite for supper."

"Come on along, Walter. We might slide in and need hauling out."

"Yeah, sure, Mr. Brewster. We might see some mice on ice."

"Mice on ice? You mean like the muskrat?"

"Yeah, like the muskrat, Mrs. Brewster, except that they're kind of cute and pitiful ridin' a cake of ice."

How pitiful-looking and cute they looked, according to Walter's sadistic judgment the Brewsters found out half an hour later when they were scrambling along the edge of the stream through Baldry's bush. Walter caught sight of them first.

"Hey, there's the little buggers comin' downstream there. See 'em?"

And there they were. Four mice riding an ice flow and obviously scared to the point of panic. They had little room to run about so they were staying close together and digging in their claws to try to counteract the changing slope of the ice as the floe bobbed from side to side. A small pile of snow that had not yet melted near the centre of the ice gave them traction and they clung fast to it.

"These is mice that had a nest in the grass alongside the bank. If they can get to shore they might do all right, seein' the weather's getting warmer now, I dunno. Don't matter none anyway. We'll have plenty of 'em next harvest anyway."

Delivered of this commentary Walter pulled a plug of Master Mason from his overalls' pocket and bit off a sizeable portion.

It was then that Charles heard a twig snap and turned to see Martin Baldry walking towards them. He was wearing his usual red toque and had his bare hands thrust into the pockets of his wool, red-and-black checked blanket-cloth coat that the Brewsters had seen him wearing since they had moved to Briarwood Farm. Even with his thick growth of grey hair he didn't look his 75 years but that's what Nettie Forsyth of the Women's Institute claimed he was. She said her mother was midwife when Mrs. Baldry had Martin during a thunderstorm.

"Well, you folks out to see the break-up too, eh? It's quite a sight this year."

Martin had had four years in High School and had the local reputation of being the best story-teller for miles around. And he had a hearty voice that projected a humorous note into every story — even if his voice was somewhat louder than it need have been.

It sure is goin' out fast this year, Martin. Walter saw that it was starting to go so he ran over to get Millie and me."

"You've sure seen a lot of spring floods, Walter." To Martin's comment Walter just smiled and gave the impression that there were things about some of the spring floods he had seen that nobody would ever see again.

"Well, I've seen a few too, in my time. Yes, I've seen a few," said Martin.

Millie could see that he was winding up to get started on a story and she encouraged him.

"What was the most exciting one, Martin?"

"What was the most exciting flood? Well, I know that one all right." And with that Martin pulled his old worn-shiny pipe out of his big pocket, saw that there was still some tobacco in it and proceeded to take his time lighting it while his audience waited in suspense.

"The most exciting one, eh? Yeah, I know that one. I was only a young gaffer then. And that was sure a funny one. It wasn't even a spring flood like this at all."

"Oh? Wasn't a spring flood? What kind of a flood was it?" queried Charles.

Martin puffed on his pipe until it was going to his satisfaction, then he sat down on a stump, scratched his chin for a moment and started in.

"Well, old Tom Snively, the farmer that lived next door to us at that time, he had a good field of peas that year. They used to feed peas to a lot of pigs in those days. A lot of folks had what they called a pea-barn. And this was a real good crop this year and he had them sown in a field that he had cultivated right up to the side of the creek here. In fact the field sloped down to the creek. But Tom wasn't liked any too well by his neighbours. He owed money around and he was a little on the crooked side, you might say. He owed money to Jeddy MacTavish's dad, Lorne MacTavish — where Jeddy farms now. Well, anyway, on this day I'm talking about I was ready to start out from home to go over to help a neighbour when it started raining again. I forgot to say it'd been raining all night and part of the afternoon the day before. But now, as I was leavin' it started comin' down again. And it started blowin'. Man, did it ever blow. Hell of a wind. Forty-mile gusts. Maybe more. But my mother she gave me a big coat that hung down almost to my feet and I left for the neighbours."

"Wonder you didn't get yourself all blowed away, Martin, little fellow like you," chucked Walter.

"I did just about, Walter. Anyway, I took a short cut up alongside the creek here. And when it started blowin' harder than ever and rainin' cats and dogs I took refuge in a big hollow tree that used to stand up along here somewhere. Big, big tree, all rotted now. I was snug as a bug in a rug there because I was faced away from the wind and rain. But just about the time I figured that I'd better get going over to the neighbours or high-tail it back home somethin' happened. When I was peerin' out, by the Holy Dumpty somethin' happened. I saw what I took to be a cock of hay come drifting down the creek."

"What time of the year was this, did you say, Martin?" asked Charles.

"Late summer, Charles. But pretty soon I saw that it wasn't a cock of hay, like it might be if it was the second cutting of hay. It was a big bundle of peas. If it had been hay that wind would have blown it all to pieces. But peas get kind of tangled up and twisted together more than hay does. Anyway, it was peas and this bundle went floatin' right past me. And then another one. Then another. And pretty soon the whole damn creek here was full of these bundles of floatin' peas."

"The peas from Tom Snively's farm, eh, Martin?" prompted Charles, wanting to let Martin know he was catching on fast.

"Well, just wait now, Charles. Yes, that's what they were. Peas from this field of old Tom Snively that sloped down to the edge of the creek here."

Millie started guessing then, too. "The heavy rain had washed them out of the field into the creek, Martin?"

"No, not exactly, Millie, not exactly. Some of them, yes, where the rising water had carried them away where they were growing close down near the creek. But it was mostly that powerful wind. Why, it just lifted those bundles of peas and blew them down the slope and dropped them into the creek. The cedars and willows on the far side of the creek, they acted like a windbreak and stopped them from blowing any farther and most of the peas ended up right in the creek, which by then was tearing along as if it was mad at something."

By this time Millie was getting considerably excited about the outcome. "What I want to know is whether Tom Snively lost all his peas, Martin."

"Well now, I'll just tell you what happened. By the time I saw all these peas come tearin' down the creek I'd changed my mind about going over to help this neighbour because I was soaking wet. So I figured I'd head back home. So I struck out, walking back alongside the creek here. And all the time I was watching this creekful of peas because it was sure something to see. So by the time I got down to where the creek runs through the line fence into Mac-Tavish's place from Snively's place. And I climbed the old snake fence — it was a snake fence in those days — and then I just stood there on the other side and I looked and looked and looked."

"What on earth at, Martin?" asked Millie.

"What at, Millie? I'll tell you what at. There were three fellows standing down at the edge of the creek. And they each had a rake. And they were the three sons of Lorne MacTavish. And they were fishing around in the creek with these long, old rakes — reaching out from the bank as far as they could reach."

"Fishin' for fish with rakes, Martin?" cackled Walter.

"No sir, they were fishing for peas, Walter. They were fishing for old Tom's peas."

"Served the old bugger right, eh?" snorted Walter again.

"Yes, I suppose it did. Anyway, there they were fishing out these peas and doing a pretty good job of it, too. Oh, they missed a lot of them but they were hauling in a lot, too. So I yelled at them, 'Hey, how's the fishing?'."

"But because of the strong wind they didn't hear me so I yelled again, 'Hey, how's the fishing?'. Well, maybe because of the wind or because they were so busy hauling out those peas they didn't answer and they just kept on working. And about that time their dad, Lorne, he clambered down the bank and came over to me laughing his head off. 'Looks like you came over to see the big show, eh, Martin?'."

" 'It sure is quite a show, Mr. MacTavish,' I said."

" 'Well', he said, 'I guess you and everybody else around here knows how old skinflint Tom is owin' money to everybody around here, including me. He owes me just over $80 for some hay he bought three years ago.' "

" 'Yes, I know, Mr. MacTavish,' I said."

" 'Well', he said to me, 'one of my boys about an hour ago saw the wind liftin' these peas and blowin' 'em over here towards the creek so he walked down here and saw they were bein' blown right into the creek so they got the idea of snarin' the peas as soon as they came through the line fence into our part of the creek. And it looks like we're doin' some harvestin', eh?' "

" 'I guess Mr. Snively must be away or something or he would have seen his own peas blowing away into the creek,' I said." " 'You hit it straight on!' Mr. MacTavish said. 'Old Tom is away with his wife so he didn't see them.' And that's the end of my story, folks."

Everybody laughed and congratulated Martin. But Charles felt there was one thing missing.

"Martin, we haven't heard what happened to the peas. Did the water do them any damage? Could MacTavish sell them?"

"Sell them? He didn't sell them, Charles. He fed them to his pigs. He figured there was over $85 worth of peas. And those peas put on a mighty lot of pork for him. And, you know, from then on every time old Tom saw Lorne MacTavish taking a load of pigs to market he'd shake his fist and say, 'There goes my goddam peas to market inside those goddam pigs of yours, Lorne MacTavish.' "

The story put everyone in a good humour — especially Walter, who went around chortling as the others watched the creek carrying the ice floes in the general direction of Lake Ontario, a few miles to the southeast. But finally they separated. Martin Baldry turned and started home and the Brewsters and Walter took a short cut across the flats towards the barn.

"Well, it's been quite an afternoon, Mill."

"Yes, it has. Good neighbours. Martin's story. And the spring breakup rolled into one."

"Given me a good appetite for supper."

"Oh, I imagine it has. Well, you're getting one of your favourites. Spare-ribs. By the way, I think the afternoon has given me an idea, Charles."

"Oh?"

"I want to think it over. I'll talk to you about it at supper time. And you can guess, if you like, between now and then but I don't think you'll get an idea as to what I have in mind."

Supper was over. For the fifth time Charles had told Millie her spare-ribs were better than the ones they had once enjoyed in the expensive Cardinal Room in the city where he had paid $15 per head for dinner, wines and brandy. And Millie had been pleased. But she also seemed anxious to impart to her husband the idea with which she had teased him earlier. And she did that when they were both seated with coffee out in the sunroom, looking out at the farm buildings, the meadow and the setting sun glinting off the new spring foliage of the elms along the creek.

"Okay, Mill," Charles began, crossing his brown plaid-slippered feet on the petit-point hassock. "Let's have it."

Millie smiled. She was sure of herself. She was positive she had a good idea.

"Well, it goes like this. How many bigshots do you know on the three city dailies?"

"How many? Oh, two, three. Homer Burns, city editor at the *Echo*. Bertram Foster, city editor at the *Beacon* and Larry Dinsmore, managing editor at the *News*. The *News* has the biggest circulation. Over four hundred thousand."

"Then that's the one to try first."

"To get a job as a cub reporter you mean, Mrs. B.?"

"No, as a columnist."

"Oh, no . . . no sir . . . not for me. How those guys flush out a column every day beats me. They're the whizz kids of a daily."

"How about a weekly column?"

"About what, Millie?"

"Oh, for instance that story that Jeddy MacTavish told us this morning. That kind of thing. It would be a column devoted to things that happen in the country. I think a lot of city people would like to read it. Many have roots in the country. They were either born in a rural area or they have relatives there."

Millie was getting more excited as she warmed to her idea and she could see that Charles was becoming interested. He was staring straight ahead, unmoving, like a figure in Madame Tussaud's Waxworks Museum. And she had seen this posture before. It was a sure sign that her husband's wheels were going around and Millie decided to leave her idea as a cud for him to chew for a moment. She watched him fumble in his pocket for a cigar, still staring straight ahead of him as if he were in a trance. He found his lighter, brought it up until it found his cigar, got it going and continued to hold the same sculptured pose. Finally he turned slowly towards her, nodded his head as if bestowing Godhead affirmation on her idea, reached over and patted her wrist.

"I think you've got something, Mill. By the Holy Doodle, as Walter says, I think you've got an idea by the tail."

"You could write up Jeddy's story as a column and maybe do another column about the . . . well, for instance, about what happens in March on a farm . . . the lambs coming and the birds coming back from the south . . . oh, there are dozens of things. Then you'd have two different kinds of columns to show him."

"By the Holy Doodle I'll write 'em tomorrow and take 'em down to Larry Dinsmore at the *News* the first of the week. He might just buy the bloody thing."

"Sure, he might just buy the bloody thing," matched Millie, with a mock inflection.

"And I've just thought of a title. How about 'Along the Side-road'?"

"Very good. Oh, very good. All the little human interest things that happen along the sideroads."

"You think I'd run out of material? I wonder."

"There must be hundreds of little stories and happenings. They just need digging out."

"I think I'd kind of like that. Yes sir, that might be kind of fun, too. Yeah, Millie, I think you've got an idea. And you know what I'm going to do? I'm going down Monday morning and throw two columns at Larry Dinsmore. By the Holy Doodle, he might just buy the bloody thing."

2

Walter Tells Two Eerie Irish Stories

Millie Brewster finally sorted out the single grey hair she had been trying to get between her fingers, gave it a yank and deposited it carefully in the wastepaper basket. Separating the strands of her hair she looked for others but found none.

Well, not too bad for an old lady of fifty, well almost fifty. Better than some women. Nora Plaxton in the city has finally gone for the full grey treatment. More or less had to. Well, how's my figure? Not too bad if I do say so. Bit of a bulge down here on my tummy. Maybe I'd get rid of it if I had 500 chicks to look after like I used to. Give me some exercise. No, I guess not. Simpler to buy a dozen month-old pullets every spring for eggs in the fall. But it looks as if I'll have to let this dress out at the waist a bit. Or diet. Or both. Maybe I should . . .

And it was then in her musing that Millie heard the dressing-room door squeak and Charles walked in.

"Oh . . . sorry, Mill. I called you from downstairs."

"Oh, I've been up here feeling sorry for myself. Grey hair. Bulge at my tummy. Arthritis in my left forearm. I'm getting old."

"I don't see any grey hair. That bulge is only the stone in that prune plum you swallowed last night. It hasn't gone on down yet — or up or somewhere. As far as the arthritis goes, that's muscular because you moved that heavy bookcase all by yourself yesterday when you were changing the furniture."

"Thank you, Charles. What's up with you this morning?"

"Oh, I've been thinking up another column to write — to take down to Larry Dinsmore."

"Sit down, Charles. No, not that chair, it needs caning. Over there."

"Maybe I need caning too, eh?" Charles chuckled at his rather feeble joke, seated himself in the other more substantial chair in the dressing room and started peering out the window. "Say, you get quite a view out this window, eh? Over the orchard and all that. I'm not in your dressing room very often to see this. From here I can see the mound of earth over the septic tank. Remember when we put that in? Quite a few years ago now."

"Can I forget? After either running outdoors to the privy or up to what we called the 'ham room' to that indoor toilet? I was just about ready to divorce you and move back to the city when we finally got the septic tank and plumbing in."

"How about now? Like a quick divorce?"

"Oh, I guess I can put up with you — though I've wondered sometimes since I've had you around the house so much from the time you resigned from the Greene Advertising Agency."

"Oh? What have I done? I'm no trouble, Mill. My God, I just go my own way and don't bother you at all."

"Charles, as Sarah Haggerty would say, you're a consarned nuisance. You even come out into the kitchen when I'm baking and tell me the recipe is all wrong. Things like that."

"Oh, come on. I don't."

"Well, anyway, maybe if and when you start writing this column for the *News* you'll be out driving around more getting your stories."

"Oh, I was going to ask you about that. If Larry Dinsmore on the *News* buys that column I think I'll retire from this part-time job I do for Horace Greene as special consultant for his Hafney Feed and Fertilizer account."

"The column wouldn't pay as much, would it?"

"No, not even half as much but I'm sick of guessing up new ways to tell farmers how to stuff little pigs full of pig starter and have them up to 60 pounds at weaning age — well, not 60 pounds but you know what I mean."

"Wait and see if you can sell the column."

"Yeah, I guess. Well, it's been eight months since we sold the farm. Instead of 100 acres we now have 6 acres. Vest pocket farm, eh? Horace Greene asked me the other day what stock I had on it. Well, I said, we've got ten ewes and a ram and we're getting about ten steers for summer feeding on the pasture and ten pullets this spring so they'll lay eggs for us starting this fall — plus two horses sixteen years old that don't have much work to do and one very old cat in the barn."

"I hope he was enlightened."

"He said why didn't we get a jackass so he could listen to it laughing at us."

"He's just jealous."

"Sure he is — ever since we sold the farm for enough money to retire on. Then he asked me why we kept Walter on when there's not much for him to do."

"Well, maybe we could do without Walter — though I'm not so sure of it. But I like Walter. He's easy to get along with, now that we know his grumbling doesn't mean anything. He claims he hasn't enough to do. I know that."

"From now on there should be more — between now and next winter."

"Well, we'll see. I think the . . ."

"Youse upstairs, Mr. Brewster?" It was Walter calling from below.

"Yes, Walter, I'll be right down. Or come on up if you like."

"Walter hasn't been upstairs here for ages."

"No, I guess not."

"My, it's hard to remember when this dressing room and the bathroom beside it here was a bedroom."

"That was sure a few years ago. Oh, we've got this old hundred-and-some-year-old house in pretty good shape, eh?"

"There's only one thing I regret."

"There is?"

"Instead of buying imitation pioneer Canadian furniture I should have bought authentic pieces around at auction sales and refinished them. I'd feel much better about it."

"There's still time. You only bought a few pieces of that kind of furniture. The other furniture we have we brought from our apartment."

"Yes, we could always sell that furniture we brought from the apartment. I think I'll start going to auction sales. They'll be starting in another couple of months. I've been reading quite a lot about refinishing old furniture and I think I'd like to try my hand at it."

"I think that'd be terrific, Mill. Oh, come in, Walter, come on in."

Walter's wraith-thin six-foot figure appeared in the doorway.

"Long time since I was up here. Sure been some changes, Mrs. Brewster. I mind when I first come here to buy this house there used to be a big brass bed sittin' in the bathroom there right where you squat on your seat."

"Oh, yes?" Millie smiled at Walter's homely description of the toilet. She had become accustomed to his artless and blunt way of saying many things.

"Yeah, but that ain't why I come in to see you, Mr. Brewster. I just been out fillin' the feed-box with oats for the horses and there was a rat jumped out when I got close to the box and I took a kick at it and missed but it put somethin' into my head."

"My God, Walter, what was it?"

"Well, you were tellin' me this forenoon about those stories you might be writin' for the newspaper."

"Yes, I don't know yet, Walter, because I haven't sold the column. But I'd like to hear some more stories like the one Martin Baldry told us."

"Yeah, I know, Mr. Brewster. I know what kind of story you're lookin' for. I ain't too dumb, you know."

"You're not dumb at all, Walter. You mean you thought of a story?"

"Well, I dunno for sure but I can tell you if you want."

"I'd like to hear it."

"Is it clean, Walter?" Millie thought she should have an advance posting to help her make up her mind whether to go or stay.

"Yeah, she's as clean as a basswood whistle, Mrs. Brewster."

"All right, Walter. Carry on."

"Well, when the Fosdicks lived over on the town line and that'd be quite a while ago Emerson Fosdick hired a young fellow just over from Ireland from near Killarney I think I mind him sayin' it was. And this Irish fellow was full of superstitions. Oh, he had these superstitions stickin' out of him all over. And it wasn't long before he decided there was a banshee in Emerson Fosdick's horse-barn. You know what a banshee is, Mr. Brewster?"

"I think it's a spirit, Walter — a female spirit if I'm not wrong. And it goes around wailing and that's supposed to forewarn a family that there's going to be a death in that house."

"Well, I never heard all that about it but it's somethin' or other that does a lot of wailin' I know that."

"So what happened, Walter?"

"Well sir, this kind of tickled Emerson Fosdick and he figured he'd have a little fun with this Irish fellow. So he got hold of a crow from somewhere — a real live crow. And he painted it red."

"Oh, Walter."

"That's as true as my birthday is on April Fools' Day, Mrs. Brewster."

"Good Heavens, so your birthday is. That's just a couple of weeks away."

"Yeah, 'tis. Well, anyway, Emerson he paints this crow red and he puts it inside the oat-box where the Irish boy gets the oats to feed the horses and he lets down the lid. So when the Irish lad he comes out to feed the horses and he lifts the lid and out comes this red crow, flappin' and croakin' and half scared to death. And it flaps right into this Irish lad's face. And then sails on out the open stable door."

Charles Brewster guffawed vigorously but although Millie smiled a little she looked a little sad, too — perhaps at the picture of the lonely Irish boy so far from Killarney who was having his leg pulled.

"Just for that I hope the Irish boy quit working for Mr. Fosdick, Walter."

"No, he didn't do that, Mrs. Brewster. He didn't know what the hell . . . I mean what the heck it was that flew out of that oat box except that it was red. He knew it was red and that's all he needed to know and he goes around shriekin' that this was the red devil banshee he knew all along was in the horse-barn. He stayed on at the Fosdick's until the end of the harvest but from that time on he'd never go into that horse-barn and Emerson had to feed the horses himself."

"That's a pretty good story, Walter."

"That the kind of yarns you want for this piece you're goin' to write?"

"Yes, if I sell the column. Know any more like that?"

"I know plenty of 'em but the next thing is to remember the sons of guns. I got a memory like an old milk strainer."

"Well, if you remember any I'd like to hear them, Walter."

"Yeah, sure. No extra charge, Mr. Brewster."

And with that Walter stopped supporting the door with his shoulder and eased himself out. Millie smiled as she watched him.

"You now have a source of stories if you sell your 'Along the Sideroad' column."

"Yes, that story alone won't make a column but I can combine it with two or three others. Oh, Walter might be able to remember a lot of stories."

"Of course if you sell the column you should start off by writing one that explains 'Briarwood Farm'. I imagine you'll be writing future columns about what happens on your vest-pocket farm, as we call it, even though I think we can find a better word than that."

"Well, it's only a small acreage. That's why I've been calling it that. Of course we could say a 'miniscule' farm or 'molecule' farm or 'tittle farm'— something like that."

"How about 'little mite'?"

"That's redundant, superfluous. If it's 'little' it's a 'mite'."

"Not necessarily, Charles. How about 'weeny'?"

"Sounds like a sausage farm."

"What about 'wee'? What about 'pee-wee acres'?"

"Hey, that's better. 'Pee-Wee Acres'. Yeah."

"Or we can keep on calling it 'Briarwood Farm', Charles, as we did when we had the full hundred acres. But what about my original question?"

"Oh, yes, about describing the farm. I think that'd make a column, sure."

"You can give some idea of the livestock we have and the orchard and fruit and vegetables we're going to have in the big garden I hope Walter is going to help us look after. And you can say something about the birds — especially the winter birds we get at our feeding station."

"I think the first column or maybe the first two or three columns should be a bit more exciting — human interest stuff — to kind of hook the reader a bit before we get down to describing anything as prosaic as 'Pee-Wee Acres'."

"I think you're right. As usual. Yes, I suppose you're right. Oh, I thought I heard Walter coming upstairs again."

And Walter was certainly coming upstairs again.

"Youse still up there, Mr. Brewster?"

"Yes, come on in, Walter."

"I'll bet he's thought of another story for you."

"Well, I asked him to so — yes, come in, Walter."

"I just thought of another story for you. Leastways it might be."

"Be glad to hear it."

"This is kind of Irishy, too, like that last one."

"That's fine. Any red devils in this one?"

"No, this is about an Irish girl. Katie Duggan was her name — a home girl as they called them in them days — and she worked for a farmer over on the ninth. I forget who the farmer was. Anyway, in the kitchen fireplace on this farm there was a bake-oven because this was way back around the beginnin' of this century."

"And they were still using the bake-oven in the fireplace?"

"Yeah, but it seems one of the stones that the fireplace was made with got splayed with the heat — got cracked like, you know?"

"Yes, I know."

"So this Irish girl, Katie Duggan, she had an Irish fellow she was keepin' company with pretty steady and he was workin' on some farm close by. And when the folks where she was workin' said they'd need a new stone to put in the place of the one that'd splayed she asks this Irish boy-friend of hers if he'd find her one."

"Which I'll bet he did if he wanted to make time with her, eh?"

"Charles, don't interrupt Walter. And don't be so crude."

"Sorry, Walter. Carry on."

"Well, anyway, this boy friend of this Irish girl he had kind of a crazy sense of humour because you know what he done? He goes out lookin' for the right size stone and the right shape and all that and by the Holy Susie if he doesn't dig a gravestone out of the buryin' ground on the hill a mile or so away."

"Oh, no, Walter. That's vandalism."

"Well, whatever that means he measured it and it was just the right size to fit into the bakin' oven in the fireplace. So one day when he knew the folks that owned this farm was away at an auction sale and his girl friend Katie was in town buyin' herself somethin' fancy at the store he goes to this house and he fits the stone into the space left by the stone that was splayed."

"A very ingenious young man, Walter."

"I dunno if he was that kind of a fellow or not, Mr. Brewster, but anyway Katie Duggan comes home from her shoppin' in town and the first thing she sees is this new stone in the fireplace. So she rushes over to have a look at it. And she bends down closer to it. Then she puts her hand to her head — like this, Mrs. Brewster, like as if she was goin' to faint."

"But why, Walter?"

"Because, Mrs. Brewster, on the front of the gravestone was the words, 'Here Lies Katie Duggan'."

"Oh, Walter. That was absolutely indecent. It's terrible."

"I dunno but that's what there was. 'Here Lies Katie Duggan.' "

"Charles, isn't that terrible?"

"Yeah, that's a little rough, Walter. Pretty rough kind of humour. What had happened was that this Irish lad had chiselled the words onto the gravestone, eh?"

"That's the idea, Mr. Brewster. I'll bet she sacked her boy friend awful fast, eh? Or maybe she quit her job fast."

"Or went stark, staring mad," commented Millie.

"I dunno, Mrs. Brewster, what happened along them lines. But anyway, Mr. Brewster, there's a story for yeh, if you think she's good enough for you to write it down."

"Sure it is, Walter. That's a good story. Keep them coming."

"Speakin' of comin'. I think I'll be goin'. I got work to do. This might not be a thousand acre farm but I can always find somethin' to keep my legs movin'."

With that Walter was gone and the Brewsters were left speechless for a moment.

"I'm beginning to think that Walter's stories are all going to be a bit on the morbid side, Mill."

"Maybe you can fit them in between other more cheerful stories."

"If I sell the column. And you know maybe we should have a little drink to the sale of 'Along the Sideroad', eh?"

"Since you are now almost a non-drinker, Charles, I'm agreeable."

"Yeah, it kind of bores me any more. But there are occasions that it seems to give the right . . . well, let's say 'signature' to a thing. And this is one. To the sale of my column, 'Along the Sideroad' to Larry Dinsmore, managing editor of the *News* — come next Monday."

3

Charles Sells His Column—
but Faces a Water Shortage

The following Monday forenoon while Charles was away in the city fulfilling his appointment with Larry Dinsmore at the *News*, Millie went down to the horse-barn. A number of antiques they had picked up at farm auction sales through the years had been stored there in the tack room. One of these days she would think of some way to display them so their friends and relations who came out from the city could examine them to better advantage. Today she just wanted to jot down a list of them for future reference.

She was just opening the door of the horse-barn when Walter came up behind her. "Say, you're lookin' turned out pretty slick this mornin', Mrs. Brewster."

"It's the same thing I've worn to the barn all winter, Walter — these old ski pants and this raggedy plaid coat. Oh, it must be this toque. I bought it in Mapleville on Saturday. That's new."

"Sure got a long tassel on it. You could hog-tie a mule with all that."

"I don't intend to. All I'm doing right now is coming to have a look at the antiques."

"Don't mind June and Judy. They won't kick when we go behind 'em like this."

"Walter, I know that. Don't forget I've known June and Judy for quite a few years. There, you hear that little whinny? They're asking me if I have any oats."

"They'll get their oats at noon-hour and their hay, too. You want some help if you're pawin' through these antikeys?"

"Not really, but you might be able to identify one or two of them. I'm not even sure what they're for."

"I guess they're all for doin' things the hard way but the old pioneer fellows managed to get along with 'em. You know what that fifteen-foot piece of wood is for?"

"Yes, it's made in the shape of a little trough — about three inches wide in the bottom and with sides on it about three inches high. You put grass seed in it."

"Yeah, then what do you do with it when you've got grass seed in her?"

"You carry it so it extends out on each side of you as you walk along in the field. There's a rope or strap or something that goes around behind your head. Then there's a little shuttle thing that you operate by sliding it back and forth as you walk along and there are little holes in the bottom of the trough and as you move the shuttle back and forth the grass seed drops down through the little holes to the ground. How's that?"

"Yeah, you got that down pretty good."

"Have you ever used one?"

"No, I used a cyclone seeder and then I got a seed-drill with a grain box and a grass-seed box. But I guess this'd work all right. Hey, here's the boss comin'."

"Charles, are you back already? I didn't expect you until lunch time."

"Well, I was going to stay downtown and have a good lunch and maybe a beer to celebrate. But I didn't."

"To celebrate? Don't tell me."

"Try and stop me. It worked. I sold it."

"Well, you said that Larry Dinsmore might just buy the bloody thing, as you say."

"He did. I handed it to him and I sit there while he reads these columns and I could see him smilin' when he gets to the part about where those boys were haulin' the peas out of the creek and then he starts laughin'. And when he finishes he takes off his glasses and puts his feet up on his desk. 'Charles', he says. 'Good stuff. All I'm wondering is whether you could keep it up or not. Could you come by these stories once a week, week in and week out?"

"Well, I told him I thought I could, by taking a little trip around the country once every two or three weeks — different parts of Ontario — maybe down to Quebec or the Maritimes, even. Then I said that of course if I did that it would take expense money and Larry said that could be arranged, he thought. So then he told me about a few little things to keep in mind about the editorial policy of the *News* and the way to slant the columns and so on and that was that. So now I'm a bloody columnist on the *News*, the big city daily, Walter. Over 400,000 copies sold every day."

"Jumpin' Whittleday, 400,000. That's doin' better than the Mapleville *Banner*."

"For a small-town weekly the *Banner* does very well. Circulation about 2,800."

"You goin' to do them stories about the Red Devil and the grave-stone with 'Here Lies Katie Duggan' on it?"

"Yes, sure, Walter. And any others you can remember. Well, I guess we better go in, eh?"

"And I think we should all have a little toast," suggested Millie.

"Good idea, Mill. Great idea."

"With sherry."

"Oh . . . yeah. Walter, come on."

"Yeah, you watch Judy there, Mrs. Brewster. You never know. Here, I'll open the stable door for you. This latch has got kind of loose. I gotta fix that. Speakin' of tellin' stories that makes me think of somethin' that happened to me one time I went down to the big city down there. Be twenty years ago, maybe. Maybe more'n that. I was walkin' along the street mindin' my own business and there was a milk-wagon standin' by the side of the street there and this old, grey beat-up horse slouchin' along between the shafts lookin' like it was sick and tired of deliverin' milk. This was on Jarvis Street, I remember now — right outside that radio company."

"The C.B.C. is on Jarvis Street — Canadian Broadcasting Corporation."

"That's the one, yeah. C.B.C., I remember now. They had a sign hung outside it. So I was lookin' this old spavin'-footed critter over when she up and acts naughty right there on the road. So that was like somethin' that happens right back on the farm where I come from in the country. And I was standin' there with my nose in the air sniffin' away when this fellow comes along and stops when he was turnin' in at the C.B.C. and he looks me over and doesn't say nothin' at first and then he says, 'What's all that sniffin' for?' Well, I told him. I said I wasn't expectin' to come across anything that reminded me of my own farm right here in the middle of the city and I kind of liked it. Then I asked him who he was. 'Well,' he says, 'I'm an announcer here at the C.B.C. Who are you?' Well, I says, I'm a farmer from a farm and a farm is some land where we grow things so you city fellows don't starve to death. Then he says, 'You like that smell?' Yeah, I says, I do. It's the best healthy smell I've smelled in the city here yet."

"Well sir, you know, that C.B.C. announcer fellow got the funniest look on his face. 'You know where you should be?' he says. Well, I says, where I should be is back on the farm throwin' hay down to the cows instead of talkin' to queer-actin' fellows like you. 'No,' he says, 'you should be out at 999 Queen Street West.' Oh, I says, have they got cows to throw hay to out there? 'No,' he says, 'that's a loony bin. That's for crazy fellows like you.' Then he turns his nose so high up in the air that he stumbles on the step goin' in to the C.B.C. and then he marches on as if he owned the damn company."

Charles and Millie had been laughing all through Walter's long recitation. With the end of it Charles was rocking back and forth so hard his jaunty go-to-the-city green fedora fell off. Millie retrieved it and shoved it down on his head.

"Walter, that's a wonderful story, it really is. I think you could find a place for it in your column sometime, Charles."

"Sure but I think I'll have the old milk-wagon horse acting naughty, as you call it, outside the entrance to the Greene Advertising Agency."

"Oh, come on, now. Horace Greene has been very nice to you since you resigned."

"I doubt if he'll be nice to me much longer."

"Why not?"

"Because I'm handing in my resignation from the Hafney Feed and Fertilizer account to take effect the first of April. April Fool's Day."

"Oh, Charles, isn't that too sudden? And don't make it April Fool's Day."

"Make it the first of May, then, or June. Oh, Horace has been all right lately. He was all right when I worked there. Just doing his job. And with that wife of his it's a wonder he's as humane as he is. Hey, what are you listening for, Walter?"

Walter was twisted into a question-mark, his hand cupped to his ear.

"You hear that poundin' sound?"

"Yes, I heard it a while ago. Sounds like somebody pounding in a steel post with one of those heavy fence-pounders."

"Sounds to me like somebody drilling a well."

"Yes, come to think of it it does, Walter. Like when Hailey was drilling our well here."

"It's coming from down towards Mapleville, Charles," said Millie.

"How about that 65-acre farm that Ben Stockley sold to Mygrange Development? Didn't Myers or Grange or somebody say they were going to develop that land first? They bought that farm long before ours and they had transits and all that out there last fall. They put in a temporary service road, too."

"Are you interested in finding out? The road to the farm runs west from Mapleville and I have a couple of things to shop for."

"And I need a coupla plugs of Master Mason," interjected Walter.

"All right, let's go. After all, we should be aware of what's going on so close to us."

With that pronouncement Charles Brewster ambled towards the blue-trimmed station wagon he had left outside the drive-shed garage and a few minutes later they turned into the gate of the Stockley farm. The old brick house was deserted. Mygrange Development

Corporation had set the date of February 1 for the Stockleys to be out and the house was now a sort of office for the Corporation. With the leafless trees and shrubs around it and the curtainless windows it looked rejected and resigned to its certain death by the bulldozer within the next few months.

At certain periods of the year when the ground was firm Charles would have driven across the field to the site of the drilling. But he could see that the mid-March sun had made the blue clay surface of the field greasy and he was afraid of losing traction. Thus the last hundred yards across the field to the workers who were knotted beside the bank of the river was made on foot, over the still-visible drill-rows of last summer's stubble. The sound of the drilling became louder as they approached as the monotonous voice of the pounding drill was warning them to stay away by shouting in increasing volume. As they came over to the seven figures moving around the drill-rig a man in black coveralls walked towards them.

"You wanta something here?" he asked, with a note of challenge in his voice. He was about thirty and a first glance showed primarily the thick, black hair, black eyes and fine, white teeth evident in so many Italian immigrants.

"Well, we live just north of here on the sideroad. We sold our farm to Mygrange Development too and we heard the drill going. So we just got curious about what was going on, to tell the truth."

The man grinned, but Charles wasn't sure how much he had understood.

"We drilla for water. Okay?"

"Yes, sure. Two other wells, I see. How big are the two I see from here with the water coming out the top?"

The Italian shrugged his shoulders. "I come to Canada." He gave the soft Italian emphasis to the first syllable. "Not know Inglese mucha."

Charles wasn't getting very far but he persisted as he pointed towards the pipes coming out of the wells already dug. "Pipes four inches wide . . . four inches?" He indicated the width with his hands. The Italian looked mystified and it was obvious there was no point in trying to extract any information so Charles motioned the others to follow him down the slope towards the creek where the two pipes rose up about three feet above the level of the ground.

"Yes, these two pipes are four-inch ones. There's a hell of a lot of water spilling out of there and running away to waste, Walter."

"Never seen so much water since it was pourin' out of the drill pipe up from your well, Mr. Brewster."

"We only have a two-inch drill pipe."

"Isn't there some way to cap it, Charles?"

"Sure they can cap it, Mill. But they're afraid of putting pressure on it in case it backs up way down in the hole and detours into another channel. That way they'd lose their water."

"What the Sam Hill will they be doin' with all this water?"

"Using it one of these days in the houses they'll be building here. Hundreds of houses, Walter."

"It sure must be a powerful flowin' stream way down there in the ground, eh? Holy Doodle."

"Yes, it's an underground river and they've struck a great flow. Like we did but bigger because of the four-inch pipes."

"That'd water a powerful lot of horses — with a few cows and sheep thrown in to boot."

The Italian had come down to join them and was looking at them suspiciously so Charles suggested they go back to the car.

" 'bye. Thank you," he said in leaving.

"Addio . . . ringraziere." The Italian waved as if glad to see them go.

The Brewsters drove back towards Briarwood Farm (as both Charles and Millie continued to call it) and on the way speculated on the time that the first houses would appear on Ben Stockley's farm. Charles gave a recap of progress to date.

"They have that service road. They built that first, apparently, to move heavy industrial machinery along before they lay out the streets. But it seems there's been some holdup in a plan they've submitted to the Water Resources Commission or whoever it is about a sewage disposal plant. Mygrange have been fighting with the officials about this and it isn't settled yet. So they can't go ahead with any building until that's finalized."

"That might take quite a while, Charles. And that suits me fine. The Stockley farm is only Unit One in their building program, the way I've heard it. Our farm is Unit Two. We might keep our view across our fields for quite a while yet."

"Hey, Mr. Brewster, you know what I've been thinkin'?"

"No, what, Walter?"

"Well, it's about the flats south of your barn. Your six acres don't take in them flats, on down south to the crik and to the west of your six acres."

"No, we just have about 300 feet of the creek, Walter. So what?"

"So it should be used for somethin'. That's goin' to grow up to weeds this summer and these fellows that own it now are goin' to have to pay to have the weeds mowed if somebody starts complainin' to the weed inspector."

"Keep talking, Walter. You're doing fine."

"And them fences is all goin' to hell, too. Somebody should be keepin' 'em up."

"Yes, they should. They should, really." Charles had caught on but he was giving Walter his head.

"Don't you git it yet, Mr. Brewster? Sufferin' cats! Mrs. Brewster, you get it?"

"I think Mr. Brewster just wanted to hear you say it, Walter."

"I'll say it, sure. I ain't backward about comin' forward. All you gotta do is see them two fellows that bought your farm and you tell 'em that they should have cattle on the flats eatin' the weeds off and you won't charge 'em as much for doin' that as the weed inspector would charge for havin' the weeds mowed — especially when the flats is full of thistles goin' to seed."

"You mean we could pasture cattle there and they'd pay us for it? No, I don't think I'd have the nerve to do that."

"You could offer to do it free, Charles."

"Yeah, as a special favor to them. You git it all now, Mr. Brewster?"

"Oh, I think so, Walter. How many head would the flats pasture?"

"Well, there's around twelve-thirteen acres there but it ain't the best of pasture bein' just natural grass and no manure on it for awhile but you could run eight or nine head there maybe. You could buy 'em at about 750-800 pounds and grass 'em from the end of May to the end of October."

"It's steers you're talking about buying is it, Walter?"

"Yeah, feeder steers. I figure we'd have to start feedin' 'em some grain when the grass starts gettin' a little scarce and we'd finish 'em off on grain in the barnyard. Then we'd sell 'em the end of November or in December — when they was ready to go to market."

"Charles, I think this is a wonderful idea, thanks to Walter."

"Don't thank me. It won't mean much work except to see that the fences is kept up. I need some work to do. The work I've been doin' all this winter you could hardly put through a knot-hole."

"Let's see now," recapped Charles. "We're planning to keep one of the steers for ourselves and have it slaughtered and wrapped and put in the freezer. How many pounds of meat would we get from a steer?"

"Well, you take a thousand-pound liveweight steer, it'd kill out to 550 pounds and after that you got a lot of insides and so on you couldn't use so you'd still have 400 pounds of meat for your freezer likely. I never weighed it on account of I never had a freezer."

"Good Heavens, 400 pounds of beef, Walter?"

"Long about there somewhere's, Mrs. Brewster. Of course, you can hire a locker from that freezer outfit in town to put whatever you can't cram in your freezer."

"Well, that'd be cheap beef, Millie. And the price of beef is sure going up."

"You're tellin' me, Mr. Brewster. You better latch onto some steers. And you're plannin' on havin' two steers on your own six acres like you say. That'll make about ten steers you'll have around here."

"How much should I clear per steer, Walter?"

"I'll tell you better next November-December."

"Approximately."

"Well, I could take a long-shot guess and say you should make maybe $50 a steer profit. It depends on a lot of things — how good the grass is and how much grain we feed 'em and if any of 'em dies or not and so on."

And with that food for thought to digest more fully Charles Brewster swung the station wagon into the driveway of Briarwood Farm. Looking down across the flats he could mentally see eight or ten feeders getting fat on the grass now belonging to Mygrange Development Company. He couldn't be sure whether they were Hereford or Angus or Shorthorn or possibly Holstein. But that didn't matter. He would be "in the cattle business", even if he didn't have a hundred-acre farm. And he would have Messrs. Myers and Grange subsidizing him.

4

April Fool and Red-fin Suckers

It was April the first. April Fools' Day. It was Walter's birthday.
And when Charles and Millie strolled down to the mailbox at the
road in the afternoon Charles suggested they should play an April
Fools' joke on him. After suggesting a number of things, none of
which seemed to have much punch, Charles made a suggestion.

"How about me writing a note to Walter from some fictitious lady
not too far away saying she's always admired him from a distance
but has never been introduced to him. She describes herself in
fairly glowing terms and ends the letter wanting to know if he'd be
at all interested in meeting her sometime."

Millie winced. "That sounds just a little too cruel. What if Walter
took it seriously?"

"He wouldn't. You know Walter. He thinks all women — well,
except you, maybe — are only suited to cooking, cleaning and chat-
tering."

"I protest. He knows I'm good at boiling sap into syrup. And for
raising baby chicks."

"I've already excepted you, Millie. Anyway, you're not raising
baby chicks this spring and not making syrup. We're buying a couple
of gallons any day now from Fred Stone at his grocery store in
Mapleville. Anyway, what about my idea? You don't like it?"

"It depends on how the note is worded, I suppose. And I guess
Walter would just throw it away. He wouldn't take it seriously for
a moment. So go ahead and see what happens if you like. Try and
write in a woman's handwriting, though."

"Maybe you'd better write it."

"Oh, no, Mr. Brewster. This is your joke. Besides, I think that
I . . ."

"What's the matter? See something?"

"Yes, look at the letters on the ground around the mailbox."

"That's queer, eh? Della Brown didn't do a very good delivery
job today."

"Four letters or circulars or something — in the mud down there.
And there's another one away over there near the ditch."

"This never happened before, Millie. She's always careful to shut the door of the mailbox tight, eh?"

"Well, we'd better not say anything this time."

"Yes, but I'm going to put my column in the box here tomorrow. I hope I can count on it reaching the *News* instead of ending up on the ground. I intend to mail it in every week. That'll save me driving down to the city every week."

"Through all that traffic."

"Yes, in rush hour it's bloody awful. Getting worse than when I was commuting every day. Well, if I'm going to write this little note to Walter I'd better get it written and in the box here."

"I hope you know what you're doing, Charles. If Walter takes this seriously this might start something that will take some finishing."

"Oh, I don't think Walter will take it seriously. He'll just grunt and say, 'Huh, some fool woman writin' me a damn-fool thing like that.' "

"What name are you using to sign it? And what address?"

"I'm just going to sign it 'Bunny' or some such thing. 18th Avenue."

"Good Heavens. That could mean anything."

"Sure, that's the idea. That address is two and a half miles north of us and I doubt if there's anybody with the first name of 'Bunny' on 18th Avenue. So nobody is going to get hurt."

"By the way, where are we going? We seem to be headed towards the creek."

"Yes, I want to show you something over here, Mill."

"When you start out that way I know that something is up, Charles. What is it this time?"

"I just want your opinion about something. Of course if you think it's silly I'll forget about the whole thing. But we can have a look anyway."

They strolled slowly across the wide lawn between the road and north side of the pond. The pond was filled to the brim because of the spring run-off and the overflow was pouring out through the underground tiling which led its surplus into the creek. At a number of places the earth along the side of the pond had been tunneled by muskrats that had burrowed into the bank. The earth had settled here, leaving depressions and cracks which would have to be filled in again with fresh earth. This happened every spring and caused Walter to exhaust his full vocabulary of rustic expressions and profanity against the depredations of the muskrats.

As they reached the archways of the old, twisted willows that reached out over the river like massive arms Charles stopped. Millie glanced around as if she expected to see something to connect with her husband's pronouncement a few minutes before. Then she noticed that Charles had raised his arm and was pointing to a spot about six or seven feetup in one of the willows.

"I think that's where I'll have it, right there, Millie."

"I think it would be a wonderful place for it. Right in that tree."

"Just high enough above the ground so that you feel you've sort of left the earth behind and yet not so high that it's hard to get at."

"That sounds like good reasoning. Conservative and all that."

"Yes, I think that's the spot for it, Millie."

"Oh, definitely, Charles. Indubitably. And now what in the name of the Elysian mysteries are you talking about?"

"The tree-house, of course."

"The what?"

"Tree-house. You've heard of a tree-house."

"Yes, a little shack built in a tree for kids to play house in."

"Does it have to be little kids?"

"No, it can be big kids, Charles. Five-feet-eight, red hair, fifty years old, ad infinitum."

"Now I'm having my leg pulled. But I got the idea after finding out that I'd sold my column. I think a tree-house up there in that old willow would give me the right atmosphere to turn out that column. And write other things, too, of course."

"You're really serious."

"Of course I am. This is a good spot for it. Walter's place is out of sight behind those spruce trees and the cedars between here and the road shut me off from the traffic."

"Just how big had you thought of making this tree-house, Charles?"

"Well, it would have to be the size that would fit in the space inside those four branches that spread out from the roots. The tree-house would be nailed to each of those branches at the four corners. In other words the house could be seven feet square approximately."

"And you'd have a ladder leading up to the door."

"Well, stairs, I guess. About six steps up from the ground to the door at the back. Then there'd be a picture window at the front, looking out over the creek and the flats and a small window on each of the other two sides. Are you with me, Mill?"

"I'm breathless. But I'm just wondering, Charles. Seven feet square, you said. What is the size of the old privy we don't use any more?"

"We use it to store garden tools and the feed for the winter birds is in there. Anyway, it's only about three feet by four feet."

"You'd be a little cramped in that."

Charles immediately saw himself writing his column in the

backhouse, as he called it, and laughed at the mental picture. "Well, there's two seats in there, Mill."

"Oh, go on with you. I was only joking."

"I think the backhouse is out. Seriously, what do you think of this idea of a tree-house?"

"I can't think of anything especially wrong with it. Would you use it in the winter too?"

"Sure, string a wire over and have electric heat. And I could have a walkie-talkie between here and the house so you could buzz me if I were wanted on the phone."

"I see you trudging back and forth through the snow drifts. But if you think it will turn you into a Shakespeare or Jane Austen or even Ogden Nash I suppose you'd better have it, Charles."

"It won't cost much. Walter can build it. He claims he's a pretty good rough carpenter."

"I was just thinking, Charles, isn't it strange how we're always wanting something we haven't got as long as it's even vaguely attainable — as far as money is concerned. If it's too far out of reach of our pocketbook we start thinking up all the reasons why the people who have those things don't really need them at all and that makes us feel better."

And with that out-thrust of homely philosophy, which made Charles scratch his ear in thought, Millie led the way back towards the house. A light snow had fallen during the night but the sun had melted it and except for one or two small die-hard drifts along the north side of the barn and among the shadows of the cedars along the river bank the green was showing through the grass. The misty yellow-green haze the willows wore in their branches right through the winter was wakening and standing out like a song against the blue spring skies. On the small stoop on the south side of Walter's cottage the cold fingers of winter had peeled off the blue paint in many spots. The winds of March had pruned the trees of smaller branches and twigs, which lay scattered underneath and awaiting a cleanup. And on the side of a mound down in the pasture flats a big grandfather woodchuck was striving to find a little toothsome forage at this onset of the season's growth period. Spring was coming back to Briarwood Farm. And it was the first spring that Charles had been free to enjoy the full days of it. And he felt the mysterious osmosis of it stirring him in a way he had never been stirred before.

They were half way to the house when Millie noticed the panel truck in the driveway. She pointed it out to Charles who couldn't figure out who it was calling on them. Then he came closer and could read the name on the side, "Benny Gilmore".

"Benny Gilmore, Drover, Markdale. Hey, that's Benny Gilmore, Millie."

"Yes, so it says. Who on earth is Benny Gilmore?"

"I met him when we were showing our bull at Markdale and got talking to him about fishing and he wanted to know if I'd like to go sucker fishing sometime when the red-fin suckers were swimming upstream in the creek to spawn. I thought he told me it was the middle or end of April."

"Hi ya, Mr. Brewster, Mrs. Brewster. I tried to get you on the phone and then I took a chance and drove over. You in the mood to go sucker fishing today?"

"Why, sure, Benny. Isn't it early in the season?"

"Yeah, maybe too early but we'll find out. I hear they're running so we might get a few of the early ones anyway. All right, Mrs. Brewster?"

"You mean if he goes sucker fishing? Why, of course. Glad to get rid of him. Don't let him get caught on a hook, though."

"Oh, we don't use hooks. We catch them in a net and then throw them into a grain sack to bring home."

"Don't make a mistake and throw Charles in. He would make quite a sackful."

They laughed and Charles went into the house to change into some old clothes and his hip waders. Then they climbed into the truck and went to pick up two other young men who were going along to help haul in the net.

An hour later Charles stood on the banks of the Rouge River guzzling a bottle of beer as a prelude to the sucker drive. Benny explained that a case of beer was a "must" on a sucker drive and although Charles wasn't that fond of beer he went along with the idea. It was followed by a second bottle. Then, when the four of them had drained the last bit of foam from the bottles Benny gave the order to start the drive.

Arrayed in rubber boots or waders, grain bags to carry the fish and a home-made net belonging to Benny Gilmore they walked along the bank downstream from where they had parked the pickup truck. This was done for a purpose. Since they were going to drive the fish upstream they would be coming back towards the truck as they followed the fish. This meant that when they netted the fish and transferred them to the grain bags they would have a shorter distance to carry the fish to the truck. Past the steep shale cliffs they scrambled and past sandbars and debris carried down by the spring flood.

Benny Gilmore led the procession to that part of the stream where it was shallow across about thirty feet of the width but dropped off to a depth of three or four feet in a channel that had been gouged out beside it by the fast flow of the water. Here Benny Gilmore waded out with his net until the water threatened to flow over the top of his waders. Charles and the two boys, sons of a man named Jamieson from Markdale, took up positions about 150 feet downstream from Gilmore. Then Benny gave last-minute instructions.

"Now, your main job is to beat the water with those sticks you've got and to heave rocks into it and jump around and splash as much as you can. You're well spread out so you can cover quite an area. I stand here with this net. And the thing is for you guys to scare hell out of them as they go upstream. That way they'll have to keep on goin' upstream towards my net. Okay, let's go."

For the next few minutes Charles and the Jamieson boys shouted, banged the surface of the water with sticks, jumped up and down and heaved rocks. A passing onlooker would have decided that they were all possessed of the devil. In the meantime Benny Gilmore held his net fast in the channel of deeper water through which the fish had to pass. Finally he stumbled towards the shore, dragging the fish with him in the net. Reaching the shore and with the others gathered around he dumped the net. Out tumbled the suckers until they became a squirming, wriggling scene on the shale rocks.

"How many you got, Mr. Gilmore, you think?" one of the Jamieson boys asked.

"I just got fourteen on my first count. Somewhere around there. How you like that, Mr. Brewster?"

Charles shook his head to indicate bewilderment. "Fastest way of catching fourteen fish I ever saw. Look at that big sucker, eh? That one right there."

"That's go four-five pounds. Some of the others are all the way from a pound and a half to three pounds."

"So there'd be about what," asked Charles. "Be about forty pounds of fish there?"

"Something like that, yeah. Oh, it's a little early in the season yet. But we're doing all right. Let's try upstream a bit. There's a deeper hole there — if my waders are high enough to let me move into it."

The shouting, dancing, banging the water act took place again and when the net was brought to shore it yielded 11 fish. But a second try brought in 19 suckers, most of them big ones from the deeper water. Three more nettings up nearer to where they had left the truck brought in another 16 suckers. And a last netting yielded 19 more.

After the last slippery sucker had been transferred to the sacks the four men took turns carrying the three sacks to the waiting truck about a hundred feet away. Much grunting and a little cussing accompanied this operation as the fish were still squirming inside the sacks and made them hard to hang onto. But finally the job was done. Then the fishermen sat down on the grass along the shore and proceeded to toast their achievement by downing two more bottles of beer each. It was warm by this time and Charles knew that warm beer wasn't a favorite of his stomach but he felt like being a good fellow with Benny and the Jamieson boys. When the empty bottles were replaced in the carton they climbed into the truck and started back.

"The only trouble with all these damn suckers is that somebody has to fillet them," observed Benny as they turned off the rough river road onto the hardtop. "You good at filletin' suckers, Mr. Brewster?"

"Oh, I've filleted bass and pike and pickerel so I guess I can fillet a sucker," replied Charles. "There's something else I'm worrying about and that is eating all these suckers."

"Suckers isn't bad eatin' early in the season like this. The meat is firm now but gets soft a little later. How many suckers you want, Mr. Brewster?"

"Oh, a couple will be enough, Benny."

His comment was answered by laughter from the other three. Then, the youngest of the Jamiesons, who so far had hardly spoken a word, said, "What the hell do we do with the other 70 suckers or whatever it is? Eh? What do we do?"

"You better take a dozen anyway, Charles. You can put 'em in the freezer. Why, your wife is goin' to be smilin' all over her face when you walk in with a dozen of these big suckers."

However, when Charles walked in with his dozen big red-fin suckers half an hour later Millie wasn't there. Then he looked out and he saw her little car was missing. So he donned one of his wife's older aprons and repaired himself to a spot near the privy where he sat on a box and cleaned the suckers on the end of a stump. He was just scraping out the bladder of the fifth sucker when Millie drove in and shortly after found her way over to where he was sitting. Immediately she started laughing.

"Charles, you look like a fish — and I suppose it has to be a sucker."

"Woman, that's the first time I've ever been called a sucker." And with that Charles threw the broken bladder in her direction.

"I mean you have fish scales all over your face. Never mind, they'll wash off. You mean you caught all these?"

"Yeah, round dozen. All the way from two pounds to five pounds."

"Oh, dear. That's a lot of fish. I hope there's room in the freezer."

"Compared to a nice sweet pickerel there isn't much flavour to suckers but maybe you can find a way to doctor them up."

"Yes, I can. I'll toss them in a batter of eggs, milk and flour and a bit of baking powder and then fry them in butter. I did that with those two suckers somebody gave us once."

"Well, get some space ready in the freezer. Where've you been?"

"Oh, yes. I'd almost forgotten. I've just come back from the Watts next door. And guess what?"

"Oh, God knows. Maybe she's had a two-headed baby suddenly."

"Oh, now, now. Look here."

"What's that?"

"A letter. Addressed to me. It was mailed a week ago from the city. From the department store. A refund for that sweater I sent back."

"Where'd the Watts get it?"

"In the ditch between our place and their gate — about a hundred yards or so east of our mailbox."

"Damn that mailwoman anyway. What the hell is going on around here?"

"There's something wrong, that's for sure. But how could it get out of her car and in the ditch?"

"Well, she dropped it when she was trying to stuff it into our mailbox, I s'pose, and the west wind blew it along to where she found it."

"I suppose. But what about those letters we found scattered all over the ground around the box?"

"I dunno. You better phone her up and ask her if she's in love."

"At her age?"

"Love knoweth no age. Ask her if she's goin' to invite us to her shotgun wedding."

Millie merely snorted and went into the house. And that left Charles Brewster sawing the head off another sucker.

5

The Brewsters Buy a Fifty-cent Dog

The season of spring was early that year in the Briarwood Farm area. Two or three fairly heavy rains during the first ten days of the month washed away much of the grimy reminders of winter, started the grass growing and turned the winter wheat which had been sown on neighbouring farms into an astonishing green no artist could hope to copy. In the barnyard cocoon sheltered by the three barns where Charles Brewster had spent an hour or so after lunch on many sunny days earlier it was now too hot for a siesta. One day he took a thermometer out to the spot where he had so often sat on a bale of straw and found it was 105 degrees Fahrenheit, when it was only about 40 degrees up near the house in the shade. But he often took a walk down through the flats, across the creek where the water was now sufficiently low following the earlier spring flooding to enable him to jump from one stone to another and get to the opposite bank. Then he followed a path worn by the cattle up the steep slope on the far side and along the top of the ridge until he came out at the sideroad and thus back to his own gate. Sometimes Millie came with him. Other times he walked alone.

It was on one of these solitary walks that he heard a dog barking in the distance. He paused, listening for a moment, and then a thoughtful expression came over his face which finally found a muttering vocal expression. "Should have a dog. Why haven't we got a dog, eh? No reason why not." The more he thought about it the more he realized that now, with spare time at Briarwood, the farm was incomplete without a dog. Propelled by this thought he took a short cut back to the house by turning himself into a toboggan and sliding down the side of the slope along the creek, leaping somewhat in the manner of a rather large freckle-faced frog across the stones in the creek and then walking on to the wooden home-made gate at the corner of the sheep-barn.

He found Millie in the sunroom, surrounded by a number of oversize books. As he paused to refuel his lungs after the rather fast trip back from the creek his wife held up the book she was looking at and read the title: "How to Refurbish Your Old Furniture."

Charles was anxious to spill the idea he had, which was almost over-flowing by this time, but he took time to nod his head and look at the coloured photograph of the old corner cupboard on the cover. Then he stretched out in a nearby chair and spread out his rather shortish legs.

"Millie, we have to buy a dog."

"Good heavens. Do we? Who's insisting? I mean is there a new by-law in the township now?"

"I've just been out for my walk and I decided I should have had a dog with me."

"We didn't have much luck with Sport, the Border Collie that kept making the cattle and sheep run backwards. And he cost us $35 because he was trained for whistle signals."

"We don't need a work-dog now. Any kind, although I think I'd like another Border Collie. You don't seem to be very enthusiastic."

"Yes, I am. I agree with you. We should have one. And I know where we can get one for a lot less than $35 too. At the Saturday afternoon livestock sale in Markdale. I think they call it the Mark-dale Livestock Arena."

"Yes, that's right. They sell everything there according to Geordie Watts. It's strange we've never been to one of those sales. They sell cattle, sheep, hogs, furniture, rabbits, pet mice, second-hand cars, tools — and dogs, of course. They might have a Border Collie in this Saturday's sale. They're a popular farm dog so we'll drive up and have a look."

As the Brewsters drove in at the entrance to the Markdale Livestock Arena the following Saturday they were amazed to find the huge parking lot practically filled with cars. Charles declared there must be five hundred at least.

He finally found a space in a far corner that he exaggeratingly suggested must be three miles from the entrance to the building — a metal-covered structure about two hundred feet long by about half that width. The Brewsters crowded past a dozen or so men and women standing just inside the entrance and found themselves confronted by a dizzy slope of rough wooden seats that went up and back from the auctioneer's stand until they disappeared at some vague place in the upper distance.

Charles noted that every seat seemed to be filled and gave the effect of a vast crowd of men, women and children ready to slide to-wards him at the press of a button. He looked at Millie and shrugged as if to admit that they would have to stand up. Then Millie started looking around her and saw a narrow space between two men. Apparently she was wearing an extremely beseeching look because the two men shifted apart a few inches and indicated that if she dared squeezing in between them she was welcome. She did try and soon discovered that the two men were very fat and that she was literally pushing aside two walls of fat to create a space. Even at that she found herself perched on the outer six inches of rough board seating. Charles thanked the men and took up a position with a standing group of men a few feet away.

As the auctioneer started the bidding on a forlorn-looking Holstein heifer guaranteed to be carrying her first calf Charles ambled over to a young man at the corner of the ring and chatted briefly. Millie didn't know what was going on but found out later that he had asked the young man if there was going to be a Border Collie sold in that particular sale. Yes, there was. Well, would there be any chance of seeing to it that it was offered early in the sale because he and his wife had to go to a wedding in about an hour. The young man would see but he didn't think there was much chance. But he would talk to the two assistants who were bringing in the various livestock and articles to be sold and do what he could.

The result of all this was that about twenty minutes later a Border Collie made his appearance in the ring. The auctioneer took the leash and tried leading him around the ring to show him off. But the dog refused to be led. He cowered at the feet of the auctioneer and looked up at him imploringly. There were many giggles from the crowd and the auctioneer started grinning. To add to the somewhat melodramatic scene the dog started slavering. The spittle started drooling on the plank floor and the auctioneer became anxious to get the sale over with.

"All right, who'll give me a start on this Border Collie dog? . . . Who'll give me a start? . . . Do I hear a bid?" There was deadening silence. "Here's a work dog that every farm can do with. No registration papers. Just an honest-to-goodness work dog. Who'll start the bidding? . . . Who'll start the bidding?" Nothing but silence. "Any kind of a bid!" . . . A man from somewhere in the tiers of seats yelled out "Ten cents!" And at that the crowd laughed. But the auctioneer picked up the bid fast. "All right, ten cents. Now who'll make it a quarter? Who'll make it a quarter? For a real Border Collie dog. Looks to be eight-nine months old. Plenty of time to train him for a real sheep dog." Somebody near the ring bid a quarter and Charles recognized Millie's voice. "Good God," he muttered, and gave her what he hoped was a dirty look. She wasn't even looking in his direction so it was wasted. She was looking at the dog and her expression was one of pity. A few minutes later someone bid thirty cents and that created another laugh. But the auctioneer persisted.

"All right, we're standing at thirty cents. Who'll give me thirty-five? Who'll bid thirty-five? Thirty-five-five-five-five, five, who'll give thirty-five? Who'll make it thirty-five?"

"Fifty cents!"

It was Millie's voice again and Charles sidled over to where she was sitting. He bent over to speak to her but she waved him away.

"All right, now I'm bid fifty cents . . . Who'll make it an even dollar now? Do I hear a dollar? And that's cheap enough for a good Border Collie work dog. Who'll give me a dollar . . . dollar, dollar dollar, dollar, dollar? All right, who'll give me seventy-five? . . . seventy-five cents . . . seventy-five? . . . are you all through . . . are you leaving it at fifty cents? Do I hear that seventy-five? . . . first and last call . . . SOLD! For fifty cents. Your name, madam?"

"Millie Brewster!"

Charles saw the clerk writing down the name and realized that whether he liked it or not he had to go forward and take the dog off the auctioneer's platform. This he did, to the accompaniment of giggles until the auctioneer's voice covered up the background noise as he started listing the merits of a Holstein calf. He lifted the dog down from the platform, almost let it slip away from him as it struggled feebly in his arms and then made for the entrance where he paid the assistant clerk for it. Outside he made for the car without even looking to see if Millie was trailing him.

"What the hell we buyin' a sick mutt like this for? More'n I can see. Look at him." He saw Millie coming up beside him. "Look at him. He's sick. Drooling all over my coat. This your idea of a dog?"

"I just had to, Charles. I got feeling sorry for him."

"Right now I'm feeling sorry for me, not the dog."

Then they noticed a man coming up behind them. Sensing that he wanted to speak to them they stopped. He was quite an old man and he was out of breath when he tried to speak to them.

"Scuse, me, Mr. Brewster . . . Mrs. Brewster. I heard your name back there. I just wanted to tell you something."

The Brewsters waited, not knowing what was coming next. The man had a quiet voice and seemed a nice person.

"I just wanted to tell you about this dog."

"Is he yours?" Charles asked. "I mean, was he yours?"

"No, but I know where he came from. I'm Joe Vernon and the people that had this dog lives not too far from me. No use tellin' you their name but they're a drinkin', smokin', swearin' lot and they beat this pup pretty bad and I've seen their kids throwin' turnips at it. But he comes from good stock. I figure that with the right people he should turn into quite a dog. I just wanted to let you know. I hope you don't mind me tellin' you."

"Of course we don't," said Millie. "I'm glad you did, Mr. Vernon. Thanks ever so much."

"That's okay. Well, pleased to've met you, folks."

When he had gone Millie and Charles stood looking at each

other silently. Millie smiled. Charles looked down at the dog. The dog looked up at him. Its big beautiful brown eyes did the rest.

"Okay, boy. You win. Let's go home and start repairs on you."

And with that he pulled a newly folded handkerchief out of his breast pocket, wiped the froth from the dog's mouth and patted it.

The Brewsters had a dog.

6

Furniture in the Ditch— Starlings in the Mail-box

The next afternoon Millie was studying a book on restoration and finishing on old furniture as she sat in the living room when Charles came out of the sunroom, his sparse red hair sticking every which-way.

"Well, I think I'd better get out this week for two or three days and look for a column or two. Take a little trip. Want to come along?"

"Oh, dear. Maybe you should just go alone on this trip, Charles. I might get in your way."

"No, of course not. For this first one I'll drive up around Lake Huron, I think. I remember hearing about some odd things up there —when we visited the people in that cottage on Tamarack Island you know?"

"Yes, I remember. Well, that's fine. By the way, have a look at your new pup there in the cardboard carton I fixed up for him."

"He's beginning to look a little less scared to death already. Eh, pooch? Eh? You starting to make friends? Eh, pooch?"

"We can't keep calling him pooch and pup and things like that. What do you want to name him?"

"Maybe we should name him 'Fifty'—after the fifty cents that bought him."

"That would be a terrible thing to do. And he heard you. He's turned his head away from you. I've thought of a name I like. When I was very little my parents had a dog named 'Laddie'. I always rather liked it."

"Okay, call him 'Laddie'. Brother by proxy of 'Lassie'. Sure, nice warm name. How do you like that, eh, boy?"

"I guess he likes it. He's trying hard to wag his tail but he's still afraid of us. Oh, here comes Walter up from the mailbox."

"By the way, we've never heard a word from Walter about that letter I wrote and signed 'Bunny' on 18th Avenue."

"That was a silly April Fools' joke, Charles. Obviously Walter took no notice of it so he isn't saying anything about it."

"Yeah, I guess that misfired." There was a discreet knock at the door. Walter was very polite about knocking except when he was excited about something. Charles opened the door and Walter appeared carrying a letter.

"For you, Mr. Brewster. And it was over by the ditch."

"Not again. Will you sit down, Walter?"

"What I got to say only needs standin'. I got a letter, too. Last week."

"From your sister? She writes about every two weeks, you've told me."

"Nah, not from my sister. I wasn't goin' to tell you but I figure I might as well. I dunno who it's from. Some woman named 'Bunny'."

"Bunny? You don't know anyone by that name?"

"No, it says she's on 18th Avenue but that's all. No name but 'Bunny'."

"That's queer, eh?"

"Crazy letter. Damn fool letter. Says she's often heard about me and how she'd like to meet me sometime. Now what woman'd be fool enough to write to an old fool like me about things like that?"

"You're not that old, Walter."

"Well, anyway, I ain't fallin' for any woman. I had a woman tryin' to git me once and that was enough. The things a woman'll do to git a man is awful, Mr. Brewster."

"Oh, it depends on the woman, Walter. You're sure you don't know of any woman on 18th Avenue with the first name of 'Bunny'?"

"Nah, course I don't. Maybe there's a rabbit up there named 'Bunny' that's writin' me letters, eh?" Walter grinned self-consciously at his own joke.

"She might be very nice, Walter, you never know."

"No sir. Ain't no woman around here landin' Walter Purdy in a bear trap. I seen too many bear traps go off and catch a man. And once a man is caught he ain't no use to nobody from then on."

"Millie, what kind of a trap did you use to catch me?" Charles asked laughingly.

Millie smiled but felt the incident had gone far enough and should be dismissed. "Walter, if I were you I'd forget all about it. Maybe it's just a joke."

"Yeah, guess you're right, Mrs. Brewster. Just some damn-fool woman."

"By the way, Walter, just to change the subject," said Millie, "We're naming the dog 'Laddie'."

"Laddie, eh? Well, for all the good he's goin' to be he might as well be named 'Nothin'."

"But he's never had a chance. He's been beaten and had turnips thrown at him and after all he's only a pup yet."

"He'll never be over that slinkin' around like he does. Never be any good."

"I'll bet he will. Want to bet?"

"I ain't a bettin' man but I'll bet you a plug of chewin' tobacco."

"I'm not a chewin' woman but I'll bet you anyway. All he needs is loving care for a few weeks."

"I guess that's what 'Bunny' figures I need, eh?"

This sparked a spontaneous burst of laughter and brought the conversation to an acceptable end. After Walter had gone Charles opened his letter. It was from Larry Dinsmore, managing editor of the *News*.

"Dear Mr. Brewster, I wonder if you could scare up a good glossy pic of yourself for use with the title of your column. I suggest that instead of just a head shot or head and shoulders that it might be a pic of you leaning over a rail fence or walking with your dog or something of that nature. We are planning to start using the column in the Saturday paper starting a week from this Saturday so would like to get the print before then. It might be better if you send three or four from which we can choose. Yours respectfully, Larry Dinsmore, Managing Editor."

"Charles, I've often told you you should have a good studio picture taken."

"I know, Millie. But the *News* doesn't want a studio shot. They want me leaning over the rail fence looking like a country squire."

"How about that picture taken of you in knee breeches when you were about ten or twelve. That wouldn't do, you think?"

"You are now pulling my leg. Well, I have a good camera — that 35 millimetre I bought a couple of years ago. It isn't a Hasselblad but it has a 1.8 lens and with a shutter speed of up to 1/1000 of a second. Maybe if I pre-set it you could take a bunch of shots. One of them should turn out all right. And I have a black-and-white film in it and that's what Larry wants for newsprint."

"The sun's out right now. We'd better get this over with."

"I have to get dressed up first. Maybe my Norfolk jacket and plaid shirt and that Alpine sports hat I used to wear just to show off but don't any more. Yeah, let's try a few shots over against the rail fence down by the pigpen."

Half an hour later found Charles leaning over the rail fence, resplendent in what he had come to call his country squire outfit.

When he had first come to the farm he had taken it seriously. He felt good in it, especially when one of the Brewsters' friends from the city came out for a visit. He seldom wore it any more but felt it might be suitable for a picture.

Millie stood on the other side of the fence a few feet away, the camera set for the right distance and with the right light opening.

"Charles, please don't look quite so . . . so angelic, I guess you'd call it. You have your eyes looking up with the most soulful expression."

"They're the only eyes I've got. What do I do?"

"Look over towards the east — towards the orchard — away from the camera. That's it." Millie pressed the shutter. "There, I think that's a good one."

"How about a couple of shots down by the road, showing the 'Briarwood Farm' sign in the background? Eh, Mill? What do you think?"

"I think so, Charles. You could hold 'Laddie' in your arms, if you like."

"Too small. Wouldn't show up. It'd scare the pants off him anyway. But I could get one of Geordie Watts' cows. I could even be riding it, or milking it."

"Come on, let's go, I have to get back to my self-help course on restoring old furniture."

"You can start on that old dry sink we bought at a sale years ago."

"Yes, then I want to start going around to auctions. The sales will be starting anytime now. You never know. I might end up becoming an antique dealer."

"Well, there's our big barn over there going to waste — 76 feet by 36 feet. That'll hold a lot of antiques."

"I'll see how I get along. I think I might like doing something like that. After all, if you're going to spend all your spare time in your tree house I'd better get myself a little hobby, too."

When Millie had taken some pictures showing Charles and the "Briarwood Farm" sign they walked west along the sideroad to the little cement bridge that had been built to take the place of the wooden bridge that had been swept away by Hurricane Hazel. It was while they were looking down into the mirror of water that Millie pointed towards the ditch at the right.

"Charles, did we leave our chesterfield at home today? Or is that it over there?"

Charles followed Millie's finger. "Not ours, Millie. But I wish I knew whose it was. We get this every spring. Damn garbage and useless furniture dumped along the sideroad here." By this time Charles was half-way to the chesterfield. "I'd like just once to get a clue to the stinkers who do this."

"Maybe there's a letter or address that might be a help. Let's have a look."

A search didn't uncover a clue to identification but it did provoke a comment from Charles. "You know, I could conduct quite a survey on the eating habits of Canadians just by going through this pile of empty soup and vegetable and fruit cans."

"Now what good would that do you?"

"Make a human interest article for the weekend section of one of the papers. I could even do a limerick about this."

"Oh, you used your limericks on poor Horace Greene."

"Listen to this for extemporizing:

> There was once a polluter named Fitch
> Who dumped garbage into a ditch;
> But one day, in a huff,
> When he tripped on the stuff,
> It was Fitch who went into the ditch."

Millie laughed obligingly. "Quite good, Charles, for a man who is out of practice."

"Maybe I should write a book of limericks. I might be a second Edward Lear. He wrote his 'Book of Nonsense' about a hundred years ago and he's still better known for that than he is for his serious writing and art work and all that. You know that one: 'The Owl and the Pussy-Cat went to sea / In a beautiful pea-green boat, / They took some honey and plenty of money, / Wrapped up in a five-pound note.' Everybody's heard that. And his nonsense limericks are well known. What about, 'There was a young lady whose chin / Resembled the point of a pin; / So she had it made sharp, / And purchased a harp, / And played several tunes with her chin'."

"Charles, this is quite a discourse you're delivering and all because we find a lot of garbage in the ditch."

"Millie, out of garbage may be born a great idea. How about me writing a book of limericks — Canadian limericks, using Canadian situations and problems and well known Canadian people."

"Those well known Canadian people might sue you for slander or libel. How would you like that?"

"I guess I'd have to watch that, eh? Well, there's one thing sure. By looking at the labels on these empty tins you can tell what brand of soup and vegetables and so on is the most popular. Maybe I could sell the idea to the manufacturers of the leading brand. I can think of a heading for a good half-page ad, too. 'Want Proof that Our Soup is the Leader Everywhere? Just Check your Nearest Ditch!' "

"Charles, you're becoming silly. I'm more interested in trying to understand what kind of people would dump their garbage and old furniture and Heaven knows what into a ditch in front of people's homes. If these are city people they have a garbage pickup the same as we have once a week out here. Why on earth would they want to bring it all the way out from the city?"

"They might be local people who don't want to afford 75 cents a week to have their garbage picked up."

"But I don't understand such people. They have no sense of public decency."

"Go on, say it, Millie. They're despicable, contemptible, dishonest, fraudulent, disgraceful, scurvy, scabby excuses for humanity who don't give a tinker's damn how they mess up other people's lives. But before we can do a thing about it we have to prove who did it. And that isn't easy. Come on, let's walk back — unless you think we can use that old chesterfield."

"What about this tree-house you're going to build? Could you use it there?"

"Too big. Maybe I'll just sling a hammock for when I want a nap over there."

As they walked back along the sideroad and approached their gate they saw a car approaching and recognized it as belonging to Della Brown, the lady who delivered the rural mail. Charles saw his opportunity right away.

"We're going to find out right now what's happening to all this mail. I'll stop her and we'll get to the bottom of this."

"Now don't be nasty. Maybe there's a reason for it, Charles."

"I won't be nasty. In fact I'll be funny." And with that Charles held up his hand, the car stopped and Della Brown rolled down her window.

"Morning, Della."

"Morning, Mr. Brewster, Millie. I'm just headed back home after finishing my route."

"I've just decided we're going to have to get a great big mailbox, Della."

"What the heck's wrong with the one you've got now? You expecting to get a ton of mail a day from now on?"

"No, but the mail I get now seems to be falling down on the ground. Either that or you're putting wings on the letters."

"A fat lot of time I've got to be putting wings on letters. So what the heck are you getting at?"

Millie thought it was time she took over in case Charles started getting a little ratty. "Della, we've found quite a few letters on the ground near the mailbox lately — even over in the ditch."

"Oh, that!" Della started to laugh and her over-ample quantity of bosom responded so intensely that Charles became a little embarrassed. "Don't you folks know about that yet and you been out here all these years?"

"Know about what, Della?" asked Millie.

"The starlings, Millie."

"What starlings?"

"Haven't you ever had starlings nest in your mailbox?"

"I don't think so. Oh, Charles, there were a few times we found some twigs and such things in the mailbox. Then you tightened the door on it."

"You mean they build a nest in the mailbox, Della?"

"Course they do. But they first of all usually take out all the letters — and sometimes they chew up the letters to get litter to build the nest with. But usually they just haul out the letters to get rid of them and then start carrying stuff to build the nest with."

"Well, I'll be damn-darned." Charles scratched his head. "And we've been blaming you, Della."

"Oh, I get blamed all the time — by folks that don't know. You know what else gets people mad at me? When I see a nest in a mailbox I haul it out and destroy it before the starlings have a chance to lay any eggs in it. And then I get all these nature-lovers givin' me blue blazes for bein' cruel to the birds. I can't bloody-well win."

The Brewsters laughed. When Della Brown got excited she didn't hesitate to let her language get a little crude at times. "This happens every darned spring when the birds are nesting. And I dunno why some of the other birds don't use the mailboxes too but them starlings know a good thing when they see it and they get the idea that you've put up a birdhouse for them. But the civil service regulations don't see it that way. A mailbox is a mailbox and not a birdhouse."

Millie was curious. "How do they get the mailbox open if we close it tightly?"

"They just got sense enough to get the end of their bill in that tiny crack that's left when you close it — that little crack at the bottom, you know — and they just keep pryin' on it until they can squeeze through."

Charles asked if there wasn't some way to get the best of the starlings.

"Yeah, the best thing I've heard of is to get a string and tie it to a pretty heavy weight. Then you tie the weight fast to the bottom of the mailbox and let it hang down. Unless you get a heck of a strong starling that should do it."

The Brewsters apologized for being annoyed at her and watched Della drive away, her torso still shaking with laughter. Then Charles made his way to the tack-room at the back of the horse-barn. He emerged a few minutes later with some baling twine and a heavy horseshoe which he proceeded to tie fast to the bottom of the mailbox and dangle below it. Then he stood back, looked at it and nodded his head sagely as if he had thought of the idea himself.

7

The Church that Gamblers Built

At seven o'clock the next morning Charles Brewster's station-wagon was seen to back out of the drive-shed, ease slowly down the driveway of Briarwood Farm to the arm-fluttering "good-byes" of Charles' wife and turn west along the sideroad. It was later seen travelling north on Highway 400, west along Highway 69, north along Highway 10 to Owen Sound and thence along Highway 6 to the old town of Wiarton on the shore of Georgian Bay. Here the occupant entered Allens' Place and had a cup of excellent coffee for which the restaurant is noted. The station-wagon then proceeded north on Highway 6, which runs up the spine of the Bruce Peninsula, for another thirty miles and then turned east along a sideroad to the hamlet of Cape Chin.

Charles Brewster stopped uncertainly beside a white clapboard house, extricated himself from the bulge of the steering wheel and manoeuvred out to the roadside. Here he yawned, stretched himself, looked up and down the dusty road, scratched his red hair, rubbed something out of his blue eyes and then walked over and knocked at the door. It wasn't until the second knock that a fragile and bent old lady opened the door cautiously. Charles made a small bow and assumed the most courteous expression of which he was capable.

"I hope you don't mind me bothering you, Mrs. MacStay. I saw your name on the sign by your door here. But I wanted to inquire about a certain church I'm looking for."

"Oh, our 'Stone Church in the Wildwood' as a lot of people call it. It's bound to be that one."

The wrinkled old face crinkled into an engaging smile as she talked with what remained of an inherited Scottish accent. "It's half a mile up the road. Easy to find."

"Oh, thank you. My name is Charles Brewster and I live down near Toronto and someone told me that the church has quite a strange history."

"Yes, I guess you could say it has. You want to hear it?"

"Sure would. That's why I came all the way up here."

"Well, come on in. I was just making a cup of tea for myself and I'll make one for you. You look safe to let in. You can't tell about strangers these days."

Charles agreed and five minutes later found himself seated on the chesterfield with a cup of tea and two homemade butter tarts on the side-table near him. Mrs. MacStay perched her tiny body on the edge of a large stuffed chair and within hands' reach of a huge cream teapot wrapped in a green tea cosy with a red rooster rushing around it apparently in pursuit of a hen that never showed up.

"Well, Mr. Brewster, it all started like this," she finally said, tilting her head back and looking up at the ceiling. "Back in 1925 we needed a church around here. Parson James was the minister at Lion's Head then, not far from here, and this was one of his mission churches and we had service in the schoolhouse. He'd been minister at Lion's Head for . . . oh, dear me . . . since 1911, I think and he was a grand man . . . oh, he was a grand man." Mrs. MacStay paused as she recalled Parson James, took a sip of tea, which prompted Charles to take a sip of tea and reach out for a butter tart.

"Well, we all decided we wanted a church of our own and we wanted it built from the dolomite limestone in the lovely hills and valleys around here. So the parson got an architect friend of his to draw up some plans and a spot was picked for the church. The owner donated the site, you see. Then we started taking up a collection and everybody gave what they could which wasn't much because nobody around here has much money — except one or two bigwigs I won't go into right now. Have some more tea, Mr. Brewster."

"Yes, thank you. You certainly remember this well, Mrs. MacStay."

"Oh, this was only back in 1925. I was a girl then. Sure I remember it. I remember how everybody pitched in to help. Farmers took time off to draw fieldstone. Other men came after their day's work to split the stone and shape it. Oh, they all pitched in. And I forgot to say that when the farmers collected the stone in the fields they hauled them to the site on a little home-made trailer that Parson James towed behind his old Ford coupe. Then came the day in 1926 when the corner-stone was laid."

"I'll bet you were right there, Mrs. MacStay."

"Oh, I was there all right — helping get a pile of food ready for the workers when they'd finished. Yes, I was sure there. Anyway, the same year, 1926, the roof was put on. Parson James jacked up his old Ford coupe and that gave the power to rotate the saw in some way, you know. You'd know about that. Anyway, the old Ford was used to saw the lumber. And then word started getting around."

"About what, Mrs. MacStay?"

"About the way everybody was pitching in to help and how we were trying to build ourselves a church on almost no money at all and all that. Well sir, Mr. Brewster . . . oh, here, have some more tea."

"No, I'm fine, thanks."

"I can get some more butter tarts or some cookies."

"No, I'm fine just the way I am."

"Well then . . . where was I? . . . oh, yes, word started to get around and wouldn't you know? Strangers heard about it and turned their cars in on our sideroad off Highway 6 and they saw the start of the church and they donated some money and . . . well, money started coming in from all over. Not any million dollars, mind you, just dribs and drabs but it all helped. And then it happened. It was the queerest thing."

Charles reached for another sip of tea. He decided he was hearing a pretty good story for his column.

"It was really the queerest thing that happened, Mr. Brewster. A bunch of fishermen from the city — from Toronto, you know — a bunch of these fellows with plenty of money, you know who went in together and bought a big island over here in Georgian Bay — they came up here one weekend and they heard about how we were struggling to build our little stone church. And they were mostly stockbrokers from Bay Street, I think it's called. So when they went back you know what they did? They put on a big poker game one night down there in the city and all the money that was made from that poker game they put into the building of our church."

Mr. Brewster shook his head. He was touched. He didn't say a word to break the spell.

"Well, that started something, Mr. Brewster, believe me. Right on the heels of that a glass company in the city offered to glaze all the windows in the church free of charge — when we got to the point where the windows could be put in, I mean. And a wealthy widow in the city offered to install oak pews. And it went on and on like that."

"When was the church actually finished, Mrs. MacStay?"

"Well, I told you it was started in 1925. And in 1928 it was all finished. And it was dedicated by the bishop of the diocese of Huron. And I can sure remember the day. I can still see that sun pouring in through those cathedral glass windows — gothic windows, I think they call them. It was streaming in and over the heads of the congregation and . . . well, it was really a beautiful day, Mr. Brewster. Say, would you like to see the church?"

"Yes, I certainly would, Mrs. MacStay. After hearing that wonderful story I couldn't go away without seeing it."

"Well, I'll get on my coat. It's still coolish yet. Say, would you like another butter tart before you go?"

"No thanks, Mrs. MacStay. You've been very hospitable. Very kind of you."

A few minutes later Charles stood with Mrs. MacStay beside him a hundred feet or so from The Stone Church in the Wildwood. It was set in a clearing which would be covered with harebells later on, according to Mrs. MacStay. The mortar work was done somewhat amateurishly but what made it distinctive was the stone bell-tower. It was an attempt at a Norman tower and gave the whole structure a "fortified" appearance — completely alien to the rather attractive lancet windows. The sun was shining upon the cathedral glass and seemed to be blessing the efforts of all those who had contributed to it.

"I imagine the church is filled every Sunday, Mrs. MacStay," Charles said. But unknowingly he had asked the wrong question. A pained look came over the old lady's face and she shook her head.

"No, I'm afraid it isn't. I'm afraid it isn't. It isn't being used now. Except sometimes for Sunday School. Just in this last generation or so there's been faster transportation and better roads and a decline in the farm population around here. People go farther afield, you know. It's too bad, isn't it? We old-timers feel very sad about it. But at least you can look at it and see the work that went into it by poor people who couldn't afford it, really — all the work and the patience and the resourcefulness, I guess you'd call it. And the faith, Mr. Brewster. A powerful lot of faith went into that church."

After Charles had driven Mrs. MacStay to her house he thanked her and then drove back to the church. He walked around it and then stood back looking at it. And he felt a great sensation of awe and respect and a strange tingling feeling more acute than he could remember ever having had before. Then he climbed into his station-wagon and drove away, with a last backward look at The Little Stone Church in the Wildwood.

Charles realized it was time for lunch and he drove on into Lion's Head. After driving down to look at the Georgian Bay waterfront harbour and at nature's carving in the side of the high rock cliffs in the shape of a lion's head he drove back up to the main street and went into a restaurant. It was noon hour but only a few diners were there so he picked a small table where he could watch the traffic going by. It was a typical small-town main street, with the passers-by in workaday functional attire and the vehicles mostly confined to trucks and farmers' cars. Here he ate a western sandwich and a glass of milk. He was finishing off with a coffee when the man at the next table turned sideways in his chair and spoke to him.

"Been here before?"

"No. No, I haven't," answered Charles.

"Didn't think so. We know all the strangers. Not many strangers around this time of year. In summer the cottages down there gets plugged up with city folks but not many around right now."

"I was just over at Cape Chin looking at the stone church there," said Charles, for want of a better answer.

"Oh yeah. Yeah, I can tell you the history of the church. Got quite a history."

"Yes, I was talking to a Mrs. MacStay there."

"Oh, Moira, yeah. You interested in old churches?"

"No, not especially. I'm going to write a column about it for a Toronto daily paper."

"Oh, you're a writer."

"Yes, you might say so."

"Lots of stories around the Bruce here. Lots of tall stories, too. You interested in tall stories?"

"Yes, I think so, sure."

"Wait'll I get myself another cup of coffee from the counter. If I wait for Nellie it'll be Christmas mornin' when I get it."

Charles watched his roly-poly figure roll over to the service counter — overalls, roll-neck sweater and greasy mechanic's cap. Probably a worker at the docks. He just might have a good yarn or two. In a moment he was back and sat down at Charles' table. Charles offered him a cigar, which he fumbled for a moment, smelled and smacked his lips.

"That's a beaut, eh?" Then, after Charles had held a match while he lit it, he sniffed the smoke flavour. "Yeah, that's no five-center, that's for sure." He sniffed it again. "My name's Arnie Bagshaw. I work in the fish plant along here when I'm workin'. Not much fish business these days but it's comin' back a bit."

"My name's Charles Brewster. I've got a farm down near Toronto — at Mapleville."

"You don't look like a farmer, sir."

"Well, I've sold most of the land. I'm doing a little writing now. And you don't have to call me 'sir'."

"That's good. I didn't want to anyway. Well, I better tell you about Dan'l and Matt. They was two brothers lived over near Oliphant and they was builders — especially barn builders. So they was out one day shinglin' a barn over near Red Bay when a real Lake Huron pea-souper came in. The fog got so danged bad that up there on the barn roof they couldn't even see each other while they were doin' the shinglin'. But they kept on a-shinglin'. Then, after a-whiles the sun burned off the fog and you know what'd happened? Well sir, they discovered that accidentally-like while they was shinglin' they'd climbed out beyond the edge of the barn and they'd nailed three rows of shingles to the fog instead of to the barn."

Charles leaned back in his chair and laughed heartily. It was a good story with a good punch-line and he'd remember it to work into a column sometime. Arnie Bagshaw was grinning at the success of his story. It was a long time since he'd run into someone he hadn't told it to before. Then after he'd sat staring into space for a moment or two he told another story that Walter laughed at but didn't think was very good. This was followed by another long one that had very little point. It was then that Charles decided he'd better be going if he was to get back the 150 miles to Briarwood Farm that night.

"Hey, just a minute, Mr. . . . ah . . . Brewster, yeah . . . I know who can tell you two or three great yarns. Old Bertie Peppler. You know where Oliphant is on the Huron side? You know how to get there?"

"Yes, I do."

"Well, you go to the store there. There's only one store and another place where they store boats and sell gas and so on. Ask 'em there where Old Bertie lives. It's on an old loggin' road that runs through the swamp and past the sand dunes and you'd never find it unless you got good directions. You ask at the store in Oliphant. It's only a couple of miles from there."

An hour later Charles found himself driving along what Arnie Bagshaw had described as an old logging road. Before he had gone a hundred yards after turning off the gravel road he decided to go back but couldn't find a place to turn around. Then he tried backing up and the car kept slipping off the road towards the swampy ditch so he went forward again. He finally came to an open clearing on a slightly higher level of ground where stood an old shack built with galvanized metal and rough wood. He pulled off the road beside the building and stepped out. Then he noticed that a very old man was sitting in the sun on the steps of the shack. As Charles approached the man rose slowly to his feet and made a sort of salute.

"Good day, sir. You lookin' for somebody?"

"I'm Charles Brewster and I'm looking for Bertie Peppler."

"I be he — except I'm Major Peppler, too. I go by both so take your choice."

"Glad to know you, Major."

"I'm from the first war. Wife dead. Kids married. I like it here alone."

"Yes, you'd sure be alone here."

"Only way to be, Charles. That your name, yeah. Only way to be in this crazy damn-fool world. Young people goin' to hell. Married folks goin' to hell. All I got here is birds and a few coons and porkys and plenty of muskrats in the swamp over there. You want to see me especially?"

"Yes, I was told to look you up by Arnie Bagshaw in Lion's Head."

"Oh, Arnie, yeah. Well, sit down on the stoop here. What'd you want?"

"He said you knew some tall stories. I'm a writer for a Toronto newspaper and I thought I'd like to hear a couple of good stories. I might have them printed in the paper."

"Oh? Tellin' folks who told 'em to you?"

"Yes, unless you'd rather I didn't."

"Can't see why I'd ruther you didn't. I'd ruther you did. Chance to get my name in the paper. Sure, you say I told 'em to you."

"All right, Major, I'll do that. And I'll send you a copy of the paper."

"That's a deal, Charles. So you want a couple of stories. All right, I'll tell you the one about Dan'l and Matt."

"Dan'l and Matt? Did they go round shingling barns?"

"Yeah, they did. I s'pose Arnie Bagshaw told you this one then about the day they et so many wild cherries?"

"No, he didn't tell me that one."

"Well, Dan'l and Matt was brothers and they was together all the time. So this spring day they was out huntin' out of season in a boat on Spry Lake, just over here a piece. And they'd been eatin' these wild cherries because they'd run out of ammunition without killin' as much as a rabbit and they was just puttin' in time. And as he et the cherries Dan'l kept puttin' the pits in his pocket, figurin' he'd plant 'em the next spring. I don't think the danged things'd take root anyway but he was goin' to try. Well sir, he looks up and all of a sudden he sees a fine bull moose standin' on the shore."

"And he didn't have any ammunition."

"Just a minute now. Hold your horses. No, he didn't have any ammunition so after swearin' a little and lookin' at this fine bull he winks at Matt and reaches in his pocket and pulls out some of these cherry pits. So he shoves some powder into his gun and . . ."

"Just a minute, Major. This was a muzzle loader?"

"Yeah, it was a muzzle loader. Didn't I say that? Thought I did. Anyway, it was a muzzle loader and he shoves some powder into it and then stuffs in some of these cherry pits and he lets fly at this fine bull moose. But the bloody moose got away."

"Oh, dear — after all that."

"Yeah, so they went back home. And a few years passed. And this spring day they went out huntin' illegal again but they didn't have much luck. 'Well,' Dan'l says, 'this ain't our lucky day but I see a wild cherry tree over there so I'm goin' over and pick a bunch to take home.' So they walks over towards this wild cherry tree and when they got up closer to it the damn cherry tree started movin' away. And they walks after it but it keeps on movin'. Then, by cripes, they saw why the cherry tree was movin'. Because it was growin' right out of the back of a big fine bull moose."

Charles laughed and clapped the Major on the shoulder. It was a good tall story.

"You git it, Charles?"

"Yes, sure, Major. Darned good story."

"You see when he was shootin' pits years before he shot some of 'em right inside the bull moose and . . . oh, you git it, eh? That the kind of a story you want?"

"Yes, sure. That's a good one."

"You say I told you when you get it writ up, eh?"

"I sure will, Major."

"Well then, there's the one about my dad who was workin' on a sailin' schooner carryin' lumber down Lake Huron. This was back in 1903. So when he got near Thessalon my dad and another fellow they had some time off so they rowed down a river that ran into the lake there. And pretty soon they seen two moose swimmin' down the river."

"Oh, another moose story, Major. Go ahead."

"That's what I figure on doin' — goin' ahead. They seen these two moose swimmin' and dad's chum he said he wanted to climb up on one of the moose's back and cut its throat. Well, it was May and my dad told him that moose meat was no good in May but anyway he gets to climb up on this moose's back. Then he tells dad to hand him the knife. But my dad wouldn't. Why kill the moose if the meat was no good? But this fellow wrestles the knife away from my dad and manages to jab it into the moose's neck without hurting it a lot."

"And this fellow — your dad's chum — he kept on its back, eh?"

"No, he slid off and clumb back in the boat. Then, by golly, they take a look at the other moose and you know what it had in its mouth?"

"Oh, I couldn't guess, Major."

"It had a big whitefish in its mouth."

"A moose with a whitefish in its mouth?"

"Yeah, so it swam to shore, too, and they both disappeared in the bushes. Well, these two fellows had to portage for a couple of miles right about then because there was a rapids. So they carried the canoe over the portage to where they could slide it into the water again and by golly they saw a campfire goin' at that spot. So they figured there was more hunters there but when they went over close here was those two moose sittin' beside the fire. One of 'em was stokin' the fire and the other was cleanin' this big whitefish gettin' it ready to fry."

As he ended his story the Major slapped Charles on the shoulder and asked him how he was doing.

"You're doing a good job, Major. You're sure full of them."

"Yeah, I got bushels of 'em. Hey, how'd you like a little slug of moonshine?"

"No, I have to drive back home tonight — unless I decide to stay overnight at a motel around here somewhere."

"I make mine out of potatoes. I got a hell of a patch of potatoes back there in another clearin'. Nice sandy land there — and sandy land is good for potatoes."

"Well, thanks all the same. Say, I've been looking at that old corner cupboard just inside the door there. That's pretty old."

"It should be old. That was my wife's and before that it was her mother's. I brung it here with me just to hold junk like's in it now — fish hooks and sinkers and cough medicine and an old pitcher and a bedroom pot, or whatever you call it and . . . oh, my God, take a look. You can see the junk in the top part from here."

"Yes, you're sure making use of it, Major."

"Makin' use of it? It's only takin' up room. I ain't got too much room in this little shanty anyway. I been thinkin' of splittin' it up for kindlin' wood."

Even Charles, who knew little about antiques, could see that this was a genuine antique. At the moment it was painted an unsightly gray and one of the doors on the lower half was off one of its hinges. But he was sure it was the genuine thing.

"How much you want for it, Major?"

"Want for it? How much'll you take and lug it away?"

"I wouldn't do that. I know my wife could make use of it and I'd want to pay for it."

"How would two dollars set you back?"

"I'll make it ten."

"Ten bucks? For that old thing? I'd be rimmin' you, Charles. I want to get rid of it. I'll only throw it away one of these days when I stop bein' lazy long enough to do it."

"Well, I'll be glad to give you ten."

"Ten bucks'll buy me a week's grub. Take 'er away. I'll help you load it in that car of yours. You got lots of room there. Come on, let's get goin' before you change your mind, though I dunno what the blazes your wife can find to do with it. She'll give you merry hell when you show up with that damn thing in your car."

8

Strawberries, Corner Cupboards and the Red and Green Man

Next morning the mid-April sun came stealing like an early-morning thief up over the cedar grove beside the creek of Briarwood Farm and finally spilled its gold across the meadow. It lighted up the healthy face of Millie Brewster as she stood out in the little paddock near the red pig-pen and studied the new garden catalogue. And its slanting rays made Walter lift up his hand before his eyes as he climbed the split-rail fence and walked over to Millie.

"Mighty early to be findin' you out here, Mrs. Brewster."

"Oh, I'm getting up earlier every morning, Walter. And I didn't want to disturb Charles by making a lot of noise around the house."

"He was late gettin' home from that Lake Huron place, eh?"

"Yes, so he's still sleeping — or was when I came out."

"Looks like you're out here plannin' somethin'— with that there garden-plantin' catalogue you're lookin' at."

"Oh, well . . . I get this way every year at about this time or before."

"Yeah, me too — for startin' the seedin', I mean. Course we don't do any seedin' of grain now but the feelin' still comes over me startin' in April or maybe even in March."

"The farmers haven't started to seed yet, have they?"

"No, but it won't be long. I used to figure that April the 10th was the sort of average time to start seedin'. Course some years it'd be the beginnin' of May or later. And I mind one year — and I can't get folks to believe this — that I started seedin' early in March and I pulled the old seed-drill in the barn all finished the last day of March."

"My, that was early."

"Yeah, might never happen again. But we paid for it. It turned rainy and drowned out quite a bit of seed so we was no farther ahead."

"Well, I've just been doing some thinking. I know we have our regular garden over there by the orchard but I think we should put in some more berry bushes. We could do with more raspberries and strawberries, too, but I'd like some black currants. And we haven't any gooseberries. I was just looking at them in the catalogue here."

"Gooseberry jam is mighty good. My ma used to make it for us kids."

"And there's a new kind of gooseberry — at least I think it's quite new — that's supposed to be good for sauces and jellies."

"How about gooseberry wine?"

"Well, now, I hadn't thought of that. I might even make gooseberry wine. But is this soil right for gooseberries?"

"Yeah, this is all right for gooseberries, I guess. Gooseberries can do better on heavier land than red raspberries that like a lighter land. But this is kind of a medium loam here. Sure, this'd be all right."

"What about currants?"

"Well, they'll take a heavier soil. You gettin' black currants?"

"Yes, but I'd like some red and white, too — a few bushes just for fun. And I'm not sure but I think I need more than one kind for pollination purposes."

"I dunno what purposes that is but who's goin' to keep the birds from eatin' 'em?"

"Oh dear, I never thought of that. The robins and starlings get most of our cherries, I'm afraid."

"Course I could stand out here all day with a shotgun but if you was to count up what you'd pay me for my time they'd be mighty expensive berries."

"Yes, I'm afraid so but I think . . . oh, there's Charles coming out now. I didn't think he'd be up for an hour yet."

"So Mrs. Brewster, what you want me to do is work up a strip across this acre paddock for the berries. Then it'd have to be fenced off to keep out whatever stock is pasturin' here."

"Yes, that's true."

"And workin' this land up from sod will take some work. I know we kept the tractor when you had your farm sale and we kept your harrows and so on but you didn't keep a plow. We'd have to borrow a plow from Geordie Watts."

"Is it all right to plant them in the spring?"

"Currants and gooseberries are best planted in the fall, I figure, after their leaves has dropped. For blackberries or raspberries, well I figure that either the spring or fall is all right. You're not goin' to get any berries this year anyway, you know — except a piddlin' few, maybe. But they'd bear next year and about three-four years from now you'd be pickin' all you want."

"Of course we still have raspberries and strawberries from the ones we planted in the regular garden over there. But they're almost finished and anyway I'd like some of these other berry fruits. Oh, there's Charles beckoning to us from the front of the drive-shed. We'd better go over."

"You goin' into the berry-sellin' business, Mrs. Brewster?"

"No, I wouldn't say that. But a couple of places in Mapleville have said that they'll take any extra that I ever have for sale. I've never had any yet but what we need for our own use."

"Well, I'm mighty partial to black currant jam. And there's nothin' nicer than a big slice of homemade raspberry pie — unless it's another slice."

"I think that what is still nicer than either one is a good cook to make it for you."

"Yeah, now you got somethin' there." Walter grinned. "Yeah, you said a mouthful. Ma, she used to be a great cook. Yeah, she used to make some mighty fine elderberry pies, too."

"Yes, now there's one thing I've never made and there are elderberry trees on our farm, too — on what was our farm, I mean. Up in the fence row on the hill. But I've never picked any."

"Makes good wine, too, elderberry does. I knew an old fellow once that got pickled on elderberry wine. He went down to Mapleville and was walkin' along the main street by the old hotel there and he mistook some young girl of about nineteen for his wife."

"Oh, now, Walter."

"That's as true as my name ain't Peter. He goes up to her and puts his arm around her and says he's come down to the village to take her back home and stop her from runnin' away with another man."

"I think you're kidding me."

"No sir, I ain't. Oh, there was quite a little hullabaloo about that. But big Johnny Warner was the constable then and he got things all straightened out when this woman accused this fellow. But after that he was mighty careful how much elderberry wine he gulped down."

"I think he should be. Well, welcome home, Charles. I didn't even hear you come in last night." Charles was standing beside the station-wagon.

"Yes, I was pretty late. Drove back from the Bruce. And I had a very successful trip."

"You get lots of them stories you were wantin', Mr. Brewster?"

"Yes, I did very well. All I have to do now is get them written up. And I brought home something else, too. In the back of the station-wagon here." He led them around to where they could see inside.

Millie peered in. Then she walked around to the other side of the station wagon and looked again. Then she looked up at Charles and she was smiling a great wide smile. "Charles, you found one. It's an old corner cupboard."

"Sure is old. And it's supposed to be an antique according to the Major."

"I don't know who the Major is but it just has to be as old as the hills. Did you see it, Walter?"

"Yeah, I seen it. It should make some good kindlin' wood for the fireplace."

"That's exactly what the Major was thinking of using it for. But wait'll you see what it looks like when Mrs. Brewster gets it restored, Walter. She'll really bring it back to life."

Walter shook his head. "I kind of doubt that, Mr. Brewster — about bringin' it back to life. It's been too long dead for that."

That broke Millie up. She leaned against the station-wagon and laughed so hard that Charles had to reach out and steady her balance. But she recovered to say: "Walter, I'll just have to remember that. I think it's priceless."

"What the hell did I say?"

"Oh, nothing, nothing. Now, Charles, we'll have to unload it but where?"

"If you're going to bring it back from the dead you'd better have it down cellar I suppose — where you can get this old paint off or whatever you have to do."

"I suppose that's the only place for it. And near the drain at the back entrance where the water and soda solution or whatever I use can drain away."

"Okay, let's go. Come on, Walter. Get ready to lift the dead body."

A few minutes later, after considerable lifting, grunting, cussing, stepping on one another's toes, bumping against door frames and hitting of heads against the top of the low cellar door the old corner cupboard stood upright in the cellar. It was in two pieces, which made the transfer somewhat easier, but now it stood with the smaller top section sitting securely in place on the lower base. Walter stood back and looked at it, a wry smile on his long leathery face. He shook his head solemnly.

"She sure ain't much to start with, Mrs. Brewster. You got a long way to go."

"Now, Walter. No more cracks, please. I know I'm just an amateur at all this. I'm just starting. But just wait till I finish with it. It'll be a joy to the eye."

"Walter, you'll never recognize it when Millie is finished with it," said Charles, feeling he had to come to the defence of his wife.

"Uhuh. What do you figure on doin' with it, Mrs. Brewster?"

"Oh, I'll first of all get a quart of very hot water and some soda, about half a teacup full. And I'll try scrubbing it with that mixture, if I can stand the fumes. That might take off a lot of that gray paint."

"You might find some more paint underneath like my ma did once on somethin'."

"Yes, I might. We'll see. It'll likely take a lot of sandpapering and maybe I'll use a blunt chisel on it too but I don't want to scratch it when I get down to the raw wood. Let me see now. How high is it, I wonder?"

"Oh, I measured it, Millie. It's eight feet high and this bottom section is four feet wide. And the part that sits on top of it is just under three feet wide."

"With three shelves at the top of it. In the bottom there are two deep shelves and one shallow one."

"And where are we going to put this great treasure or are you going to sell it?"

"I think it would look good in the corner of the dining room. The bottom section would hold things like serviettes and bowls and so on that aren't used too often. And I think I'll take the doors off this upper part and use it to show off some of our better ironware pieces — things like that. Say, I just remembered. In all the excitement I didn't even ask you what you had to pay for it."

"Well, it came a bit expensive, I'll have to admit."

"Fifty dollars."

"Oh, no, not that much."

"Twenty-five anyway."

"No, a bit less than that."

"Fifteen."

"Ten dollars."

"Ten dollars? For both sections?"

"Well, sure. The Major was going to sell it to me for two dollars. In fact I could have taken it away for nothing, I guess. He said it took up too much room in his little shack. But I felt like a heel even giving him ten."

"I would think you should. It'll be worth a lot of money when I get it restored."

"How much you figure, Mrs. Brewster?" Walter was getting curious.

"I don't know prices very well yet, Walter. Maybe $50. Maybe $75."

Walter whistled. "That's better than growin' gooseberries for a livin'."

"It'll take a lot of work. I realize that. But we'll see. Charles, where on earth did you run into this bargain?"

"Oh, I went in to see Bertie Peppler — the Major, he calls himself. He has a little shack in the woods not far from Oliphant. Lives all by himself. A man in Lion's Head told me he had a lot of tall stories and he sure had."

"Let's hear 'em, Mr. Brewster."

"You can read them in my column, Walter. But I'll tell you what I ran into. The Major told me to drop in and talk to another man on the way back to Wiarton about a character who used to live near there. And the story he gave me about this man was sure something. Old Uncle Dal, this fellow called him."

"What was so unusual about it, Charles?"

"You may not believe it."

"Try us."

"Well, according to the man I talked to this Uncle Dal used to work on the sailboat of a prominent Toronto yachtsman years ago. But it seemed he had one problem. He could never remember which side of the yacht was port and which was starboard. He used to get them mixed up. But one day he figured out what to do. He faced the front of the yacht, the bow, and after he'd determined that starboard was to the right and port was to the left he put a red sock on his left foot and a green sock on his right foot. All he had to do then to steer properly was to look down at his socks."

"Charles, this is silly."

"I told you you wouldn't believe me but I'll finish the story anyway. When Uncle Dal retired back to the Bruce peninsula he took this queer notion with him — of wearing one red sock and the other green. And he took off from there. First he painted half his house red and the other half green. He painted the pickets on his fence alternately red and green. He painted his rowboat red and green. He painted the chairs on his verandah red and green — right up and down the middle. What's the matter, Walter?"

"This is the darndest fool thing I ever heard of. He was ready for the nut house."

"No, he wasn't. He just wanted to be different. He painted red and green stripes around the trunks of his trees. He painted his old car red and green. Then he went inside the house and painted all the furniture red and green. One half the walls, floor and ceiling was painted red and the other half was painted green. Then he started on himself. He painted one of his rubber boots red and the other one green. He painted half his hat red and the other half green. He painted his cane red and green. And of course his socks stayed red and green."

"Is that the end, Charles? What about his nose and eyes?"

"Well, I dunno, Millie, but that's quite a story, eh?"

"It sure is quite a story. And you think we're going to believe it?"

"You'd better believe it. I talked to two or three of the neighbours near where he lived and they said it was true."

"The house still there, Mr. Brewster?"

"No, it was burned down or fell down or something a few years ago. But you can still find red and green boards around in the grass."

"I'll bet he had his coffin painted red and green, too."

"I didn't think to ask about that, Walter. Maybe he did."

"Well, that's quite a yarn anyway. You're doin' all right on these trips of yours."

"Yes, I think they should make good columns. I should make a column about you restoring old furniture, Millie."

"Don't you dare — until I know how."

"Are there a lot of different theories about it?"

"Oh, I suppose you could say that. It depends on whether the wood is soft or hard, too. This corner cupboard is pine, of course, and that's the wood the early pioneers used because it was so easy to work with. They had to make rough furniture fast when they moved to a piece of land to settle down. It's what is known as country, or cottage furniture. And it was made to be painted."

"We're getting a free lesson, Walter."

"Yeah, but I might get charged so I better go along and rake the junk off the flower beds. They're dry enough to go at now."

"Before you do let's go up to my study for a few minutes. There are two or three things I'd like to talk to you about."

"You goin' to fire me? You can just as soon do that down cellar here."

"No, I didn't have that in mind, Walter. This place wouldn't be the same without you."

A few minutes later Charles and Walter were seated in what had come to be known as "the study". It was across the hall from the dining room at the front of the house and was the room that Mr. Henderson, the real estate agent, had described as the parlour. Now both the Brewsters used it. The biggest area on the two outside walls were lined with books almost to the ceiling. Along one of the inside walls was an immense storage cupboard holding scrapbooks of Charles' former work, trays of coloured slides, the slide projector and other personal items. Two couches were in a v-shaped position in the corner and two stuffed easy chairs were angled beside them. Charles dropped as if he were quite tired into the nearest chair and then confirmed it by saying he still felt the effects of driving back from the Bruce Peninsula so late the night before. Walter slid into the other chair and stretched out his long thin legs until he somewhat resembled a comfortable spider.

"All I wanted, Walter, was to check about things around the little farm here. You won't have any seeding to do this year anyway, eh?"

"No, I'm goin' to miss that. I used to like tryin' to be the first out seedin' on the hill up along the fifth. That's an early field — slopin' to the south and east like that. I was first out most years seedin' on that field."

"Well, this year I'm afraid you won't be. I understand that My-grange Development have rented the land to someone to work for them until they start building houses there."

"I hear they're puttin' twenty acres of it into sod — growin' sod to sell for people's lawns in the city. That way city people can have a lawn right away because they're too lazy to put grass seed on it themselves."

"Ah, well, that's the way they want it. Walter, what's doing right now? You're cleaning up the debris after the mess the winter made of things, eh?"

"Yeah, and cleanin' up under them weepin' willows is a son of a gun, Mr. Brewster, what with the ground covered with limbs and dead stuff and the Lord knows what."

"Yes, I know. What about the garden? Is it ready to work up yet?"

"Yeah, she'll be ready soon. I hope June and Judy haven't for-gotten how to walk down a row pullin' three sections of harrows."

"It'll give them something to do, eh?"

"Yeah, they'll be gettin' soft. But I'll be goin' over the garden with the drag harrows and I figure that's all it needs to get a seed bed. Then we can start plantin' — unless we get two feet of snow."

"Oh, I don't think so. By the way, we should be getting some pullets and cockerels pretty soon, shouldn't we?"

"Yeah, we should. You're figurin' on gettin' some month-old pullets, eh?"

"Yes, I don't want Millie to start raising day-old chicks again."

"It ain't worth it. All you want here is a few hens to lay eggs for yourselves — and for me, I guess."

"How many pullets would we need?"

"Oh, s'posin' we had about ten. They should lay six-seven eggs a day. That be enough?"

"I think so. I only have eggs two or three times a week for break-fast. You like a couple every day I know. But Millie only eats about three a week. There'd be enough left over for any baking she does."

"You might as well get a heavy breed. They don't lay as good as a light breed but you'd have the hens left over when they quit layin' or cut down on their layin' to make meat of."

"And for extra poultry meat we should get about twenty cock-erels, I guess."

"Yeah, I s'pose, for a year's eatin' when they're fat enough. That along with the old hens would make about thirty or so. That's about one every two weeks. Then, you'll have your side of beef startin' next fall if we get these feeders to put in your six acres and in the flats if those fellows that bought the farm are willin' to have you eat the weeds off."

"That reminds me. I have to go and see either Frank Myers or

Milton Grange about that. Well, that's about all, Walter."

"Yeah, except I should know pretty soon if we're puttin' cattle in on the flats. If we be I gotta start fixin' them damn fences. Right now them fences has got spots in 'em where they wouldn't hold in a jackass."

When Walter had gone Charles Brewster slouched back farther still in his easy chair. He pulled over the hassock, put his feet up on it and stared out the window. The view was over the front lawn to the road, past the forsythia bushes and the group of white birches. But instead of all this he saw the oak tree that grew up in front of his window when he lived in the apartment house in the city. He recalled that it was while he was watching it come into bud during the burgeoning month of May that he had started dreaming about having a little farm in the country. And it was the following May, after much searching, that he and Millie had found Briarwood Farm. Charles Brewster smiled a happy smile. Now, quite a few years later, he could look back on it and find it all good. As for the future? He crossed his fingers. The future looked good, too. It looked very good.

9

Walter Gets Mad—but Settles for Banana Cream Pie

While Charles was having lunch with Millie the next day he suddenly started choking. Gripping his throat he clambered to his feet and went lurching about the kitchen like the proverbial drunken sailor. Then he leaned over the sink and his eyes started to water. Reaching around clumsily he patted his back and Millie took that to mean she had a chance to pound him, which she did, until he stopped choking and waved her away. Slowly he recovered his breath and faced her, tears streaming from his light blue eyes.

"Damn suckers," he muttered. "Damn suckers."

"I thought you filleted them, Charles."

"So I did. Must've missed some bones."

"Has it gone on down?"

"Didn't come up so . . . guess it has . . . hope it's gone somewhere."

"And we were enjoying them so much. Are you all right now? Do you want any more?"

"Damn right. I'm going to finish that sucker if it kills me."

And with that determined pronouncement he swayed back to the table, sat down and faced the half-finished sucker.

"I thought you'd like them. I tossed them in a batter of eggs and milk and flour and a bit of baking powder. Then I fried them in butter."

"All right, all right. You told me all that once. I didn't say I didn't like them, woman."

"Take it easy, Charles. Concentrate on eating. By the way. I wonder what's happened to Walter. He said he'd be back from Mapleville in plenty of time for lunch."

"I guess he got talking to somebody." Charles was silent for a moment and then he apparently started feeling remorseful. "They're fine . . . good . . . don't taste like bass or pickerel but . . . taste fine." He was busy examining every bite before he put it into his mouth. "Not bad when they're firm like this in the spring. I just missed that bone when I was filleting them. I'm all right now."

"I was going to tell you that Walter cleaned out the old brooder house yesterday when you were writing your column. I helped him put up the canopy with the electric element and we put some straw on the floor and a feed hopper and a drinking fountain. That's all we need for the few pullets and cockerels we're getting."

"Walter is getting them tomorrow, eh?"

"Yes, at Grove's Hatchery. Mr. Grove offered to bring them out but I think Walter is out of Master Mason chewing tobacco. He's bringing out some feed, too."

"Month old, eh? Well, the pullets will be laying about the middle of September. And the cockerels should be quite a size by then. We should sure eat next winter. And there's that big vegetable garden we're planning this year. By the way, I want to plant two or three of the rarer vegetables. I'd like to try some eggplant and some kale and some vegetable spaghetti."

"My land, what started all these gourmet ideas, Charles?"

"Oh, they're not gourmet, especially. I've had eggplant — fried in butter — and I like it. And I haven't the faintest idea what vegetable spaghetti is so I want to find out."

"You can use it for a salad or as a sort of spaghetti. Speaking of salads, we should be able to pick the fiddlehead ferns any day now. I'd better be on the lookout for them. If you don't get them when they're small they get tough. Now there's a gourmet dish. People in the Maritimes send them to New York restaurants and they're frozen and considered quite a delicacy out of season."

"Well, along with our own beef we won't starve. Maybe we should get some more geese."

"No, thank you, Charles. No more geese. I had a bad experience with wandering geese, you know."

At this Charles leaned back in his chair and started laughing. This brought on another choking session but he recovered to agree with Millie that there would be no geese on Briarwood Farm that year.

"How about ducks or turkeys, Mill?"

"Maybe next year. I think I'll leave them to the specialists."

"How about guinea fowl?"

"No. They fly all over the place — right over a barn, so I've heard. They're mainly good for making a noise when there's danger around. I hear they make an awful racket then."

"Well, no danger around here, Millie. When we bought this farm Walter told us it was a 'peaceful claim' as he called it. And it has been so far. Well, that sucker was not bad eating. I'll have to go sucker fishing with Benny Gilmore every year."

"I know something else you have to do every year and you haven't done it yet."

"Take a bath?"

"No, make out your income tax. And here it is almost the end of April."

"What do you think this is? Right here at my elbow. I've been working on it, Mill. But I'm a writer. I'm not a voodoo expert. I can't figure out half of it. And the government makes it sound so simple. Listen to this: 'Stripped of all its mystery, a tax form is simply a piece of paper on which you do four basic things — identify yourself, list your income, reduce your income by subtracting allowable deductions and calculate your tax.' "

"Charles, that sounds very simple."

"Okay, Millie, it's all yours."

"I suggest you get Charlie Noble at your bank in Mapleville to help you make it out. His bank is doing very well out of us since we put some of the money from selling the farm in there. He should be a whizz at it."

"Good idea, Millie. I'll take it down this afternoon. Oh, here's Walter coming in. I wonder what held him up in Mapleville."

Walter knew what had held him up and he proceeded to let Charles know the moment he sat down to the plate of fish and mashed potatoes that Millie had been keeping warm for him.

"I been havin' a hell of a lot of trouble, Mr. Brewster."

"In what way, Walter?"

"I lost the front license plate off the truck."

"It fell off?"

"Yeah, and you was the one that put it on, you mind?"

"Yes, that's right. I remember I had trouble getting the two screws in but I thought I finally got them in pretty tightly, Walter. Where did it fall off?"

"Huh! That was what I spent an hour findin' out. But the way I found out it fell off was when the police stopped me and I got into an argument and told him off and he was goin' to take me over to the police station and throw me in the cooler but I talked him out of it because I told him you didn't put the bloody plate on right in the first place."

"Did you find the plate, Walter?"

"Yeah, I found the bloody thing up on 18th Avenue. And next year I'll be the one to put them on." And with that Walter speared a piece of sucker and mouthed a big forkful of mashed potatoes with a fierceness that proclaimed his complaint at an end. And it left Charles and Millie with nothing but sheer astonishment. They had never heard Walter declare himself quite so belligerently and didn't know quite what to do about it. But finally Charles cleared his throat and made a feeble protest.

"Sorry about that, Walter. I guess that was my fault. I'd better let you put on next year's plates." Then, to change the subject, he picked up a copy of the last *News* which carried the first of the columns he was writing under the heading "Along the Sideroad."

"I guess I didn't show this to you, Walter — the first column I've written for the *News*. The paper came last Saturday but I kept forgetting to show it to you. There's the picture that Mrs. Brewster took of me leaning on the rail fence down by the pig-pen."

Walter grunted as he took a cursory look at it.

"This column includes the two stories you told me — about the crow that was painted red and the tombstone with the words 'Here Lies Katie Duggan' on it."

"You got my name there, seein' I told you the stories?"

"Yes, I have. I said the stories were told to me by Walter Purdy."

Walter grunted again and chewed on his sucker.

"You can read it later. By the way I'd like to walk over with you and see how the tree-house is coming along."

"It's comin'," Walter muttered.

"Yes, well . . . I appreciate you building it — with all the other work you have to do."

"That supposed to be funny? I ain't got a lot to do — except fix them fences before you get your feeders if you're goin' to get feeders."

Millie had been busy in the living room. Now she came back to suggest that maybe Walter would like a piece of banana cream pie she'd made that morning. Walter grunted approval and Millie went to get it. She didn't comment that she had planned to have the pie for supper but had decided after listening to Walter's complaints that maybe he'd better have a piece of her pie for both meals.

A few minutes later Charles stood with Walter on the ground beside the creek surveying the tree-house. Charles nodded his head sagely. "Yes, Walter, you're doing a good job. It's coming along fine."

"Hell, I ain't got nothin' done but the frame so how can you tell?"

"Oh, I can tell. Yes, I can tell. I can see just what it's going to look like."

"You got better eyes than a sharp-shinned hawk then. I s'pose you can see yourself sittin' up there in the tree, too, eh?"

Charles laughed quietly. "Well, in a way I can. I can hear myself tapping out my column right now."

"By the Holy Susie, if you can hear that you must be a bat as well as a hawk. You're a ten-days' wonder, Mr. Brewster."

"You think those uprights are strong enough, eh? We might get some strong winds across the flats from the northwest there."

"They're four-by-fours. That should do for a buildin' less'n seven feet square. Of course if you want me to get steel beams just let me know."

"Now, now, Walter. This is fine. I see you have the lumber all pre-cut for the siding. Those boards don't look quite long enough."

"They don't, eh? Well, s'posin' you get down and measure 'em. Mr. Brewster, it seems to me I ain't doin' so good around here."

"In what way, Walter?"

"Oh, hell, you're doin' a lot of complainin'. Now, look here. If you don't like my services around here I can soon start walkin' up the road. I can get along on my money. I can go and live with my sister — even though I might not like that because she takes fits."

"Walter, you're still upset about the license plates. I said that was my fault."

"Yeah, okay, Mr. Brewster. I just don't like the idea of . . .". Walter didn't complete the sentence. He was busy looking down towards the barns. "What damn fool let the team out of the stable?"

"I did, Walter, when you were away. I thought they should get out and get a little exercise."

"That's all right — out in the barnyard. They shouldn't be out here where you're goin' to use it for pasture. It's too soft there yet. They'll punch holes in it."

Charles sighed. He muttered what was intended to be a half-meant apology and headed back towards the house and Millie. She was down in the cellar working at getting the gray paint off the old corner cupboard but came up when she heard him come in. She found him slumped in the corner chair, his head thrown back on the embroidered antimacassar.

"What on earth is wrong, Charles? You look as if you'd just seen a ghost."

"If Walter's a ghost he's a fighting ghost today."

"What now?"

"Oh, he got upset because I asked him about his work on the tree-house — just little points I wanted to clear up. Then he got mad because I'd turned June and Judy out into the pasture near the sheep-barn. He said it was too early yet — that they'd punch holes in the soft ground. Then he said that if I didn't like his services around here he could soon start walking up the road and go and live with his sister who has fits."

"Good Heavens. Of course he was upset about the license plate falling off up on 18th Avenue. That got him started. But it isn't like Walter to get all this upset."

"Yeah, I know. He was swearin' away like an old trooper, instead of just the usual rural cuss words he always uses."

"But he wouldn't walk out and leave us."

"I dunno. I just left him standing there and came in."

"But we have to do something. We can't do without him. He's invaluable."

"What do I do? Do I give him the deed to the farm and ask him if we can stay on and work for him?"

"I think he's just bluffing. I don't think he has the faintest intention of leaving, Charles."

"But supposing he did. I've learned quite a lot about stock and the other work around here but I don't feel that I want to be responsible for everything — especially now that I have to go chasing around the country a bit looking for material for columns."

"Well, maybe we can find out right now. I just saw Walter coming to the kitchen door. He'll be out here in a minute. So let's just sound him out carefully. Let Walter have the first word when he comes in."

As it happened Walter seemed at a loss for even the first word when he found his way out to the sunroom. He stood awkwardly in the centre of the room, his cap off, smoothing down his graying hair and looking down at the floor. Charles suggested he sit down and when he did it was on the edge of the chair, looking very abject. In fact everyone looked a little ludicrous, as if they were acting out an Irish tragedy. But Charles finally broke the tension.

"Well, I guess I made a bloody bungle of things today, Walter."

Walter crossed his legs, cleared his throat, opened his lips in a slightly twisted smile and said nothing. Then Millie tried to come to the rescue.

"Well, there's one thing about it. When you men have a bit of an argument you have a smarter way of settling it than we women do. We women hold a grudge for a long time and won't even speak if we meet in someone's house or on the street. I think you men have the right way of doing it. I'll bet that you could just shake hands and forget the whole thing right now."

"Walter, I think she's got something there. I'm sorry if I seemed to be complaining about things. It must have been that darned sucker I had for lunch."

Walter was on the spot. He squirmed around in the chair, looked out the window, uncoiled his legs and coiled them again and twirled his cap.

"Maybe that's what's wrong with me, eh, seein' I had a piece of the same sucker."

Everybody gave a low nervous laugh and then Charles walked over and put out his hand.

"Okay, Walter?"

"Yeah, sure, Mr. Brewster, sure. I guess this is from livin' alone too long, eh?"

"Oh, I wouldn't say that, Walter."

"That's what my sister tells me — when she isn't havin' fits, I mean. She says I shoulda got married to a woman long ago."

"Plenty of men don't. It's a matter of what we like to do."

"Well, I got kinda mad when I was up on the 18th there flounderin' around in the ditch tryin' to find that license plate."

"Yes, I know. That was my fault."

"Walter," interrupted Millie, "how'd you like a cup of tea and a piece of banana cream pie?"

"That'd go down pretty good — though it wasn't so long ago I had a piece of pie."

"Oh, that doesn't matter. If you like it as much as all that it pleases me so I'm glad to see you eat it."

"And I, Walter, at this time would like to say that I think your job is worth an extra ten dollars a month."

"Nah, Mr. Brewster. Nah."

"Oh, yes. We appreciate what you do around here and I've been a little slow about realizing it."

"Nah, Mr. Brewster."

"Oh, yes. Retroactive to the first of April."

"That good or bad?"

"That means it dates back to the first of April. It started then."

"Oh, I see, yeah. Well, you don't have to do nothin' like that. Startin' right now would be fine. But if you'd rather do it this way I s'pose it's all right."

And with that Walter lifted the corners of his mouth, sat back in his chair and began to look as if he had just taken over the ownership of Briarwood Farm. When he had gone and taken the tea and pie away inside him Charles inhaled and then exhaled with a great exaggerated blowing-out of his chubby cheeks.

"It looks like Walter will be staying on, Millie."

"You didn't think he wouldn't, did you?"

"I guess not."

"Charles, what was Walter doing up on 18th Avenue? I thought he went down to the village."

"He was supposed to. Yeah . . . why was he up on the 18th, eh?"

"You don't suppose . . . ?"

"Looking on the mailboxes for somebody named 'Bunny'?"

"Good Heavens, I hope not, Charles."

"What I hope is that there isn't actually somebody on 18th Avenue named 'Bunny'."

"You started all this, you know. You wrote that little note on April Fools' Day and signed it 'Bunny' on 18th Avenue and had this fictitious 'Bunny' writing that she'd always admired Walter and would like to meet him sometime."

"Yeah, I know. Well, let's just hope there isn't anybody on 18th Avenue named Bunny. Holy Susie, as Walter says. I could get my neck into a noose about all this."

10

A Horse Cemetery and a Waterless Well

The morning of the fifteenth of May was much like the days that had immediately preceded it. The thermometer stood at around 65 degrees Fahrenheit. The sun rose in the east as usual and seemed to be having fun dodging around and behind a dallying ballet of blue-gowned clouds. The grass was a spanking new green. And the world in general seemed serene and filled with peace and tranquillity.

And then the Brewsters heard it. The sound ravaged the silence. It surrounded their house and shut them into a foreign enclave in which nothing seemed familiar. It was unlike any machine-made noise they had ever heard, including the industrial township machinery used to grade their sideroad and excavate the ditches.

As it appeared to come from some point out on the road Charles and Millie Brewster sprinted down the lane (as fast as Charles' rather short legs would permit an approximation to that movement) and looked across the road into the farm fields beyond. And there it was. The largest earth-moving equipment they had ever seen and making more noise than any machinery they had ever laid eyes on. At least it seemed that way to the Brewsters. But soon they dismissed to a great extent the noise and simply looked at each other. Finally Charles managed to say: "What the hell's going on here?"

Millie was less profane. "What on earth can this mean, Charles?"

"I dunno. Have you heard anything about Jim Duncan selling his farm?"

"No, not a word. I remember him saying, just before we sold ours, that he wouldn't think of selling his 300 acres."

"My God, he must have sold it. You don't need earth-moving equipment to work a farm."

"But what are they doing?"

"Too soon to tell but they seem to be removing that hill — cutting it down or something. Who would want to remove a hill? It isn't that big a hill or mound or whatever you call it."

"Where can we find out?"

"At the township office, Millie. They'd have a plan over there
about what's going on. We could have found out weeks ago, if we'd
been curious enough but nobody even suspected that Jim Duncan
had sold his farm. But I guess he must have."

After a few minutes' speculation as to the mystery the Brewsters
walked slowly back up their driveway and met Walter up near the
house.

"Oh, I don't get all het up about nothin' that goes on in these
parts any more," Walter said calmly. "We could have a hunk of the
sky fall into the flats down there and I'd hardly wink at it. It's somethin' turrible what's goin' on around here."

A call to the Township Planning Department a few minutes later,
after Walter had gone, explained the mystery. A golf club in the city
had bought the farm and were turning it into a golf club. It was as
simple as that. They were selling their old club which was to be
used for a housing development and the selling price was six million
dollars. At that point Charles whistled and hung up.

"Six million bucks?" Charles whistled again and shook his head.

"Six million for Jim Duncan's 300 acres, Charles?"

"No, for the old golf club in the city."

"So I'll bet he got plenty for that 300 acres, if the golf club had
all that money to spend," said Millie.

"I guess he would. I wonder how much."

"But why wouldn't we have heard something about it? The
councillors must have known. Other people must have known."

"It looks as if it was the best-kept secret in the township. I guess
they thought it might shoot up land values around here."

"Charles, why don't you phone up Lloyd Dunwoody, the clerk at
the township office. You know him. Find out about it."

And Charles phoned a second time, the result being that he
found out quite a lot, including the cold fact that the necessary
technical information regarding the zoning of land covered by lot
number and concession number had been published in the Mapleville *Banner* some time before. When Charles hung up and reported
this to Millie her comment was that they must both be pretty dumb.

"But I haven't been reading the *Banner* as closely as I used to.
They have so much sport in it now and I don't know much about
sport."

"Yes, and maybe that's the section where they had the paid ad
about the golf club development. But I still don't know why someone
around here didn't tell us about it." Charles shoved his hands in his
pants' pockets and stared at the floor as if hoping to get a clue there.
"Of course it isn't going to do us any harm, Mill. Wouldn't you
rather have an 18-hole golf course across the road than 500 houses?"

"Yes, a golf course should be very nice. The grass will always be kept mown and we'll always have a view across it."

"Oh, it could be a lot worse. I asked what Jim Duncan got for it and I got a pretty vague answer. He said he'd heard somewhere around $4,000 an acre but he wasn't sure. Let's see, for 300 acres that would be what? . . . a million and two hundred thousand dollars? That can't be right."

"Of course it's right."

"Holy Doodle. A million? . . . and two hundred thousand?"

"That's exactly a million more than we got for a hundred acres. Well, I don't begrudge the Duncans. They're nice people and they're getting older and now they won't have anything to worry about."

"By gosh, land is sure going up around here, eh?"

"Now don't get greedy, Charles."

"No, I'm quite satisfied. I never expected to ever have the $200,000 we got for our 94 acres — plus the six acres we have left and the old house here and all that. I don't give a hoot if the next farm sells for $10,000 an acre one of these days."

"Good for you. I feel the same way. Now let's come down to earth and start the day's business."

"I'd still like to know what that big earth-moving thing is doing out there pushing that hill around." Charles was looking really worried.

"You'll find out. Landscaping, probably. I imagine they'd do that first. I know what I have to do right now and that is feed the 10 pullets and 10 cockerels we have in the brooder house."

"Yes, you're back farming again, Millie."

"I rather like it. It isn't much of a chore. And we can look forward to having our own eggs this fall."

"Well, I'm cutting grass this forenoon so Walter can go on working on the tree-house. He says I can't help right now."

"I'll expect some inspired columns in the *News* when you start working in your tree-house."

"Yes, I will, too. And that reminds me. I have to go over to see a man on the town line this afternoon about a column."

"What about?"

"It seems there's a horse buried under every tree in his orchard."

"Good heavens. How many trees? And why?"

"I don't know. Somebody in the village told me about him and I phoned him yesterday and I'm seeing him this afternoon."

"Well, it sounds interesting in a gruesome sort of way. By the way, has Walter told you that Tabby can hardly climb up and downstairs in the barn now?"

"Yes, she's pretty feeble. Of course she's as old as the hills."

"In the winter when we thought it was too cold for her in the barn and brought her up here she wasn't a bit comfortable. She was too accustomed to the barn."

"Yes, that's where she wants to be. Walter says I'll have to shoot her one of these days — when she just can't get around but I don't think I can do it."

"Oh, no. Let Walter do it. You can't, Charles."

"Yes, he's used to that kind of thing. Well, I'd better get busy doing something and let you feed your big flock of pullets."

About the middle of the afternoon Charles knocked at the door of a large stone farmhouse on the town line a few miles east of Briarwood Farm. The door was opened by a tall, middle-aged man with a pleasant, ruddy face and smile-crinkles around his eyes. He reached out for Charles' hand and shook it strongly.

"Come in, Mr. Brewster, nice to see you. I'm Ches Cowper as you know. Slip your jacket off, if you like. We're pretty informal here. Have that chair, it's more comfortable than this."

Charles wasn't accustomed to such an overflow of courtesy. He could only come up with a vague expression of thanks as he sank down in the chair.

"Well, now. Will you have a cup of coffee? I'm afraid we don't indulge in spirituous liquors here. Bad for the liver."

"Yes, I'll have a coffee, thanks. Just clear."

"Ah, me too. Why spoil it with cream and sugar?"

Mr. Cowper went to the kitchen door and gave an order for the coffee. Then he seated himself in a chair where he faced Charles at an angle easy for conversation.

"You wanted to know about my orchard burying ground. Well, it isn't mine, really. I mean I didn't bury the horses. That was done by the man who farmed here about forty-fifty years ago. I met him once just before he died. He was a great talker. Never stopped. My wife says I'm a close second. Well, anyway, he raised heavy horses. Clydesdales. And he raised the best. His Clydes were known all over the world. Both mares and stallions. And they took prizes at fall fairs everywhere. I understand you have horses on your farm, Mr. Brewster."

"Yes, when I sold off most of my farm last year we kept the two Percheron mares. They're getting pretty old now."

"Well, I like heavy horses, though I don't raise them myself. Anyway, the story goes that when a visitor came to this farm he was led out to a vantage point where most of the prize horses could be seen in the pasture. And then this fellow would slowly cut a hunk of tobacco from his plug, insert it into his mouth and start chewing — and talking."

"About horses, I'll bet."

"Right, Mr. Brewster. About horses, always. And about all his visitor could do was keep nodding his head. And it was said that sometimes when he was talking pedigrees and pointing to the horses he'd turn around and find that his visitor had disappeared."

"Just got tired of hearing him talk."

"Right. Well, anyway, this man thought so much of his prize horses that when the first horse he bought passed away he buried it beneath one of the apple trees in his orchard."

"It would be quite a problem digging through the roots of the tree, wouldn't it?"

"I would think so. And I haven't the answer to that. I would think it would take a lot of digging and with some damage to the roots. But apparently he did and that story was corroborated by a man I met in Mapleville one day. That's where he wanted his horses buried and bury them he did. So in time through the years the trees became the tombstones for his horses buried in the ground underneath. Oh, here's my wife with the coffee, Mr. Brewster. Sally, meet Charles Brewster."

Charles stood up and vocally acknowledged the introduction as Mrs. Cowper placed a tray holding a coffee-pot, serviettes, cups and a platter of home-made assorted tarts on the round table between the two men. She was an attractive woman in her middle forties and exuded the same genuine feeling of pleasantness and healthy candour as that of her husband.

"You have a lovely house here, Mrs. Cowper," Charles said and meant it. "Both inside and out."

"Thank you. We love it here. We moved out from the city you know but unfortunately we only bought two acres with the house. The entire farm was for sale but we couldn't afford it five years ago. But we'd never again move back to the city."

"This stone house is quite old."

"Just over a hundred years. And it's so solidly built it should be here for a long time yet. Well, now, I'll run along and let you men talk. It's been nice meeting you, Mr. Brewster."

"Nice meeting you, too. And thank you for the coffee."

When his wife had gone Mr. Cowper lost no time in picking up his story.

"Where was I? Oh yes, I was saying that in time these horses were buried under the apple trees out in our orchard here."

"Has anyone ever actually found any of the skeletons?"

"Yes, apparently the orchard was plowed between the rows a few years ago and under the very first tree the plow turned up part of the vertebra of a horse. And the same thing happened under the next tree and the next. So you see the horses weren't buried very deeply — mainly because of the roots, I suppose, as we were mentioning a while ago. Anyway, the man who was plowing it gave up and let it stay in wild grass, as it is now."

"Well, that's quite a story, Mr. Cowper."

"The orchard horse cemetery, eh? That's about what it is. I can tell you another short story about plowing up something, too — about a watch."

"I'd like to hear it," said Charles, sipping his coffee and munching on a raspberry tart.

"Well, you might find it hard to believe this but it's been authenticated. And it's about a farmer about 60 miles east of here whose father lost his watch while he was plowing back in 1917. It was a good watch, too — a Hamilton railroad watch. And the date he lost it was October 19, 1917. Well, this man died two years later at 11.50 a.m. — ten to twelve noon. So the son took over the farm, worked it, married, had a son who in turn, when he was old enough, took over much of the running of the farm. And in 1957 he had occasion to plow in the same field where his grandfather had lost his Hamilton watch. And the date was October 19th — the same date as when the watch was lost in 1917."

"That's some coincidence, eh?"

"You haven't heard anything yet. He was plowing, as I said, and he turned part way around in the seat to pull the cord that lifts the plows out of the ground at the headland when he saw something on the black earth that made him stop the tractor and climb off."

"Now don't tell me, Mr. Cowper."

"Yes, it was a watch and he took it home to his father who, of course, recognized it as the Hamilton watch his father — the boy's grandfather — had lost in 1917."

"Well, I'll be darned."

"It was dull and rusted and dirty and had been twisted out of shape a bit, of course. But when this boy's father looked at it he realized that the shoe of his father's plow had run over it and stopped the watch going at the moment it fell out of his pocket or wherever he was carrying it in his clothes. But he was able to make out the position of the hands. You know where the hands pointed?"

"I'm afraid to guess. You better tell me."

"They pointed to 10 minutes to 12 o'clock. And that meant that they foretold the time when the grandfather would die two years later."

Charles shook his head. It seemed impossible to believe. And it would be a great story for his column.

"You've never been tempted to explore under the trees, Mr. Cowper?" asked Charles, still intrigued by the story of the horse burial.

"Nah, I'd rather not. It's been proven that there are the bones of horses under many of the trees so the other trees probably have horses buried under them, too. I'd just as soon leave it that way. Pax requiescat! Have some more coffee."

"No, I'm fine, thanks. I appreciate you giving me your time."

"Oh, this is my day off. I'm an accountant in the city but I've been there a long time and I reserved the right, when we moved out here, to take a day off during the week. I'm also a week-end painter of sorts. That's one of my efforts over there."

"Oh? An apple orchard in full bloom. That your own orchard?"

"Yes, I just did it this past week so I hung it up there to give everybody who comes in a chance to take a whack at criticizing it. What do you think?"

"Oh, I'm no critic. But I think it's a darned good painting. It's an oil."

"Yes, I prefer water colours but I'm not very proficient yet. I think that's not a bad painting myself. You're a writer, Mr. Brewster?"

"Oh, well. A journalist . . . scribbler . . . public relations man . . . what have you."

"Why don't you write a book?"

"Right now I'm writing a weekly column for the *News*."

"Yes, I read your first column a few days ago. Darned good. About painting that crow red and scaring the daylights out of the Irish boy. Well, use those stories I told you today if you like. Might as well let other people get a chuckle out of them."

Shortly after Charles took his leave of the Cowpers and drove back along the sideroad to Briarwood Farm. All the small farm orchards along the way were in bloom. The whites and pinks of the apple and pear trees seemed to light up each little enclosed area. At any other time of the year you could pass the orchards and hardly notice them. Now your eye was drawn to each one and it was lovely. It was like classic ballet, Charles decided — a stage crowded with beautiful young girls clad in white-frocked, diaphanous gowns. He wished he had the talent to write a good poem about it — instead of the catchy limericks he often wrote. Maybe he should try sometime, he decided, as he swung the station wagon into the driveway of Briarwood Farm.

However, this ambition was soon wiped out by the figure of his wife and Walter standing out in front of the drive-shed and, as he pulled up beside them, apparently in serious conversation. Walter was gesticulating in a forceful, un-Walterlike manner and appeared to be shaking his fist in the general direction of Mapleville. Millie was nodding her head as if she agreed with every punctuation mark of what he was saying.

"What are you two looking so solemn about?" he asked as he shut the car door.

"Our water has given out, Charles."

"Our water has what?" Millie had made this announcement with such a distressed inflection that she might well have been stating that the oceans of the world had dried up.

"We have no water, Charles. No water. The well is dry. Not enough for a cup of tea."

"And it's them blackguards down there that's doin' it, Mr. Brewster."

"You mean where we saw them drilling for water that day we went down there."

"Sure, they drilled until they hit our bloody underground river. They're suckin' it all up."

"That's not so good." It was all Charles could think of to say at the moment. Then he added that he had better get down to where the drilling was going on and see what he could do.

"You better give 'em double hell, Mr. Brewster."

"I'll see, Walter. That isn't always the best way."

"You better not take me with you. If I got started on 'em I'd beat the tar out of the whole lot of them."

Millie decided she had better have her say. "I think Mr. Brewster is right, Walter. After all, according to law they're likely within their own rights. If they are we'd better try and get their cooperation."

Walter gave Millie a searching look as if to tell her that she didn't know beans about such things. Charles offered a peacemaker smile to them both, got into the station wagon and went in pursuit of cooperation or some other factor that would help to fill his empty well.

11

Silver Siding and Golden Bantams

Mid-afternoon of the following day found Charles Brewster kneeling beside his well. From a certain angle he was a figure compressed into a chubby body, foreshortened legs and without a head. The reason why there seemed to be no head was because that part of his anatomy was cut off by the platform on the well as he stuck his head down into the dank, dim atmosphere and tried to discern whether or not his water was rising. Finally, he hauled a flashlight from a back pocket and sent its beam down to scan the possible level. He pulled it back and staggered to his feet because his doubled-up legs had cut off an adequate blood supply but there was a smile on his florid, blithe countenance.

Millie came out just in time to get within the penumbra of that smile and it triggered her question. "Is it coming at last, Charles?"

Charles nodded. "She's a-comin'," he said, with a rustic inflection. "She's a-startin' now so let's hope she keeps on a-comin'."

"The man you talked to down at the drilling site said it would be about the middle of the afternoon before the water would show up in our well. So he was right."

"Yes, he said it would take this long after he capped the well they were letting run free to test it and to wash out the sand. But what happens when they start using the water for houses? That's the important thing. I'd better get in touch with the Water Resources Department or Department of the Environment or the King of Canada or some such power and find out just what our rights are — or are not. We might have to drill down deeper — to get below the depth to which the Mygrange Development Company has gone."

"Then the Mygrange Development Company would drill down below the point to which we had drilled and so on ad infinitum, Charles."

"Millie, look behind you."

Millie jumped as if a snake could be lurking in the grass. She turned to find Laddie, the Border Collie, stretched out on his belly a few feet away making a brave attempt to wag his tail.

"Oh, Laddie. Look at him, Charles. I tried to get him to follow me off the verandah but he wouldn't budge at first. He's scared stiff."

"Yes, he hasn't an ounce of courage in him. Those kids at that farm where they used to throw turnips at him did a real job of killing whatever spirit he had. It's going to take us a long time to get it back."

"Oh, Laddie. It's all right, Lad. We're pulling for you. It'll take time but we're on your side."

The dog again moved his tail as if he desperately wanted to wag it but wasn't sure if it was allowed or not. Millie bent down and stroked him gently and the dog responded by stretching out on its side but there was still fear in its brown-gold eyes. Then it lifted its head and licked the back of her hand.

"I guess we're going to have a barkless dog, Millie. I can't imagine Laddie ever getting up enough courage to bark at a car or a cow or anything."

"You want to bet?"

"No, that's one bet I won't take. I hope I'm all wrong. Hey, who have we here coming up the drive? Isn't that Bobby Duncan?"

"Yes, it is. On his way home from school probably. He's a nice lad. I wonder what he wants."

"Golly, he sure has a bushel of freckles, eh?"

"Shush, he'll hear you. Hello there, Bobby."

"Want to buy a banty?"

"A what, Bobby?" The question was so abrupt that Millie didn't comprehend at first.

"A banty rooster. I got one for sale. A banty hen, too."

"A bantam rooster and a bantam hen. What do you think, Charles?"

Charles chuckled and stroked his jowls. "Well, I dunno, Bobby. We haven't thought about it."

"I got too many, pa says. He says I better sell three or four, maybe more."

"I see. Well now, where would we keep them, Millie?"

Bobby had the answer to that. "Just let 'em run loose around the barnyard like I do. Or you can throw 'em a little grain once in a while. You won't have no trouble feedin' 'em. And the hen is layin' and she's startin' to want to set. So you might have a few more banties."

"Oh, we might. Well, I'm not so sure we want a lot of banties."

"You can just take the eggs away then so she can't hatch out. You can eat the eggs, you know, except they're pretty small."

Charles cleared his throat, looked thoughtful and turned to Millie for support. "What do you think, Millie?"

"I don't know just what to say."

"I'm only chargin' a dollar apiece because I got too many, pa says."

Millie didn't have the heart to turn him down. "I think maybe we could take a rooster and a hen off your hands, Bobby."

"Okay, I'll bring them over in an hour or so. I think you'll like them."

It was then that Charles sensed that he might be able to acquire a little information. "By the way, Bobby, your father has sold the farm, eh?"

"Youp, last fall that was but we weren't supposed to say anything about it for a while. They're goin' to have a golf course."

"They're doing the landscaping now, eh?"

"I guess so. They sure got a lot of machinery over there."

Millie wanted some information, too. "Where will you be moving, Bobby?"

"We're goin' to stay there — for right now anyway. They want pa to drive a tractor mowin' the grass when they get the golf course ready to play on. And this summer he'll be workin' at plantin' trees and buildin' some bridges across the crik and things like that."

"Well, we'll still have you as neighbours then."

"I guess so. Well, I'll be back in a while, Mrs. Brewster."

And with that Bobby started off down the lane and left the Brewsters staring at each other.

"Looks as if we are going to be the proud owners of a bantam hen and a bantam rooster, Millie."

"Oh, I couldn't turn him down. And it might be fun. And they shouldn't be any trouble if they're just running around loose."

"Wait'll they start raising baby bantams. You'll have a whole flock of them."

"Oh, no, I won't. Of course, I think it might be interesting to have the hen hatch out one setting of eggs. I think a few bantam chicks would be kind of fun. Of course if she's moved to a new location like this she might lose her urge to set."

"Yes, you might be lucky."

"Go on with you. I'm the poultry-woman, remember. And just wait till you see them when Bobby brings them over. I think you'll like them."

And Charles did like them, when Bobby arrived with them later that day. He took the hen out of the grain sack first. She was rather subdued in colouring,, a blend of brown and tan with reddish flecks throughout. Then Bobby gave Mrs. Brewster the hen to hold and he took out the rooster. Mrs. Brewster gasped. He was scarlet and gold and emerald, with flecks of blue and bronze. Around his neck, which he held up with proud ramrod stiffness as he chittered his disapproval of the treatment he was getting was a ruffle of gold veined with startling red. And his serrated comb was fire-red and topped his head like a flaming, jaunty cockade. Charles was just as impressed as Millie. And Millie was ecstatic.

"I think he's the most beautiful thing I've ever seen. Did you ever see such amazing colours, Charles?"

"They're terrific, eh? What do we do with them right now, Bobby? We could put them in the shed where we used to have the geese?"

"I don't think they'd go back home if I just put them down and let them run loose, Mr. Brewster."

"We can always try it but we don't want the trouble we had when our geese started waddling back and forth from here to our neighbours. Okay, let's put them down and see what happens."

With that they placed the bantams on the ground. And nothing unusual happened, except that the hen kept clucking as if anxious to climb into a nest and the rooster looked rather arrogant and then crowed. But they didn't fly away. After they had apparently surveyed their new environment they started pecking quite unconcernedly and Millie remarked on how tame they were.

"I guess that's because I've made pets of them. I pick them up all the time, Mrs. Brewster. I hope they don't follow me when I leave."

"Well, here's your money, Bobby. You've made a sale. Have you names for them?"

"Oh, I've been callin' the rooster Peter and the hen Patty."

"I think those are very nice names, don't you, Charles?"

"Sure I do. Peter and Patty. That's fine."

"Well, I better go now. I have to help with the chores."

"When are you having your farm sale, Bobby?"

"June the 9th, Mr. Brewster. It's on a Saturday. There's quite a few antiques for sale but we're keeping quite a lot of furniture, ma said, in case you're interested, Mrs. Brewster."

"Yes, I think I would be. I'll be at the sale."

"Okay, I guess I better go now. Thanks for the money, Mr. Brewster, and I hope you like the banties."

"Oh, I'm sure we will. 'Bye, Bobby."

The Brewsters turned from watching Bobby Duncan start down the lane to observing the actions of the bantam rooster and hen. At the moment they seemed to be quite at home.

"But what about tonight, Charles? They won't know where to roost."

"Oh, they'll find a place — unless they decide to head home when it starts getting dusk. They're kind of cute, eh?"

"I thought you'd like them. Now if she'll just lay some eggs and set on them we'll have some baby banties. So then I'll have banty chicks, 10 pullets and 10 cockerels. And it looks as if we have another visitor, Charles."

A car that had been coming up the driveway swung around the circle, stopped in front of them and a man in his middle thirties stepped out. He was well-dressed, looked over-fed because he was too stout for his apparent age and judging by the expensive car he was also well-heeled.

"Afternoon, my name is Tomkins. Ron Tomkins. You're the Brewsters?" Charles acknowledged that they were.

"I hear you have some old farm buildings you're not using now. I was talking to a man in Mapleville. I just wondered if you wanted to sell the siding off them and make a little money — pretty good money, in fact."

Charles looked him over for a moment. "No, I don't think I'd be interested."

"Are you using the buildings now?"

"Oh, some of them."

"That them back there?"

"Yeah, they're back there."

"Mind if we have a quick look at them, Mr. Brewster?"

"I don't see why but you can if you like." And with that he told Millie he'd be right back and led the way to the farm buildings. He stopped in front of the old pig-pen. He could see the furtive eyes of Mr. Tomkins light up like a traffic signal. Then he watched him feeling the thickness of the siding, seeing if it would crumble in his fingers and giving it a general appraisal as he stepped back to have a look at the length of the boards. Then he lit a cigarette and said: "I'll give you fifty for it, Mr. Brewster."

"You mean for the pig-pen?"

"No, no, you keep the pig-pen. For the boards — the sheathing. Those old boards."

Mr. Brewster decided to pull a leg. "You mean you'd be glad to take off these old boards and leave the frame there so I could put other boards on?"

"Well, if you wanted to, sure."

"What the hell use would it be as a pig-pen without any sides on it? You think the pigs would like that?"

"I didn't think you used it now."

"I might want to. What do you use old boards like this for?"

"Silver siding. For wall covering in houses — especially in librar-ies or rec rooms, you know. It's a kind of fad with some people."

"Uhuh. So you'd sell them for so much a thousand board feet."

"That's the way we sell them, yes."

"Wouldn't they be kind of stinky? I can imagine having people in for the evening and before long I can see somebody starting to sniff and start thinking they were in a pig-pen."

Mr. Tomkins gave an agreeable little chuckle. "I've never heard any complaints that way. How about it? Want to sell 'em?"

"I don't think so. Silver siding, eh?"

"Silver snail siding some call it."

"Silver snail siding. Well, Mr. Tomkins, I think I'll just keep my silver snail siding. I kind of like the sound of that. Why, I might want to do the whole inside of my house with it one of these days. As for the fifty dollars, I imagine you probably sell it for six times that. So thank you, just the same."

Mr. Tomkins looked considerably deflated. "I'll give you a hundred dollars, no more."

"No thanks, Mr. Tomkins."

Together they walked back to the car and Mr. Tomkins drove away. Millie was pulling out some pigweed from the gravel in front of the drivehouse.

"Well, I had a chance to sell the silver snail siding from the old pig-pen."

"I hope you didn't. I've been reading about that in a decorating book I brought home from the library. It's very expensive to buy."

"Oh, I didn't sell it."

"I might just use that one of these days."

"Don't tell me you're going into the pig business, Millie."

"I certainly am not. And I don't think I'll tell you right now what I have vaguely in mind."

"You're starting up a distillery."

"Heaven forbid."

"A storeroom for heroin, Millie?"

"Something much more wholesome."

"I don't think you intend to tell me."

"Not at the moment, Charles. I may change my mind."

"Quite a mystery. As a matter of fact it's been quite a day. We got our water back in the well, we bought a pair of bantams and we have a chance to sell the outside of our old pig-pen."

The Brewsters didn't know it right then but they were to be faced with another mystery after supper that night. Walter went back to his cottage by the river as usual and Charles and Millie started talking about antiques.

"Of course, Charles, when it comes right down to it, there are only two things you can do with old furniture if you want to bring it back to life. You either paint it up or strip it down."

"Much the same thing as women do, eh?"

"Now don't be crude. As I was saying, the stripping down and then trying to decorate it can be quite a job and if it isn't done right it never does look like anything."

"You were telling me the other day that there are professional people who strip furniture."

"Yes, it's some kind of chemical process. They dip the furniture into a big cold vat and let it stay there for as long as it needs — anywhere from a few minutes to a few hours. Then they hose it down and then do it all over again in a hot tank to get off the fine particles."

"And it does the job, eh?"

"Oh yes, after drying for three or four days it's ready to be refinished or painted or simply waxed or oiled."

"Why don't you do that?"

"I just like the idea of doing the work myself, Charles. Besides, it's rather expensive. It's about five or six dollars for a chair and a chest is about twice that. And a table would be somewhere around twelve or fifteen dollars, I would think."

"Well, there is something about doing it yourself. It's putting that work in it that gives a sort of pride in having it that you probably . . . Millie, are you listening?"

"Can that be Walter? Coming over from his cottage?"

"Yes, I . . . guess so, but . . . holy smoke, he's all dressed up. The only time he gets dressed up like that is when he goes to visit his sister and that's about four times a year and it's always Sunday afternoon."

"He's going down to the drive-shed — to get the truck, I suppose."

"He didn't say a word about going out anywhere tonight."

"No, but I remember now that when he came in to supper he was shaved. I thought it was so he wouldn't have to do it in the morning but that couldn't be it. Walter often misses a day in shaving anyway — sometimes more."

"Was he acting strangely at supper?"

"I'm trying to think. I don't know that he was."

"Well, why the hell would he get all dressed up and go out on a week night?"

"You could always go out and ask him, Charles."

"No, that's his business. But it must be something he thinks is important."

"Maybe he's joined the Lions' Club."

"Hey, maybe he has a girl."

"Oh, Charles, what rot."

"What about 'Bunny'?"

"But there is no 'Bunny'."

"I'm beginning to wonder. By golly, what if there is? Sufferin' rattlesnakes, as Walter says. Wouldn't that be something now?"

12

Cats, Rats and Cattle

June came rushing across Briarwood Farm with her banners singing a riot of colours. The severity and rigours of winter were forgotten. Far back in memory was the wintertime day when the car wheels spun vainly on the icy stretch of the long hill leading to the fifth concession road — and the moonlit night when the towering snow-drifts on the sideroad brought many a car to a stop and held it prisoner until the township snowplow rescued it when the strong winds stopped blowing. Where the water of the creek was now shimmering across sunny sandbars memory recalled the frigid days when it was a long, winding chain of steel-blue ice.

From an old mullein stalk a bobolink now rises, singing on the wing and leaving behind it a stave of rollicking, reedy notes, as if to tell that when local, land-locked mortals were floundering through a tiring path of snow it was having a glorious holiday in South America. Now, too, the meadow lark again shows its black gorget-on-yellow from a fence post as it whistles its skewy, slurred notes and then drops down to the ground and crawls along a tunnel of grass to its nest. The hulk of a crow stalks along the ground and finds the nest of a kildeer. It seizes one of the eggs and bears it away unbroken while the helpless mother strikes feebly at the marauder and puts on a pitiful display of having a broken wing to try to draw its attention away from the nest.

A woodchuck whistles from a hillside hole. The robins go frantic about their erring youngsters who tumble out of the nest before they can fly. Tiny baby rabbits, rat-sized, are killed off by a stalking cat. A grackle's nest is attacked and a dozen other grackles rally to its aid — shrieking raucously and dive-bombing the tree where the ravage is taking place.

The cropland turns colour as the oats and barley and pasture grow their green carpets on the black earth. The corn is up and stretches in precise rows like miles of little green sentry-soldiers. The strawberry vines form a lush matting and shelter the green berries which will burst into mouth-watering goodness and redness later in the month. And out on the pastures the neighbouring farmers' cows, released from their winter prison a week or so before, do everything but play leap-frog as they celebrate their freedom. And a succession of practical things were June-happenings on the Brewster farmstead. The flock of sheep, with every joint showing now that their wool has been clipped off, bleated continuously for their straying lambs. The twenty pullets and cockerels in the brooder house were slowly discovering that they were developing wings that could be fluttered like two tiny semaphores. In the well the level of water continued to be satisfactory and the Brewsters crossed their fingers every time they thought of how they were at the mercy of the Mygrange Development Company's future demands. The fields of fall wheat planted on the neighbouring farms along the sideroad were enclaves of startling green. The creek red chub darted through the shades beneath the gnarled willows. Millie Brewster's flower beds turned into crazy-quilts of bloom. In the garden a dozen vegetables stuck their periscope noses out of the ground and then slipped up into the light.

And down at the creek Charles Brewster sat in his tree-house and pondered. He wasn't just down "at the creek". He was over the top of the creek. He could stick his reddish-haired head and freckled neck out the window and look down at the quicksilver of the flowing water any time he wished. In fact during the first few days in which he spent certain periods of the day in his tree-house he found his head sticking out of the window too much of the time. He was taking much longer to do his column and certain other things he found himself writing than he should be taking. In fact it took a surprise visit from Millie to start him realizing this. He didn't hear her climb the steps from the ground, didn't hear her turn the knob in the door.

"Excuse me, Charles."

"Eh? . . . Oh! . . . Yeah!"

As he uttered these somewhat meaningless ejaculations he was bumping his head on the side of the window as he sought to pull it back into the room.

"I'm sorry. I should have given you warning. I was going to whistle but I thought you'd think it was a starling."

"Oh, no need to. Sit down in chair number two. What'll you have? Highball, beer, sherry? Sorry, we haven't a license here."

"We'll have coffee. I brought over a thermos."

"Oh, that's great. I guess I should bring over a thermos with me every time. Or I could have a little hot-plate over here to plug in and make coffee. I could even cook bacon and eggs and toast on it, eh?"

"If you had a bed you could even move in and be out of my way."

"Don't give me ideas. Well, that's fine. Nice cup of steaming hot coffee."

"And I brought you a little thing I snipped out of the Mapleville *Banner*. It's a notice in the classified section about a Rummage Sale they're holding. 'Good chance to get rid of anything not worth keeping but too good to throw away. Bring along your husbands.' "

"Oh, that's cute, Mill. I better stay away from that one."

"I think so. How's the column going?"

"Not bad but I'm spending too much time with my head out of the window observing nature."

"That's not a bad idea, either. Well, the reason I came over is to tell you that Horace Greene phoned and he wants to know if you can go in tomorrow. He wants to talk about the Hafney Feed and Fertilizer account."

"Oh, nuts. Look, I have to resign from that. I want to write other things. I'll resign when I go in tomorrow. And Horace will throw a fit so I better take a resuscitator with me."

"What other things do you want to write? Limericks?"

"Oh, a lot of things. I've just finished a limerick, by the way. Want to hear it?"

"Of course I do."

"I just happen to have it with me." Charles cleared his throat.

> "There once was an M.P. of note
> Who thought he'd the world by the throat;
> But he ebbed with the tide,
> His young bride by his side,
> When the vote punched a hole in his boat."

"Charles, why don't you try writing real poetry? I know your limericks are very good but I've seen two or three serious poems you've written and they aren't half bad at all."

"I wasn't going to tell you but that's exactly what I am doing."

"Good for you. And you don't want to show them to me yet."

"Not yet. Hey, there's a big truck pulling in — going on down towards the barn."

"I'll bet it's the feeders you're getting."

"Holy Nellie, that's what it is. I'd better get on my overalls. They'll want some help unloading them. Where's Walter?"

"I don't know. Probably down in the barn. How many are we getting?"

"Ten head. We'll put two in our own pasture and the others in the flats. I got permission from Mygrange to use the flats so the cattle can eat off the weeds along with the grass and not have to get somebody to mow the weeds. Well, I better go."

And Mr. Brewster went. A few minutes later he was helping unload the ten steers at the entrance to the pasture. The drover, Mel Kirby and his son, John, had erected a ramp leading down from the back of the truck to the ground and the ten steers were prodded to make the descent. This they did with much bawling, skidding, snorting and baleful looks. But eventually they were all down on the grass which was to be their home and also their food supply for the following five months or so. Immediately they started cavorting, a sure indication that they had come from inside winter quarters and were seeing the wide open spaces for the first time in months. They spun in circles, kicked and bucked as if they were putting on a show at the Calgary Stampede, threw their heads up, pawed the ground and ran at random across the pasture. Meanwhile the Kirbys, Charles and Walter stood back and commented. Then Walter wanted to know where Mel Kirby had bought the feeders.

"Down east about 180 miles — down near Ottawa. I buy a lot of cattle there. Sure of good stuff." With that Mel slapped his cattle cane against the side of the truck so violently that Charles jumped. It turned out that it was simply the usual accompaniment to Mel's conversation. "Yeah, you can grow them into good beef by this fall."

"How much they weigh?" Walter wanted Charles to know that he knew what he was talking about.

"Weigh 7860 pounds for the load. That figures out to what? About 786 pounds apiece except that three or four weigh less and three or four weigh more."

Walter pressed on. "That one over there ain't up to too much."

"She'll fill out. That one throwin' itself around over there makes up for the small one."

Charles decided that since he was paying for them he should be showing a conversational interest. "And how much gain should we reasonably expect, Mr. Kirby?"

"Oh, depends on your pasture. This pasture looks fairly good though it's hard to judge it right now, eh? And you have to count in the grain you feed them later on, especially if the pasture runs short, eh? But you can likely count on makin' fifty bucks an animal — somewhere around there."

Walter asked him what he thought of Holstein feeders instead of a beef breed.

"Well, I'll tell you," replied Mr. Kirby. "I don't see a hell of a lot of difference when it comes to eatin' the meat. Nothin' wrong with Angus or Shorthorn or Hereford but I eat Holstein beef meat most of the time. And I got no complaint, eh? I got no complaint at all." Mr. Kirby slapped the side of his big truck with his drover's cane and changed the subject. "You're in the writin' business so I hear, Mr. Brewster."

"Yes, I write a column for the city News."

"Yeah, somebody was showin' it to me a couple of weeks ago. You had a piece about how somebody painted a crow red and put it in the horses' oat box and when this Irish lad lifted the lid it scared the hell out of him, eh?"

"Yes, Walter here told me that story."

"Well, I can tell you a little story — and she's true, too — about how I got rid of rats in a feed mill I used to own."

"I'd like to hear it, sure."

"Well, this was an old mill that I took over and ran for a few years and as soon as I started operatin' it I could see that the fellow that owned it was losin' money because the rats were eatin' up his profits. Why, the place was crazy with 'em — rats as big as little dogs."

While the others were laughing Mr. Kirby lit up a cigarette and continued. "Well, I tried everything. I set traps, I put out poison seed and poison meat and poison cheese around the mill. No good. Then I got ten cats but I think the rats were bigger than the cats and started chasin' the cats around instead of the cats chasin' the rats. I dunno. Then somebody told me that if I caught a rat and singed it and let it go that that'd scare the other rats away. But I figured that seemed kind of cruel, even to a rat, so I didn't do that. And then one of my customers told me about an idea he said his dad had tried once and it worked. So I caught six rats alive — by usin' a cage with a door that tripped when the rat got inside. Then I took these six rats and I dipped 'em in tar and stuck hen feathers all over them."

There was general laughter as the others formed their own picture of rats running around with hen feathers. Then Mr. Kirby resumed his story. "Well sir, things started to happen right away when we let these six rats loose. No sooner did the other rats get a look at these rats that were tarred and feathered than they just about went nuts. They'd never seen anything like such crazy-lookin' creatures before. They started gallopin' all over the mill lookin' for the nearest way out. And it wasn't long before every last one of 'em was cleaned out."

"What about them there rats that were tarred and feathered?" asked Walter.

"Well, I'll tell yeh," concluded Mr. Kirby. "When these six rats got a chance to take time off and look at each other they got such a shock that they got out of the mill, too."

Everybody laughed and Mr. Kirby gave the side of his truck an extra-hard whack with his cane by way of emphasis. "You like that story, Mr. Brewster?"

"Yes, that was quite a yarn. Well, I'd better pay you for the cattle and the trucking."

"Got the bill right here. I don't think you'll find that out of the way."

Mr. Brewster used the side of the truck to write out a check for the amount and with a "glad to be of service to you", the Kirbys climbed into the cab of the truck and departed. Walter and Charles turned to see that the cows were simmering down. They were heaving and puffing from their post-winter exertions but soon would be settling down to eating the lush growth of grass.

"Well, Walter? There they are. You think the fences will hold them in?"

"Yeah, I put in twenty extra steel posts and two new wooden anchor posts at the corners where they were gettin' rotted. Diggin' them holes was no damn fun, either. I kept hittin' stones and every time I hit a stone I'd cuss. You hear me cussin' down at the house?"

"No, I didn't hear it, Walter. Well, the cattle should be under control then if you've done such a good job on the fences."

"Oh, them buggers won't get out. They're not bad lookin' feeders, either, except that runty one and maybe it'll come along."

"I want to bring Laddie out here and get him used to the cattle, Walter."

"Eh? That dog you got would take one look at these cattle and howl his way all the way back to the house again."

"Oh, he might get used to them. He's starting to get a little spirit into him already. He's wagging his tail now and walking around without slinking so much."

"Speakin' of dogs, how about cats?"

"How about them? How do you mean, Walter?"

"Well, that story about tarrin' and featherin' the rats brung it to my mind. We're goin' to need a couple cats around these barns. That old cat couldn't catch a two-day-old baby mouse right now."

"Yes, I know. She won't live much longer."

"I know where I can locate a couple of cats if you want 'em, Mr. Brewster."

"I guess it's never much trouble locating cats. People are glad to give away their kittens anyway."

"These is grown cats I'm talkin' about — ready to kill mice and rats."

"Where is this, Walter?"

"A farm up on the 18th sideroad."

"Oh? The 18th, eh?"

"Yeah, I could drop up tonight and pick 'em up."

"Well, I suppose that's all right. Would they stay around in a strange place?"

"I can shut 'em up in the barn for a couple days and if I feed 'em they'll likely hang around."

"I don't like to have you go all the way up to the 18th especially, Walter."

"Oh, I'm goin' up that way anyway after supper so I'll bring back a couple of them cats, Mr. Brewster." And with that Walter shut the gate into the pasture and walked towards the barnyard.

Shortly after supper that night Millie saw Walter headed for the drive-shed. A surprised look came over her face as she motioned Charles to look.

"Well, I'll be damned," was Charles' pithy comment.

"He's all dressed up again. This is at least once each week since we first saw him going out with his best suit on, Charles."

"His only suit, you mean. By golly, this is quite a mystery. He seemed to want to go up and get those cats when he mentioned to me this afternoon that we should have a couple of cats in the barn."

"You said he was getting them on 18th Avenue?"

"That's what he said, Millie. I'm beginning to wonder what the heck is going on around here. I think we should find out where he gets the cats. He didn't say which farm."

"I'm beginning to think you feel he actually has a girl friend up on 18th Avenue, Charles."

"I don't know what to think. It's just a little queer, that's all. When I signed that letter 'Bunny' as an April Fools' joke, I simply put 18th Avenue on it. That doesn't mean a damn thing. There just can't be any connection. We're just imagining things. There's nobody on 18th Avenue with the first name of 'Bunny'."

"Well, there's some attraction up there, that's for sure. Or up that way somewhere. Walter doesn't get all dressed up in the middle of the week like this for nothing. Something darned queer is going on."

13

Trout Lapland and
Bay Street Automatons

About ten o'clock the next forenoon Charles Brewster's station wagon could be seen travelling down the Parkway towards the city and to the Greene Advertising Agency. Charles drove fairly slowly. When he was commuting, nearly a year before, he had felt impelled to drive up to and over the speed limit whenever traffic permitted in order to get to the office in time. Now he indulged himself and smiled as he remembered how often he used to get mad at the hold-ups in the rush-hour periods. Once he had had an accident. A car had tried to switch lanes and in so doing had cut him off too sharply. The result was an accident to both cars. Fortunately no one was hurt seriously. The other man's insurance company had paid for the repairs to Charles' car but it had meant a long wait while the car was being fixed and he used a courtesy car. And it had bothered his nerves for quite a while.

But today it was different. He was on his way to resign from his part-time job as consultant on the Hafney Feed and Fertilizer account. He felt as free as one of the song sparrows on his farm. This was Charles Brewster's day. And he still felt that way when he was ushered into the office of Horace Greene.

"Well, well, Charlie, good to see you. Sit down. Have a cigar. You're losing weight, boy."

Charles sat down, took a cigar and acknowledged that he had taken off twelve pounds since Christmas and was now smoking a pipe most of the time. But he allowed Horace to light his cigar.

"How are things going, Horace?"

"Oh, so-so. Good and bad. But the Hafney account you're looking after is in good shape. They're well pleased. That new logo you figured out made them real happy. You're a darned good creative man, Charlie. And your knowledge of what you've learned on that farm of yours is coming in real useful. The copy shows that you've acquired a genuine practical knowledge of farming — real down to earth stuff."

"Well, I'm glad they're satisfied with it. To tell the truth, Horace, I know you wanted to see me about the account today but as well as that I . . . well, I've decided that . . ."

"Chuck, just a minute. Here, have a look. Some roughs of six institutional ads we're getting ready for the meat department of Hafney."

"You mean you've got the meat account as well as the feed and fertilizer?"

"Not yet, m'boy. Not quite yet. This is just a come-on campaign — to show them what we can do here, as opposed to the agency they're using now. How's that look?"

"Well, it . . . looks pretty good . . . yes."

"I didn't call you in on it. I let the creative department go ahead with it because this series doesn't involve farming especially. But I think we'll land that meat division account within six months. And it's worth three-quarters of a million bucks."

Charles whistled appropriately, drew on his cigar and cleared his throat.

"Horace, as I was saying, I've decided that I'd better not . . ."

He didn't finish. Horace held up his hand. "Chuck, would you like a little nip? I keep a bit of Grant's Scotch in my drawer here."

"You know, Horace, I hardly ever touch the stuff any more. It seems to kind of bore me. I get interested in other things."

"That's fine, Chuck, that's fine. By the way, I've read the last three or four columns you've been writing for the *News*. Pretty good stuff."

"Thank you. And that's one thing I wanted to see you about today. I have to do quite a lot of travelling to get the material and it's keeping me pretty busy. I guess you can see that, Horace."

"Why, sure, it would. But it's a good hobby. Now, as I was saying, I think that when we get this meat division account of Hafney's you can come in on it — writing public relations stuff to get a liaison between producers of meat, processors and the consumer. That's needed right now so . . ."

Charles held up his hand — up high, as if he were stopping traffic, which he was in a sense. "Horace, I'm trying to tell you something. I want to resign from the Hafney Feed and Fertilizer account."

"You want to what?"

"I want to resign from it. I know you pay me well for it but I'm making something out of my column and . . . well, I just want to have no other responsibilities."

"But you're just nicely broken in. You only started when you resigned from the firm last summer. What do I do for someone to write the stuff you do?"

"I'd like to resign at the end of June."

"Good God, man. That's only a month away or less."

"There are always writers, Horace — good advertising creative men. You can find somebody else. Go after Ted White over at the Dunmorgan agency. He knows the rural scene pretty well. I think he could work into it."

"Oh, hell. Charles, this is . . . this is preposterous. You can't do it."

"Yes, I want to, Horace. The end of June."

"All right . . . all right . . . do it . . . quit . . . leave me holding the bag. You don't give a damn about leaving the firm where you spent a lot of happy years. You got your real start with this firm, remember. You got married on the strength of it. I told Millie, when you were engaged to her, that you'd have a steady job here and she wouldn't have anything to worry about. And you didn't, either. Oh, we had our little differences, especially when you first moved out to that farm. But nothing a good talk didn't settle. Now how about it, Chuck? You can't quit."

"I'll stay until the end of July instead of the end of June."

"Well, that would be some help, Charles. Maybe we can influence you to stay longer — with a raise in pay if the meat division account comes to us, eh, boy?"

"Oh, I doubt it, Horace. I'm getting so hooked on country life that the advertising business leaves me a bit cold, I'm afraid. However, we'll see."

"Charles, let me take you out to lunch. I know where you can get the best Trout Lapland with a rich creamy dill sauce."

"Trout Lapland, eh? Nah, at home I can have Sucker Briarwood, with sauce à la Millie."

"How about the best scampi you ever ate — with shallots and mushrooms and tiny shrimps and a final flambé of Pernod and brandy — with a shake of hollandaise sauce."

"Horace, you're losing me. Besides, it costs too damn much money. They charge anything they like these days in expensive restaurants and I'm damned if I'm going to let people gouge me out of twenty-five bucks or so for a meal — which makes them richer and richer and makes me poorer and poorer. I'd rather have a good steak and kidney pie out at the farm."

"Charles, that farm has sure done things to you."

"Sure, it's given me a sense of balance . . . a sense of equation. I'm an individualist now. I'm bloody well damned if I'm going to spend two or three times what a meal should cost just to be seen in a fancy restaurant. I'm down to basic thinking now. I'm my own man, Horace. So thanks just the same. I appreciate it. And I'll get in touch with you next week. I'll have that copy you wanted by then for the Hafney beef feeding program."

And with that Charles went out into the street and became ingested, through a process of pushing, shoving and prodding, into the tornado of traffic on one of the main streets. He went into a new skyscraper that had only been completed a month before. Here he could stand behind an immense plate glass window that he decided was a hundred feet long and twenty feet high and see a microcosm of life in a city of two million people — ambitiously called souls. From his five-million-dollar command post of glass, steel and stone he could cover the criss-cross of earthlings as they fled across the intersecting streets in a sort of double-dare game with the four-wheeled traffic. Since it was the heart of the financial district the population, as it seemed to Charles, appeared to be trying to dress themselves so those outside the pale of this enclave would be aware that they worked in an atmosphere overstuffed with affluence. The dwellers were shaped as people anywhere. They were thin, short, tall, fat and non-adjustable in the relationship of the various parts of their anatomy. But they had used a not inconsiderable part of their emolument to so clothe themselves as to make the best use of their disparate parts. In many cases the result was not too effective but the main thing was that the cost of the cloth and the fitting by tailors and dressmakers proclaimed itself.

It was the aspects, the mien, the visages that interested Charles. It appeared to him that everyone seemed rather ill. They looked either sad and beaten, as if they were losing every round with life and were slowly giving up or were so mad at life that they spent their hours in the financial section taking out their anger on the ticker tape by glaring at it as belligerently as possible. There were two minor classifications outside these groupings. There was an occasional sweet old lady who had been pressured for various reasons into this violent neighbourhood and she was like a tiny white candle being transported tremulously to some safer border. And there were hordes of vacuous and/or vapid teenagers who darted and zig-zagged hither and yon like water-bugs on a swamp pond. They appeared to be trying to attract the eye of the male potential pursuer by wearing such a scanty covering around the hips that it gave intermittent excitatory views of not only the upper thigh but the movement of the two feminine bulges in their rear. It was a sort of sex contest of fiercely competitive proportions. It was a chorus played out before the gray backdrop of the Exchange temple.

Charles stared at the spectacle for over an hour. It was strange that he had never reacted before in the way he did now. Then he realized that he had never had time to do that. He had been too busy four blocks away at the agency. At times he had been a part of it but not as an over-all observer. Now, after only a few months away, he was back in the canyon where the walls rose nearly a thousand feet sheer above the pedestrians and he felt nauseated. He tried to tell himself that he was over-reacting, thinking of it as a sort of revolting 20th century Sodom. But he couldn't overcome his initial revulsion and started walking away from it on a quiet side-street. A little farther along he came to one of the older and more gracious hotels where he knew the food was excellent. Here he had a glass of cold beer, a steak and kidney pie and deep apple pie with old Canadian cheese. An hour later he was driving back up the Parkway, as if trying to flee as fast as possible from his forenoon in the city.

Millie greeted him, after he had put the station wagon away and gone into the house, with a knowledgeable greeting. "You look as if you're glad to be back from the jungle, Charles."

Charles over-sighed and threw up his hands dramatically. "You can have it. But I've gone and done it. I've resigned from Horace's bloody Hafney account. But after he'd pleaded a bit with me I told him I'd stay on until the end of July — a month longer than I intended."

"Well, I'm glad you've resigned. We haven't as much money coming in as interest as Onassis and that Jackie-daw woman, as you describe her, but we're doing all right. You don't need the Hafney account. Have you had lunch?"

"Yes, at the King Eddy cafeteria. Best civilized place to eat in Toronto. They don't drench food with all that damn French and Hungarian and God-knows-what sauces. And they don't grab your wallet as well as your money on the way out."

"Much better food than what you get at home?"

"Hell, no. Millie's cafeteria is at the top of course. I didn't think I needed to say that. By the way, are the two cats still around or did Walter say?"

"Yes, they were here an hour ago, anyway, when Walter was in to lunch. And the banties as Bobby calls them are still around. Peter and Patty. And Laddie is still here."

"How are you, Laddie? Come 'ere, eh? Come on. Over here!"

"He's wagging his tail at least. That's more than he did when we first got him. Look, I think he is coming over."

"That-a-boy, Laddie, come on. Yeah, look at him. And he isn't scraping the floor with his belly the way he used to. Ah, that-a-boy. We're going to make a real live dog of you yet."

"Walter keeps on saying he'll never be a barking dog, though."

"Oh, I don't know. Eh, Laddie? You never going to bark? Well,

I'm betting on you, see. I'm betting my bottom dollar that one of these days you're going to start barking like a real dog when a strange car drives in."

"Of course he will, Charles. By the way I was talking to a Mrs. MacCormack on the phone. She has antiques in her house over in Markdale and she tells me that there will be a lot of antiques offered at Duncan's sale a week from this Saturday."

"She'll likely be bidding against you then."

"No, she says she's through buying antiques. She's just over seventy years old and she's not buying any more. She says she's an antique herself now and she doesn't need any more around the house."

"Well, you'd better pick up a few at the Duncan sale then — and hope that too many dealers aren't there to run the price up."

"You mean I can actually blow myself to anything I see there that I like?"

"Well, within reason, dear. I don't think you'll ruin the exchequer but you've earned the right to indulge yourself. You've worked hard around this place."

"Thank you, sir. Well, Mrs. MacCormack says there'll be a sort of preview the day before — to give people the chance to look them over beforehand. So I'll be there to decide what I want to bid on the next day."

"How's the old corner cupboard coming along?"

"Almost finished. I ran into a problem when I was stripping the paint off. The original paint applied was the old type of red milk paint — like the little old red schoolhouse, you know. Casein paint, made with milk and natural earth colouring."

"And that penetrated right into the pine, eh?"

"Yes, and so far that I just couldn't get it out of the little crevices in the wood. So, in my sort of amateurish fashion I guess, I covered this residue with a paint mixed to the shade of the pine. I just wiped it on and after a few minutes I wiped it off carefully so the grain would show and the natural pine colour. Then I felt that a flat varnish was needed over this to protect the finish so that's what I've done."

"And it looks good, eh?"

"I think so. Oh, I guess I didn't tell you. I took the doors off the top part of the cupboard — and I had some trouble getting the screws out, too. But I thought it would be better to leave the top open so as to display whatever I put in there."

"Which will be our better chinaware, I think you said."

"Oh, I have another idea for it now but that's all tied into the old pig-pen."

"What the hell has the corner cupboard got to do with the old pig-pen?"

"I told you the other day I have something in mind. I'll let you know in good time, Charles."

"Yeah, do that, eh? The suspense is killing me."

Remarking that his go-to-the-city clothes were killing him, too, Charles went upstairs to change and Millie descended to the depths to see her corner cupboard — as if she had fears of it changing under her non-professional application from the gray colour with the grain showing through to a violent orange or indigo.

Out in the cow stable Walter was looking out of one of the small southern windows at the ten feeders in the meadow when Charles entered.

"They got themselves real settled down, Mr. Brewster, it looks like. They're chewin' away as if the grass was only goin' to last a month."

"I hope they're wrong, although I heard someone on the radio predicting a very dry summer."

"I kind of figure that way myself. We're goin' to need all the grass we can get."

"How are the two new cats you got, Walter?"

"There they be right behind you on that bale of straw. Right at home. Mighty purty coloured cats, too."

"Hm . . . tortoise shell and white and the other one black and white. Yes, they're full grown, eh?"

"Yeah, and one of 'em came trottin' out from between the bales with a mouse a while ago. That's a good start. But the old cat, Tabby, she ain't too well pleased about all this."

"What do you mean, Walter? She's jealous of the two new cats, you mean?"

"I guess she'd like to be but she ain't even got strength enough to be jealous though I guess she feels that way. She just mopes around and keeps out of their way. And the two new cats they're pickin' on her some, too."

"Fighting with her?"

"Oh, not exactly fightin' but they show their claws at her. They know she ain't got long for this world and they're the new bosses now."

"I guess we'll have to do something about it, Walter. We better get rid of her, as much as I hate to."

"She ain't no good to herself, even. She's been just about blind for a long time. We best shoot her and be done with it."

"I can't shoot her, Walter. I just can't shoot anything. I get chicken."

"Oh, hell, I'll shoot her if that's all you want. You ain't got a gun, eh?"

"I've only got that old antique flint-lock thing. I don't think that would help much. You've got a .22 gun."

"Yeah, I ain't got no .22 bullets, though. I better slip down to Hardings tonight and get some bullets."

"Okay, Walter. By the way, don't say anything to Mrs. Brewster about it."

"I guess not, eh? Women is weepy."

"We can tell her in two or three days. I don't think she'll hear the shot if we take the cat out in the barnyard."

"Nah, she won't hear nothin'."

"Walter, did you have to pay anything for the two cats? If you did I'll fix it up with you."

"Nah, they give 'em to me. They was glad to get rid of 'em. They had nine cats. Now they got seven."

"You got them up on the 18th, eh?"

"Up on the 18th, yeah."

"Where is it? Would I know the farm?"

"Nah, I doubt it — between the 8th and 9th concessions. Way northeast of here."

"I feel I should phone them and thank them at least, Walter."

"Nah, you don't have no need to. I done all that when I got 'em."

"Between the 8th and the 9th, eh?"

"Yeah, now don't you go trottin' up there wantin' to thank 'em or somethin'."

"Well, but . . . why not, Walter?"

"Because there ain't no damn need to, that's why, Mr. Brewster. There just ain't no damn cause for you to, that's all. No cause at all for you to."

And with that Walter stalked out of the stable into the barnyard. And Charles walked out another door and towards the house wondering what the hell kind of a bee Walter had in his bonnet.

14

The Death of the "Old Cat"

The next forenoon when Millie was busy in the orchard feeding her pullets and cockerels Charles slipped out of the house and down to the barn. Walter was waiting for him with the agate basin of warm milk he had brought down from the house a few minutes before. He wanted it to coax the old cat down the steps from the barn floor to the cow stable beneath. Tabby wasn't deaf and for many years she had come to her food when she heard a tapping on the basin. Since she was hidden away somewhere up on the barn floor Walter had decided this was the best way to bring her out of hiding and down to the stable.

"Yes, here she comes, Walter, down the steps. She still wants her milk."

"Look at her, eh, Mr. Brewster, comin' down."

It was pitiful to watch her trying to ease herself down the steps. She knew the milk was there and she wanted it. She knew she should be down there beside the milk in the agate basin. Even though she was blind and would never again see the basin nor the milk in it, nor the person who poured the milk into it, she knew it would be there in the same spot it had been in for many years.

In silence and suffering she made her way down. One front paw was first lowered to the step below. Then she squirmed sideways until the other front paw slipped off the step. Then she tried to drag her hindquarters down but her legs were so stiff with rheumatism that all she could do was to let the back part of her body slide off the edge of the step and drop down on a level with the rest of her body. And so she reached the step beneath. And, eventually, she reached the bottom step and the cement stable floor.

Charles hadn't realized her body had become so uncontrollably useless. She wasn't usually in sight when he went out to the stable. And it had been mainly during the three previous months that she had so rapidly declined in her strength. Now it came as a shock to him as he watched her.

"The other cats aren't around, eh, Walter? If they are they'll bother her."

"Nah, they're out in the sheep-barn. I seen 'em a while back."

Charles remembered the day old Tabby had first come to Briar-wood Farm. That was eight years before and she seemed quite old then but lithe as a panther. Many times he had watched her while she crouched as motionless as a tortoise-shell statue near some hole from which she suspected a mouse might emerge. Suddenly he would see her back slowly arch. Then she would spring and trot away a few feet with the mouse in her mouth. A few seconds of soundless motion, the death squeaks of the mouse and it was all over. It was something to admire — the slow, patient waiting, the supreme coordination of every movement as she made the kill, the casual way in which she trotted off with the mouse dangling from her mouth.

Now as Charles and Walter watched her she sipped daintily of the warm milk as she drooped her beautifully coloured body over the edge of the agate basin.

"You remember the day she tangled with the big rat, Walter?"

"Ho ho, that was some fight. That damn rat was almost as big as she was."

Charles remembered how Walter had heard the rat jumping around in the steel drum in the pig-pen. The barrel had had pig-feed in it but was then empty. The rat must have smelled the remnants of feed at the bottom and thought it could get out again or it had possibly fallen in and then found it impossible to jump high enough to reach the top edge of the steel drum and escape. And the smooth sides of the drum made it impossible to climb up.

Charles remembered how he and Walter had carried the drum outside the pig-pen and brought Tabby. Walter had said it was unfair to put the cat in the barrel with the rat. In any case she would probably have sprung out again because a cat wants space for her movements, especially when dealing with a rat the size of the one with which she was faced. They had laid the drum on its side, thinking the rat would come out. But it had apparently known that danger lay at the open end of the drum and had stayed as far back as it could. Then Walter had tried to put the cat inside — thinking that, as the drum was on its side, she would tackle the rat. Still she refused and jumped out.

Finally Walter had tipped up the drum so that the rat was forced to slide out onto the grass. Instantly Tabby had sprung upon him. There was a dizzy whirling of rat and cat for only a few seconds, each fighting for a death grip. And then the motion had stopped as quickly as it had begun. Tabby had the big rat by the back of the neck. It was still squirming but she got a fresh hold and there was the sound of teeth crunching into the grey neck. The huge rat's struggles had grown weaker and she had lugged him away, growling over her possession as she went. An hour later Charles and Walter had seen what was left of it beside the pig-chute at the south of the horse-barn — one tail that measured seven inches long and slimy bits and pieces of other parts of its body. Later Tabby had been violently ill.

"I wonder how many kittens she's had through the years, Walter," Charles commented as they watched her very slowly getting some milk into her body.

"Holy Susie. I dunno. More'n I could count up to maybe. She's sure had a lot of batches. Maybe a hundred kittens. Maybe more."

"You should know. You had the job of drowning most of them. Millie or I didn't have the nerve to do it and we had to do something with 'em."

"Yeah, I just chucked the kittens in a grain sack and put a stone in with 'em and chucked 'em in a deep hole in the crik."

"I remember you saying more than once that if we kept all the cats we wouldn't have any milk from the cows to ship."

"We'd have been out of the milk-shippin' business, that's for sure."

As Charles watched old Tabby now the realization came over him that never again would she give birth to a kitten nor catch a mouse nor reach the great beams under the barn roof with sudden rushes and leaps the way she used to. She was old and sick and close to death. As the men stood looking at her she raised her head and backed slowly away from the agate basin. She dragged her feeble body over beside the stable wall where she sensed she would be out of the way. And there she tried to wash her face. That, too, was a sad thing to watch. To do it she had to lift one front paw and lick it, as was her custom, then use the wet paw to rub over her face. But in making even that slight exertion she would start to fall sideways and have to put her paw down again to recover.

"I guess we might as well do it now, Mr. Brewster."

Charles nodded. He watched Walter take a short .22 bullet from his pocket and fit it into the firing chamber.

"You carry the gun out to the barnyard," Walter said. "I'll carry the cat out."

"Oh, out there, eh?"

"It's as good a place as any."

"Yes, I guess."

Walter reached down and picked her up. He was hardened to death on a farm through all the years of seeing things die and be killed, having to shoot a horse with a broken leg, cut the throat of a pig that was to be sloshed in boiling water and cut up for winter pork and things like that. But in spite of all this Charles noticed that he was moved by what was happening. He lifted Tabby as gently as he could. Then he cradled her in his arms and held her close against him so she wouldn't roll off if he made a misstep.

They went out into the rectangular sunlit space of the barnyard. Charles stood back against the stone wall of the cow-stable. Walter took the cat over to the mounded manure pile in the centre of the barnyard. There he placed the cat gently on some fouled straw on the side of the manure heap. She didn't offer to move. Walter came back to Charles and took the gun. They were about twenty feet away from the cat.

Walter raised the gun. The old cat tried to lift herself to her feet but she sank down into the manure a little and gave up trying. But she kept moving her head around slowly as if she would have liked to find out where she was. Walter cocked the gun but waited for her to keep her head still. When she did Walter squeezed the trigger.

Old Tabby gave a sudden, small erratic movement as if she were about to jump up. Then she sank down on her side, twitched for a moment, again sank down on her side. Her body twisted into a sort of coiled position. Then her limbs very slowly straightened out and she lay still on the manure pile.

The "old cat" was dead!

15

The Man who Dug his own Grave

Next morning the seven o'clock sun seemed to be shining more brightly than it had ever shone before as Charles Brewster swung his station wagon out into the sideroad and started for Ottawa, over 200 miles away. He had decided that some of his columns should include human interest stories from other parts of his province and someone had told him that some areas around the capital city were replete with interesting material. He expected to be away until the following night because of the distance.

The road was good, the traffic was light and by approximately noon Charles found himself just outside Ottawa. He pulled in at a roadside restaurant which proclaimed, on a gaudy billboard, that it was the *cordon bleu*! By the time he had finished a third of the boot-leather slice of beef and choked until he sneezed on a piece of cement pie (listed on the menu as maple custard) he was glad to stagger out into the June sunshine. He had decided to look up an old friend who ran a community paper on the periphery of Ottawa and just might be able to steer him onto some stories. He found the address by following an Ottawa street map and a few minutes later was talking in the back office of Harry Minden, a sandy-haired man in his mid-forties with a ready smile, a vigorous handshake and crumpled, comfortable suit.

"So now you know what I'm after, Harry. Any good leads?"

"Yes, two or three, Charlie. You better go and see Eli Fanshaw. He has a good farm across the river and about 12 miles farther on and he has a story I've often heard him tell about a man who dug his own grave."

"Sounds interesting, Harry."

"It's sort of two stories in one but I'd like him to tell it. And you can go and see Max Tyner if you have time. Eli Fanshaw can tell you how to get there. He's always good for a few stories."

"Well, I appreciate this, Harry."

"Say, this column you're doing sounds interesting. I'd heard you sold your farm for quite a lot of money. So now you're just doing as you please, eh?"

"Oh, more or less. I still have the house and six acres left but I just can't do nothing. By the way, I had a quick look at your last issue while I was waiting for you. You've got a lot of advertising there."

"Yes, I'm doing all right. In fact I'm short on editorial space so I think I'll go for another four pages to balance the advertising. And I've got a good staff and that's something these days. I'm lucky."

They shook hands again, promised to keep in touch and Charles left. He had little trouble finding Eli Fanshaw's farm and Eli himself — a little gnome-like man with a narrow face and beak nose but with good-humour lines that made Charles like him right away.

"So Harry sent you, Mr. Brewster. You're from Toronto."

"Yes, about twenty miles out of Toronto — near Mapleville."

"I haven't heard of it."

"No, you wouldn't have. Well, I hope you don't mind me dropping in on you."

"Of course not. Glad to have a visitor. Now, let's see. We can walk through this little field here. That's where the grave is."

They walked side by side and on the way Eli began to tell the story.

"This happened over a century ago but it's a true story that's been handed down through our family all that time because it happened right on this farm, you see. I'm a descendant of the man who owned the farm then." Eli paused, looked around him and then suggested they circle around a spot that looked to be wet. "Well, it seems there was a Scotchman who was walking along the sideroad just south of here. You'd pass it on your way up, just half a mile down there. He was walking along and all of a sudden he got sick — real sick. But he managed to drag himself along as far as this farm and into the barn. Not the one you see there now. That was only built thirty years ago."

"You don't know the Scotchman's name."

"No, I don't. I don't remember ever having heard it though some of my folks who've since died must've heard it I suppose. Anyway, the hired man on the farm tried to look after this fellow but he died awful sudden. Well, it seems that my forbears — who worked the farm then — were away for the weekend or for a couple of days or some such thing so the hired man, not knowing what to do and possibly being pretty upset and confused about all this happening so suddenly, dug a grave for him right in the middle of this field you're in now. The hired man had no idea who he was and couldn't find any identification on him so he did what he thought was best at the time."

"Is that the site of the grave up ahead there? I see two huge stones about four feet high and ten feet or so apart."

"Yes, that's the spot. When the farm was being cleared of stones they left those in the field. Even the big old equipment they had in those days for lifting stones and taking them over to the side of the field to make a fence wasn't powerful enough to transport those two big boulders. Anyway, that's where the Scotchman was buried. But lo and behold, Mr. Brewster, just a few days after the grave was dug the dead man's identification was established. Somebody in Ottawa had seen a notice of his sudden death in the paper and came up to the farm here, found out what happened and claimed the body. Well, the grave was opened and the Scotchman's body was taken away. I don't even know where it was eventually buried."

"Poor fellow, eh? His relatives were probably all back in Scotland."

"I'm not sure. They probably were, Mr. Brewster. Anyway, would you believe it? Only a few days later the hired man who had dug the grave for the Scotchman got sick very suddenly. And inside of two days he was dead. But before he died the local doctor diagnosed the disease as cholera. He'd caught it from the Scotchman. So, anyway, it was decided that because of the fear of a cholera epidemic or some such thing that he should be buried immediately. So you can guess where he was buried."

"Yes, in the grave he had dug himself for the Scotchman, I imagine."

"In other words he had dug his own grave."

"That's quite a story. A sad story but most unusual, Mr. Fanshaw."

"There's a sequel to it if you care to hear it. Oh, here we are at the grave. Huge stones, eh? One at the head and one at the feet. And the hired man is buried between the two. We've always worked around it. You can see where it's only cultivated up to about three feet each side of the two big boulders. There was originally a wooden marker with the hired man's name on it but it got rotted away and his relatives couldn't apparently be traced. He was an itinerant man who worked here and there, you know, as so many of them did in the old days."

Eli Fanshaw leaned up against one of the huge boulders and Charles followed suit and waited for the sequel to the strange story.

"Only a few months ago, Mr. Brewster, maybe a year ago, I guess it was, some children were walking through this field one Sunday morning on their way back from pilfering apples over in my neighbour's orchard over there. Well, as kids will they wandered over to the grave here, maybe with the idea of sitting back against one of these rocks and eating the apples. Now, if you'll turn sideways there you'll see that the earth above the grave has dropped down about two feet, almost three — more than you'll usually see in a grave for some reason. Anyway, these kids were sitting around beside the grave for a while and then they happened to look over the edge of the elevation. And what did they see but an old man with a great, long grey beard lying stretched out on his back right on the spot where the original grave was."

"Holy Smoke. That'd make them move in a hurry."

"Yes, it sure did. They dropped their apples and ran away screaming their heads off."

"There must have been a simple explanation of it," ventured Charles.

"Yes, there was. Later on it was discovered that a very old resident of the area was in the habit of going to this spot in the field quite often on a Sunday afternoon for a snooze in privacy — and the most level place he could find to stretch out was right on top of this grave."

"Well, I'll be darned." It was the only comment Charles could think of. "That's quite a story, Mr. Fanshaw."

"I can tell you another one about a grave but it isn't quite as interesting as those I've told you."

"I'd like to hear it."

"Well, about twelve years ago I guess it was a middle-aged farmer who lived down near my brother's farm near Cornwall breathed his last. He'd only been married two or three years and according to the gossip his young wife had led him a merry chase by seeing other men and that had something to do with him dying so soon after marrying her. Anyway, just before he died, according to his sister, he told his wife that he'd come back to haunt her."

"Which he did, eh?"

"Well, about a year after he died and was laid to rest on a fairly steep hillside on a sideroad, a car with his young wife and her current new boy friend in it had to swerve suddenly to avoid a truck. So it went into the ditch and on through the wire fence around the cemetery. And the car came to rest on its side and right up against the tombstone of the husband who slept underneath it. And both the woman and her boy friend had very serious injuries."

"I guess she remembered what he said, eh? — about coming back to haunt her?"

"I guess she did because when she came out of the hospital she put up a 'For Sale' sign on the house right away and as soon as it was sold she left that part of the country and was never heard from again. And she's never come back. Oh, and she didn't take her boy friend with her, either."

Charles laughed. "Well, I appreciate you telling me these stories, Mr. Fanshaw. By the way, this is a great farm you have here, just from what I've seen. Everything is neat around the farm buildings and the fences are good and . . . well, it just looks like a good farm."

"Well, thank you. If it is it's because of my dad's influence. He liked good farming. He thought a farmer should try to be worthy of his land. He sent me to college and I sent my son to college. Both of us have the B.Sc. degree. Not that that's necessary to be a good farmer but I think it helps you appreciate what you have and to use good farm methods."

"I think farmers are getting more . . . well, more sophisticated than they used to be, don't you think?"

"I suppose that's the word for it. They're not known by city people as hayseeds any more. The urban population has almost decided to accept them as fellow human beings, I think." Mr. Fanshaw grinned. "Maybe they've learned that we feed them. No farms, no food. No food, no life. At least some of them are beginning to catch on."

"The trouble is it takes so much money to get into farming these days — for a young man just starting out, I mean."

"Yes, unless his parents have a family farm, which he expects or hopes to inherit sometime, it's almost impossible for a young man to set himself up in farming. It's at least a hundred-thousand-dollar enterprise these days. But it's the greatest profession in the world. And I said 'profession'. It isn't just something a man does when he discovers he's no good for anything else — as some people used to think. Working with the good earth is an honourable profession, Mr. Brewster, don't you let anybody ever tell you it isn't."

As Charles drove back towards Briarwood Farm he couldn't help thinking about what Eli Fanshaw had said — that working with the good earth was an honourable profession. He began to wish that he had had the background to get into the farming business when he was much younger. Instead he had become mixed up with advertising and then became so involved that he had stayed there. Now it was a bit too late. However, he now lived in a farming atmosphere and maybe that was the next best thing — far better than living in a city apartment which, to him, had always seemed like being in a hospital.

At Gananoque he detoured a few miles from the Macdonald Cartier Freeway to visit an old fishing pal of many years' friendship. He had caught many a fine string of fish with Fred Bremner up in the French River region and they had always had fun together. But he hadn't heard from him in years. He realized he didn't even know if he was still alive.

But Fred Bremner was very much alive and Charles was soon sitting beside him out in a little sunroom at the back of his house, having a bottle of cold beer.

"You're looking real good, Charles. I mean it. You've taken off some of that pot, too."

"Yes, I've lost a dozen or so pounds in the last four-five months. So do you look good, you old dog. How's the wife?"

"Oh, I didn't tell you when you first came to the door, Charles. I lost Janie last summer — just about a year ago. This damn cancer. I was going to let you know about it at the time but I was pretty well cut up about it and neglected to."

"I'm sorry, Fred. She was a great girl."

"Yes, she was. Well, look, I'd just as soon not talk about it. What are you doing up this way?"

"I'm after stories. I'm writing a column now for a Toronto newspaper once a week. So I've been down near Ottawa and thought I'd drop in here on the way home."

"What kind of stories?"

"Oh, tall stories, human interest, success stories, anything."

"You're just too late. Delmer South died a couple of weeks ago. He was the best story teller around here. He was great at it. He knew more stories than there are scales on a sucker."

"Maybe you remember some he told you, Fred."

"Well, let's see, do I? I should, by golly, I should, I sure should. But I'm just no good at remembering stories, Charlie."

"I'm not myself but you should know a fishing story or two. Lord knows you and I have heard enough of them."

"Yes, that's true. Hell, I must be getting old, eh? My memory's slipping. But there's one thing that I've been keeping my eyes on around here the last five years or so. I don't think you'd call it a funny story but it's funny to me. I guess you'd call it a human interest story."

"Let's have it, Fred."

"Well, it may not amuse you at all, but . . . as you maybe know we have a lot of people who have been moving out here from the city — from Kingston and other places and they commute back and forth. I think they're crazy to drive that far but that's their business. But they're buying old farmhouses and renovating them."

"Oh, that's going on all over, Fred."

"Yes, but, now you take this one family. They moved in and they built a partition down the centre of the big kitchen — and the wife used the extra room for her washer and dryer. Then she decided the three upstairs rooms were too small, so she had one of the partitions taken out. Then her husband decided the third-floor attic was too big so he had a partition put up making two rooms out of it and the other room for a study. And he had a verandah put on."

"Well, that's what they wanted, Freddie."

"Yes, but wait now. After seven years they moved back to the city and a new family came in. So what do they do? They decorate the house all over again, even though the other couple had only done it two months before — to help sell it, you know. Then they had the floor lowered in the cellar and moved the dryer and washing machine down there. Then they had the partition taken out of the kitchen so as to make a nice big farm-size kitchen of it. Then they took the partition out of the attic so the husband could have a sort of nice, big hobby room there. About the only thing that was left as it was before was the verandah. And by golly they just got finished with all this when the husband was transferred to Montreal and they sold it."

Charles laughed.

"Wait a minute. I'll give you the gag line, Charlie. They had trouble selling it because they had to put the price up to pay for all these renovations but they did sell it finally. A new family with six kids moved in about a month ago and the first thing they did was put back the partition down the middle of the kitchen. The wife had a bad heart and she didn't want to walk up and down stairs to do the laundry. And because they had so many kids they put the partition back in the attic so as to make extra rooms for some of their six kids. And that's the story up to now."

"The price of that house should be pretty high by now, with all those changes."

"Sure it's high. But people are sure crazy, eh? The builder who did a lot of the work told me he expects the next buyer to want the bathroom taken out and an outhouse installed the way it was before the renovations started."

"They're all crazy except thou and me, Freddie. And there were times when your wife thought thou and I were a little crazy when we stayed out in the rain fishing and came back to your cottage soaked through."

"Yeah, I guess. Well, it sure is nice seeing you again. And I'll tell you what I'll do. I'll try and remember some of the yarns Delmer South used to tell and I'll write them to you in a letter, Charles, and that's a promise."

They shook hands and Charles drove back to the Macdonald-Cartier Freeway and continued on to Napanee, an historic old town sitting astride the river. He drove along the main street, through the bustling business section, up the hill on the west side and pulled in at an attractive motel where the owner showed him to an excellent room overlooking the Napanee River to the south. Charles didn't look out the west window until the motel owner had left but he then discovered that he was looking out over the cemetery. How-

ever, it was starting to get dark by then so Charles decided it would-
n't matter very much. From what he could see it appeared to be a
not unattractive and well-kept area.

Charles had a bath, slipped on a fresh shirt, sat looking out the
south window and across the river for a while and then made his
way to the attached restaurant. Most of the diners were just finishing dinner and he was able to get quick service. Following the vicious
battle of his teeth against the leather beef and cement pie at lunch
that day — which caused him to eat only a small quantity of each —
he felt hungry. His eye was drawn to "Home-made minestrone
soup" and he ordered it, hoping it would not only have the flavour
but plenty of vegetables and all the things that go into the making
of such a fine soup. His eye was also transfixed by "sirloin steak —
generous portion". Thus he gave his order to the attractive teen-age,
black-eyed smiling waitress in a Black Watch tartan skirt. He also
ordered a glass of red wine and thought of Millie as he sipped it.
Millie rarely drank anything but wine. Tonight she would be having
dinner with Walter. In fact dinner would be over by now and he
wondered what she would be doing — probably reading a book on
furniture restoration. Then Charles remembered that Millie would
have been at the preview of the antiques at the Duncans' that afternoon to find out what she might like to bid on at the sale the next
day.

Miss Black Watch marched up at that time with the minestrone
and it looked good. And it tasted better as Charles stirred the ingre-
dients and found plenty of the basic macaroni and navy beans,
zucchini and Parmesan cheese. As well he found chopped celery,
chopped onion, tomatoes, parsley, shredded cabbage and other nice
things. And the beans had almost certainly been soaked overnight as
they should be because they were firm without being too hard. The
thought that went through his mind was that he should have ordered
a demi-carafe of Chianti to go with it but he wasn't in the mood to
experience the dry, cutting harshness of Chianti. Just as the last
spoonful of minestrone disappeared the waitress brought his steak,
medium rare and he saw that the generous portion advertised looked
to be more than generous. The waitress was looking at him as he
savored his first bite and she smiled with assurance as well she might
because it gave promise of being one of the most satisfying steaks
he had ever eaten. And it was. When he had finished the last juicy
morsel Charles sat back, folded his arms over his now-filled paunch
and slowly and flourishingly lighted up a big cigar. (He still liked
a good cigar even though he was smoking a pipe much of the time.)
In reply to Miss Black Watch's query as to dessert he lifted his hands
imploringly and patted his tummy.

Leaving her a generous tip he went back to his room, looked at

TV for half an hour, undressed and pulled on his nightgown (which he had come to prefer to pyjamas) and climbed into bed. After thinking over the happenings of the day, the people he had met and the stories he had heard he turned over and in a few minutes was snoring gently.

Leaving the motel next morning shortly before eight o'clock, after enjoying feathery-light scrambled eggs, whole-wheat toast and coffee he arrived at Briarwood Farm at about 11.30 and found Walter and Millie talking together out in the driveway. Walter greeted him with his usual rustic comment.

"We been thinkin' you all of a sudden got elected to parliament down there in Ottawa and wasn't comin' back, Mr. Brewster."

"I didn't even see the parliament buildings, Walter. I was just on the edge of Ottawa. How are things, Mill?"

"Well now, let me see," said Millie, leaning over as Charles bent to kiss her cheek. "The cattle all got out and in trying to get them back in Walter broke his leg and . . . the horses kicked the stalls down and . . . oh, yes, the roof blew off the south side of the barn . . . didn't it, Walter?"

"Oh yeah . . . yeah, roof blew off and . . . cattle all got out and . . . you can see I broke my leg. We had a bad time, Mr. Brewster."

"Yes, I can see that. Well, I better not go away again."

"Nothing happen to you, Charles?"

"No, life was very pacific."

"What's that s'posed to mean?"

"Quiet, Walter. Peaceful. I got some stories for my column, saw some nice people and had no car trouble. And I guess I'm home in time for lunch."

"Yes, it's ready now. And I hope you're going to go over to Duncan's sale with me. It starts at one o'clock."

"Did you go to the preview yesterday?"

"Yes, and there are some quite good antiques. Mrs. MacCormack was there and she coached me on which were the really good ones."

"You going, Walter?"

"Nah, I went with your wife yesterday. I better stay here and see that the cattle don't get out again. Anyway, with this broke leg I'm havin' trouble gettin' around."

Chuckling over Walter's essay into humour they all went into the house and sat down in front of Millie's Welsh rabbit — made with Charles' favourite sharp Canadian cheddar.

16

Ye Olde Antique Sale

It was a lovely June Saturday afternoon and so ideal for farmers to work at their haying that Walter declared there would likely be a small crowd at Duncan's sale. However, the farmers were aware that Jim Duncan had some good milkers and they included a number of young bred heifers that would be freshening in the fall and that helped draw the crowd. The Brewsters were there in good time but even at that they just managed to squeeze the truck into a parking space fairly close to the house so they could more easily load anything that Millie chose to buy at the sale.

The auctioneer, Clare Prentice, had decided to sell off the farm machinery first, then the antiques and such furniture as the Duncans wouldn't need even though they were staying on in the house for an indefinite period, and finally the livestock would be sold. To help in getting better prices for the antiques a man named Stanley Ramsey had been asked to assist by very briefly describing the antiques as they came up for sale.

But first the "junk" as it was called was sold off the wagon. Since Millie had examined the antiques the previous day she and Charles took time to watch the bidding as Clare stood on the wagon. It was always fun. The first thing sold was a very old wheelbarrow filled with odds and ends of scrap iron and other sundries which were practically worthless. The consignment sold for a mere twenty-five cents and the bidder was the most surprised of anyone at having it "knocked down" to him at this price. He was still more surprised when, as he tried to trundle it out of the crowd, a wheel fell off and everything slid onto the grass. But the selling went on after a good laugh. Three old shovels of assorted sizes sold for a dollar. A set of tree-pruning shears brought $3.50 and someone yelled out that the buyer could have bought a brand new pair for $3. A hay knife brought a dollar, a good brace and bit sold for a little more and a set of platform scales brought $7. A real bargain was a large-size mailbox which sold for fifty cents. The new price, somebody told the buyer, was about $8.

And so it went on until the hay wagon itself was sold. From

there Clare Prentice led the way to where the farm machinery was ranged in a semi-circle. While a seed-drill, two sets of plows, a set of double discs and a spring-tooth cultivator were being sold Charles led Millie over to where he had spied something in which he was interested. Millie took one look at it and then looked questioningly at her husband.

"What on earth is it, Charles? It looks like an elm log. Now what can you want of an elm log?"

"It is an elm log, you're quite right. But it's also a log roller — for rolling the land, flattening down the lumps, you know — something like a packer. They used them in the old days before they were able to get iron rollers."

"Wouldn't it be awfully heavy?"

"If it weren't heavy it wouldn't do a job. Let's see, that length of log is about twelve feet and it's about three feet in diameter. And it hasn't been used a lot either. You can still see some bark on it here and there."

"And it's made to be pulled by horses, Charles."

"Yes, you see the framework mounted above it at the centre? That's held in place by that projection which is set into each end of the log — and supports the seat on top there. Then the projection extends out to hold the tongue in place."

"Well, it's primitive but if it did the job that's all that was needed. Are you going to bid on it, Charles?"

"Oh, I think so, if it doesn't go for too much. We can drive June and Judy over here to haul it home. We may never use it but I just like the idea of having it. Real pioneer stuff."

Apparently the farmers who finally assembled to start the bidding on the log roller didn't have much appreciation of its value as far as agricultural Canadiana was concerned. The bidding started at fifty cents and went up slowly fifty cents at a time to five dollars. At this figure Clare Prentice gave a brief reminder of the roller's historic value and the bidding went up slowly once more until it stood at $8.50.

"Sold to Charles Brewster. And you got a good buy there, too, Mr. Brewster."

Charles hoped he was right because he could see some of the farmers smiling as they moved on to the next implement to be sold. Millie fortified him by whispering that she thought it was a good buy.

Finally came the time when Clare Prentice stood up before the first antique to be sold with Stanley Ramsey, the expert, beside him.

"This is a gunstock chair and there are a number of variations on the design you see here," declared Mr. Ramsey with authority. "This happens to be the gunstock type because of these extensions at the base of the back support. They come in both round or U-shaped seats but not always caned. This particular one isn't. The gunstock type chair is more prevalent in Canada than elsewhere and was probably made between 1870 and 1880. And it's made of walnut and varnished."

The bidding started at $10 and went up rapidly to $30. Millie kept in the bidding and finally got it at $45. Mrs. MacCormack was standing beside her and whispered that she hadn't paid too much because the chair was in unusually good shape.

Three other "Canadian" chairs were then sold. They were black, stencilled in gold and according to Mr. Ramsey were a "late survival of an earlier painted style of chair, with turned rungs; and this chair is older than the bamboo-turnings on the legs with a slight splay to the foot that characterized later chairs; at one time favoured in hotel ballrooms in the olden days and often lacquered in gold." They were sold at $40, with a responsibility on the bidder to take the three chairs.

A farm cradle made from cast iron and iron wire about the turn of the century was sold next. Millie decided she wasn't interested but listened to Mr. Ramsey describe it as "a swing cradle of the same type that once ensconced Winston Churchill as this type was reserved for heirs of the Duke of Marlborough". It was suspended between two uprights. Millie didn't bid on this and it sold for a high price.

Three items of butter-making equipment were sold next. A wooden paddle was sold first. "This item was also known as Scotch hands," stated Mr. Ramsey. "It was used mainly to work the butter to remove the moisture. Now in this butter-mold I'm holding up now you may think this crack or notch at the edge is because it's damaged. Nothing of the kind. This is intentional and was used to drain off the excess water or for separating curds and whey. The notch was cut by a bow string. The butter-mold you see here is made of hard wood — maple, in fact. Sometimes they are made of butternut. This is a particularly good one, with the individual mark of the maker. In this case it resembles a sort of crowfoot pattern. Now, as for this burl bowl I want you to see that it's in excellent state of preservation. You can see that as I hold it up for you — no cracks in it."

Millie was determined to have the butter-making equipment and she got them. The mold cost her $28, the wooden paddle $14, and the large burl butter bowl set her back $90, which made her wince but Mrs. MacCormack whispered that it was worth it. Charles took the articles as they were handed down from the auctioneer and added them to the gunstock chair acquired earlier.

A Franklin stove was offered next. Mr. Ramsey described it as made in Hamilton, Ontario, about 1862, the name H. Stewart being associated with the stove industry in conjunction with Burrow and Milne. "The name of the stove is 'Onward' and I'd like to point out the fine condition of the two mica doors and the fact that there isn't a crack in it."

The bidding on the Franklin stove was brisk. It was in perfect condition and everyone seemed to want it. Millie finally bought it for $95. As soon as it was lifted over in the general direction of Charles he stood guard over it while he tried to hang onto the chair, the butter mold, wooden paddle and butter bowl. He left the bidding to Millie as the crowd moved away a little to where an early storage chest was being sold. "About 1880," suggested Mr. Ramsey. "Although this storage chest or commode or wash-stand if you will goes back to the mid-19th century or before. You'll see it has a drawer above and two doors with a storage compartment beneath. The space below was primarily for the purpose of holding chamber pots. Many of them had marble tops which were removable and that type is very expensive these days. They were often used as a wash-stand, with a splash back. This particular piece is made of veneered mahogany with a touch of trim around the base."

The bidding started at $5 and soon went up to $20. Then it slowed down but reached $30, which was Millie's bid. After a long harangue Clare Prentice encouraged some further bidding but Millie finally got it for $38. It was lifted over to where Charles sat and he remarked that he was beginning to think he should put up a little building around himself and start up an antique store on the spot.

Six preserving sealers were put on sale next. "These sealers or Mason jars as they are known by," declared Mr. Ramsey, "because Mason invented the hermetic sealing jar with the porcelain-lined screw cap sealed by a flat rubber ring, are getting very scarce. These jars on sale today are known as the Boyd's mason jar."

The six jars sold for $5 each but Millie did not bid on them.

Next to be sold were a number of small brass sleigh bells, a glazed chinaware table jug with a "Made in Staffordshire" identification on it, a large spinning wheel, often known as a "walking wheel" (but Millie already had one), an apple corer or parer, an antique china teapot with an overglazed hand-painted decoration (which Millie wanted but decided she'd better refrain), and a number of smaller pieces (which, again, Millie decided against because of fiscal reasons).

Then the auctioneer held aloft a tin lantern with panels of glass. As soon as Charles saw it he wanted it and he watched to make sure Millie would bid on it. In his appraisal Mr. Ramsey said: "This lantern is a combination of tin and glass. The glass is known as early glass, 'crown' glass and often is faulty with bubbles and flaws from the method used to blow and spin the glass. This lantern is very old and you don't find many of them around. It's quite a large one and I think you'll agree that it would look just fine on a post outside the door."

That was exactly what Charles had decided the moment he saw it, and as Millie looked over at him he nodded his head to indicate that she was to bid on it. The bidding started at $10 and went up rapidly to over $20. Then it slowed down for a while but crept up once more to $32. Millie looked over imploringly at Charles and he was still nodding his head as if he had palsy so she kept going. And finally Charles had his tin lantern for $34. There was a slight cheer from the crowd as many of the bidders had been watching the interplay between Millie and Charles. The lantern was handed down and he placed it lovingly beside the articles already acquired.

A number of smaller antiques were sold in which Millie wasn't especially interested — until a kitchen cupboard was put up for sale. Clare Prentice described it as four feet high, three and one-half feet wide and one and one-half foot deep, and could be used as a counter combined with drawer and storage space. Mr. Ramsey took over with more explicit details. "This cupboard is made basically of pine with maple trimmings. When it was new it was probably finished in contrasting colours but as you can see it's now varnished to a dark red-brown. It's a plain utilitarian piece and if you look at the back boards, which I haven't had a chance to, you'll probably find some clue as to the date of manufacture, probably around 1860 I'd say, as a guess. These cupboards were also made in maple or hardwood and bring a lot of money."

Millie wanted the cupboard. She could see herself restoring it after removing the heavy varnish. And, while she waited for the bidding to move up to get an idea how many people were after it, she started bidding when it got up to $23. It went up from there, a dollar at a time, until it reached $42 and she was beginning to wonder. She looked over at Charles and he nodded sympathetically and with a little smile so she decided to hang on. She finally got it for $50 and began to feel guilty, until Mrs. MacCormack whispered that it was high enough but not out of the way. The cupboard was carried over to where Charles stood in his island of antiques, which was getting farther and farther away from the spot where the last of the antiques were being sold.

Millie didn't buy anything else. There was a lovely milk glass piece in blue shaped like a chicken in the nest and created originally to contain potted meat, candy, chocolate, custard powders or some such thing. Millie wanted it but clenched her teeth and didn't even bid, even though Clare Prentice kept looking in her direction because she had been a good buyer throughout the sale. A copper tea kettle was the last item sold and the crowd drifted away — the men to go to the cattle barn for the sale of milk cows and the women to have a cup of coffee at the refreshment booth which had been set up by the Women's Institute.

As soon as the crowd split up and thinned out Charles brought the truck around and succeeded, with the help of Millie and two men who had nothing better to do, in getting the purchases loaded. Then they drove out the lane and back to Briarwood.

Walter was hoeing the garden but he saw them drive in, walked over and stood looking at what the Brewsters had bought. Then he scratched his ear and said "Holy Susie!" He looked again and said "Holy Susie!" again. Then he enlarged on this a bit. "I seen better junk than this sold at my old man's sale donkey's years ago — and for just about nothin', too."

"It brings more now, Walter, because it's older," commented Millie.

"Can't say as I'd bring more now that I'm older."

"You're not made of pine, Walter."

Walter scratched his ear some more at that and helped them unload the furniture purchases. Most of the items were carried into the house and down cellar, where Millie knew she could gloat over them without having to listen to any comments.

Just before supper that day when she was out watering her flower beds Walter turned off the motor of the power mower where he had been cutting the area between the house and his cottage and came over to her.

"I guess it's time I showed you somethin', Mrs. Brewster."

There was a note of mystery as well as apology in the way Walter spoke and Millie asked him what he meant.

"Well, you better come down to the granary and see for yourself, I guess."

On the way down Charles came over from his tree-house and joined the mystery parade. Walter led them up the barn ramp, into the barn and on into the granary. As soon as they entered Millie heard a petulant clucking sound in the far corner.

"It's the banty hen, Walter — Patty. And there's Peter right beside her."

"While you're at it you better look under her."

"Now don't tell me."

And with that Millie went over, opened the little door through which the grain could be lifted by bag or transported by auger into the granary. It gave her more light because it was quite dark in the windowless interior. Then she looked down at Patty, as Charles craned his neck over her shoulder. And she saw what she knew she would see — three or four little chick-heads peering out from beneath the ruffles of Patty's feathers. In the meantime Peter decided he had better display a little parental braveness so he leaped into the air and flew at Charles. Walter reached out while he was in mid-air against Charles' pant-leg and batted him down. He slunk away a few feet to decide whether he should come back fighting another day while Patty kept up a continuous clucking that was both belligerent but also held a note of fear for the safety of her chicks.

"What do you think of that, eh, Mrs. Brewster?"

"I don't know what to think. I didn't really want any banty chicks, Walter."

"Now, Millie. That wasn't quite what you said, you know," Charles reminded her. "You said that maybe just one batch of chicks might be all right."

"Sure," added Walter, "and this would be her second batch if I'd let her keep the other eggs."

"What other eggs, Walter?"

"She's been layin' up here quite a while. I found some eggs up here one day and she was settin' on 'em so I knowed they'd be no good for eatin' so I heaved 'em out on the manure pile. Then when she started layin' some more I got to thinkin' that maybe you'd kind of like to see some banty chicks hoppin' around the place so I says, 'All right, go ahead and lay a clutch and hatch 'em out and I'll take the blame.' So that's what I done."

"And I'm glad you did. I know I was pretty indefinite about it when you asked me, Charles, when Bobby first brought over the bantams but I'm glad we have them. How many are there, Walter?"

"There's eleven right now and they should be outside. I can get that coop we used to shut up the old gander in and put it over by the drive-shed. You can keep 'em in there."

"We can't just let them run freely, eh, Walter?" Charles asked.

"If you do you'll have 'em wanderin' away and then you'll have a goshawk or somethin' after 'em. There's nothin' a goshawk likes better'n a young baby chick."

"Goshawks are those sort of blue-gray hawks — bigger than crows."

"Yeah, that's them. So you better keep the old hen — I mean the banty here — cooped up for a while and just let her chicks go outside the coop. They'll stay right around close by."

"Well, whatever you say, Walter," agreed Millie. "And I'll have to feed Patty, of course, but the chicks will pretty well peck their own feed, won't they?"

"Oh, you better give 'em some chick starter, too, same as you did your Leghorns but they'll soon be on their own, I figure. I don't know much about banties. Far as I'm concerned I never went in for raisin' hens the size of these critters."

Peter, Patty and the eleven chicks were housed in the former gander coop where some straw had been placed. Upright slats formed the front of the coop so that the chicks could run in and out. This kept the parents very worried but it was something they would just have to get used to, according to Walter. Then, after a container of feed and one of water was added Charles, Walter and Millie stood back and watched. Immediately the chicks started darting out through the slats in the open air and Patty became very upset as she strode back and forth behind the slats, quite unable to cope with this new situation. Peter went further than that. Twice he flew up against the slats to try and give the impression that he wanted out right away so he could do some fighting on Patty's behalf. Then, he backed away, possibly with a bruised wing, and sulked in the corner. The Brewsters and Walter left to go to supper with Peter sulking and Patty clucking. As for the chicks, they were darting around on the grass looking like eleven little stripe-faced clowns.

17

Nostalgia in the Tree-House

It was about a month after Jim Duncan's farm sale. Charles went out for a stroll along the sideroad one morning. He walked west and was about half-way to the new cement bridge that had been built to take the place of the old wooden one swept away during the Hurricane Hazel catastrophe many years before when he saw something blue along the top wires of his road fence. Crossing the ditch he went over to the fence and discovered that it was a Great Blue Heron, or "crane" as it is often called by country folk. It was motionless and after looking at it for only a moment he realized it was dead. The long neck was thrust between the top barb wire and the top strand of woven wire below it. Apparently it had become so entangled that it had choked to death. Then he noticed that the neck was punctured in three or four places by the barbs of the wire.

He tried to release it and finally did, by holding the wires apart. The heron fell to the ground and lay there with its eagle-length wings outspread and long legs sprawled grotesquely apart. In spite of his agitation Charles couldn't help but notice the length of the yellow bill. He had never realized, either, when he had seen the herons in flight or fishing in the creek, that they had so much grey in the colouring and so much white around the head and down the long neck.

A car drove past and Charles reacted instantly. The thought went through his head that if he were discovered beside the heron he would be accused of killing it. And this was against the law. So he stood perfectly still, trying to look nonchalant until the car had passed. Then he saw another car coming. It was turning out of Jim Duncan's driveway and he motioned to the driver to pull over to where he was. When Jim had climbed out Charles pointed to the heron. "Ever have that happen before, Jim?"

Jim was silent for a moment as he looked down at the bird. "I'm not quite with you, Charles. It's dead, I know, but what happened?"

"It was flying low, I suppose, and ran its head in between this barb wire on top and the wire below it and got jammed in between them or something. It's hard to tell."

"I guess the barbs on the wire let the neck go in but held the bird from pulling it back because the barbs caught on its skin, eh? No, I've never seen that before, Charles. By golly, it's a big bird, eh? Look at that wing-spread."

"What do I do with it? I think it's against the law to kill a heron so maybe I should let the police know about it, eh?"

"I s'pose, Charlie. They could tell you what to do. They won't accuse you of killing it, that's for sure. They know you and Millie are great for protectin' wild life. More'n I am, I'm afraid — especially those confounded starlings and grackles. I get mad enough to wring their necks, at times. But they're smart all right. I figure they're the gangsters of all the birds — the way they swagger around and grab a livin' and all that. However, this ain't helping you do somethin' about this bird."

"I'll phone the police at the Township Office and find out what to do, Jim."

"To tell the truth this is a coincidence. I was just on my way over to see you."

"Well, that's fine. Come on in."

"Now that I haven't any livestock I don't know what to do with myself, Charlie. Look, let's put that bird in the trunk of my car and I'll drive it in to your place. It's a mighty awkward bird to lug by hand."

"And after that I'll invite you to have a cup of coffee over in my tree-house, Jim. There are a few things I'd like to talk to you about so we can have a little chin-wag."

Seated beside Jim Duncan half an hour later, after phoning the police at the Township Office, Charles pointed out the window of the tree-house towards the fields that had once been part of Briarwood Farm.

"Makes me kind of sad every time I look up the hill towards the fifth there, Jim. Makes me wish I had it back again."

"With my farm sold I'm in the same boat now, Charlie. I hate to see my land go out of farming but I've had this rheumatism for the last seven or eight years and I just can't get around the way I used to. And Bobby is only eleven years old. He can't take over the farm for a few years yet."

"Well, my reason for selling was different. I had to get out of that rat race in the city. Like another cup of coffee?"

"No, this is fine. Say, this tree-house is quite a thing."

"Yes, I get kidded about it. Tree-houses are supposed to be for kids and all that."

"Oh, that's just an old wives' tale."

"That reminds me. I read the definition of a groundhog the other day."

"Don't we all know what a groundhog is without a definition?"

"I guess so but according to this definition a groundhog is a wood-chuck with an old wives' tale."

Jim laughed. "Yes, not bad. Hey, they're combining grain up on your hill there."

"Yes, they just started yesterday."

"Golly, the summer is going fast. This is the middle of July. Doesn't seem any time since they were putting in the spring crop there. But farming is sure different from the old days. Until a few years ago I farmed with horses — until I got the tractor — and they pulled an old sulky riding plow. And of course we had the old horse-pulled cultivator and drag harrows and one-furrow plow for plowin' the garden and the roller and . . . what else? . . . well, we threshed out in the field, of course, and all the neighbours came to help and we had a big threshing dinner out on the lawn with fifteen or so farmers sitting down at long plank tables. I can still see that big straw stack sitting up in the field after the threshing machine pulled out to go to another farm.

"I can remember when I was about as old as Bobby is now . . . how I'd be in bed at night and I'd hear the old steam engine coming along the sideroad here pulling the separator and the water wagon behind it. It'd go 'chug-chug — chuga-chug-chuga-chug'. Then it'd come to a little hill it had to go up and I'd hear this 'chug-chug-chug-chug-chug-chug' as it had to work harder to get up the hill. It'd keep getting closer and closer and I'd go over to the window and look and . . . by golly, pretty soon I could see the sparks comin' out of the stack from the burnin' wood. And it'd turn in the lane then, because it was headed for our place and they moved the machine at night because they wanted to get it all set up level and the drive-belt on so they could start in the mornin' as soon as the dew was off enough that the grain wouldn't plug up the separator. I can hear and see that old steam engine comin' along, Charlie, as if it was only yesterday."

"That'd be a pleasant memory, Jim."

"Yeah, it is. Kids these days will never hear that — except they might hear the engine running a bit at a fall fair where they've got an old antique steam engine."

"I missed all that. I grew up in the city."

"Well, we can't all grow up both places. I don't know where I'll move to once I have to vacate the house I'm in now. It looks like they're going to let me stay until they get the golf course ready to play on and that'll be a couple of years because they have to build the club house yet and finish making the golf course. Twenty-seven holes, it's going to be — an eighteen-hole course and a nine-hole course. They've offered me a job runnin' around on a tractor pullin' a set of tandem mowers to keep the grass cut. But that won't be for a while yet. Startin' next week I'll be workin' to help build four wooden bridges across the two creeks that run through my farm there — so the fellows that are playin' golf can get across without jumpin' the creek."

"I hear it's going to be quite a swanky course."

"Huh. I hear they're goin' to charge $2,000 to join it and then about a thousand a year for the fee to play golf. That's too rich for me. Farmers don't make that kind of money. But farmers sure get a lot more for what they grow and raise than I ever did — and a lot more than my grandfather ever did."

"What would he get for his pigs, for instance? Any idea?"

"I know exactly. We have an old diary of his kept in the 1880's. Back in 1880 he used to get $5 a hundredweight for his hogs. That was liveweight, of course. You know what hogs are now, dependin' on how you hit the market — more'n ten times that, for dressed weight hogs right now. William Davies was the biggest pork packer in Canada then — between 1870 and 1880. At his establishment in Toronto he used to kill 50,000 hogs a year."

"Your grandfather would see a lot of changes if he woke up to-day."

"Well, he died in 1918, ten days before the first world war ended. He always wanted to live to see how that war turned out. Anyway, in this diary it tells about a brand new invention — this was about 1880 — for drying apples at St. Catharines. It dried 150 bushels of apples a day and it was simply an upright box built over a furnace. The temperature got up to 170 degrees after they'd been cut into quarters by an assembly line of girls and it took about five bushels of green apples to make one bushel of dried apples and they sold for 13 cents a pound."

"Dried apples were quite a thing then. Now they have the atmosphere controlled apples that keep them as good as new almost, eh?"

"Do you know that in 1880 there were 84 varieties of apples grown in Ontario? Now there's what? — about four or five main varieties. And those old apples sure had some quaint names that you hardly hear of these days — Freckled Mollie, King of Tomkins County, Peck's Pleasant, Lady Apple, Early Joe . . . Seek-no-Further and . . . Maiden's Blush. Names like that. Most of the varieties fell by the wayside because of the Canadian climate, of course — and public preference."

"My old orchard still has four or five varieties that you mentioned in it."

"Yes, you've got a pretty old stand of trees there. Oh, I just remembered that granddad talks about eggs back in the 1880's. There was a Mr. Wilson of Seaforth then who was known as the 'Egg King of Canada'. He kept ten teams of horses busy collecting eggs from country stores and these were packed in barrels, 70 dozen eggs to the barrel, and he shipped them to the New York market. And you know how much a dozen he got? Nine cents."

Charlie whistled. "Well, they had their problems in the old days, too, Jim. But they made do as best they could. And I guess we all owe them a debt bigger than most people realize for kind of showing us the way—away back in 1880."

"Yeah, that's true. Say, this is quite a change for me—sitting here this time of day palavering away like this. How're the two banties Bobby sold you getting along?"

"Oh, we have eleven banty chicks now, Jim. We're in the banty business."

"Oh, dear. The reason I told Bobby to sell some of them was because we were getting too many."

"That's all right. Millie thought she'd get a kick out of it, I guess."

"Say, you bought quite a few antiques at my sale. And I'm glad to see they got a good home because they're the real thing—genuine, Charlie. They were handed down from my granddad's time and some of them came from his father. But we've had them around for so long and besides we'll have to move one of these days so we thought we might as well sell them off."

"Well, Millie is enjoying them, that's for sure."

"I'm sure glad about that. You got the commode. I remember that in our bedroom when I was a kid. It had a big water jug and bowl in it and the chamber—known as the 'pot' in those days, I guess they didn't know what else to call it. I remember my dad and my granddad, too, going down in the morning, real early, to light the fire in the kitchen stove. He'd put the kindling wood in first—wood that he'd shaved very carefully from a cedar log the night before—then he'd put in a couple of hardwood pieces of wood on top of that and then, by golly, he'd throw some coal oil on it. I can still see the way that coal oil gave a little roar and then blazed up."

"That sounds pretty dangerous, Jim."

"Sure it was dangerous. But he wanted to get it going fast to start the ice in the water pail thawing out and ... well, getting the kitchen a little warm for the rest of the folks when they got up."

"I sure missed a lot, I can see that. It sounds as if you and your granddad were pretty close pals."

"Yes, I was only about a dozen years old then—younger than that I guess. But I remember him making me basswood whistles. He was good at it. He could make a basswood whistle like nobody else around. I used to swap them at school for such things as marbles and licorice whistles and once for a Player's cigarette. I remember taking that cigarette with another lad that had one, too, and we went up to a culvert not far from the school and hid in the weeds and started smoking it. Well sir, Charlie, we both got sick as dogs. We were choking and throwing up and I don't know what all. But maybe it was just as well. I haven't smoked a cigarette from that day to this. I smoke a pipe once in a while but that's all."

"I've started smoking a pipe. I used to smoke cigars, as I guess you know, but I rather like a pipe now that I've got used to holding it in my mouth without it falling out."

"By the way, Charles. This is changing the subject but what about Walter these days?"

"I dunno. What about him? In what way?"

"Well, Harold Corrigan, over on the town line was talking to a friend of his, Stanley Bowles who lives over near Markdale. I don't think you know him but he knows Walter. And Stanley was telling Harold, who told me, that Walter was seen at a square dance in the Community Hall with a woman a week ago Saturday."

"Walter was seen with a . . . Holy Susie. Walter with a . . . ?"

"He didn't know the woman at all but that is something new for Walter."

"Yes, it sure is, Jim." Charles decided he wouldn't say anything at the moment about the way Walter was going out "all dressed up" lately.

"I've known Walter since he bought the farm here, long before he sold it to you. As a matter of fact I knew him when he worked for a farmer on the ninth concession. And I've never heard of him appearing in public with a woman."

"He hasn't said a word to me, Jim." And this was true, of course.

"How old is Walter?"

"He was sixty the first of April this year—April Fools' Day."

"Well, it's never too late to fall in love, so they say."

"No, I guess not. He's never said anything to me that was very much in favour of women though. He's told me a dozen times that he met a woman once that 'tried to climb in bed with him and he had quite a time kicking her out', as he puts it."

Jim laughed. "Well, I better be heading back. This was kind of a nice talk we've been having. I like talking about the old days. I hope you didn't mind."

"No, I've enjoyed it. I should do a column about someone like you who knows what went on in the old days."

"I'll let you have granddad's diary if you like. I want to get it back of course."

"I'd appreciate that. Yes, I would, Jim. It should make a good nostalgic column."

Jim Duncan got up from his chair, wincing a little from the rheumatism in his hip and leg and rubbed his thin, weatherbeaten face.

As he shook hands apathetically Charles could feel the roughness of his calloused fingers. Then he backed slowly down the steps to the ground and started back to his car. Charles turned to look out through the window again. As his eyes travelled slowly across the lower part of the landscape, then clockwise up the sloping of the hill and across to the sideroad a look of veneration, a sort of reverence came over his face. He sat with his chubby hands under his chin and took it all in, let it absorb him. Finally, without taking his eyes off the landscape, he reached down into the drawer below him and took out a sheet of paper and spread it in front of him. On the page was quite a long poem. "The Last Crop." He had been writing it over a period of days in his spare time. Now he sat back in his swivel chair and read it aloud.

"It's not too bad, I think," he murmured when he had finished. "Yes, I don't think it's too bad. At least it's an attempt to say what I feel. And, one of these days I'll read it to Millie and get her opinion, eh? And I'll try writing some others . . . see what old Charlie Brewster can do with it, eh?"

18

The Well goes Dry — and the Farm Freezer gets Filled

Charles and Millie were sitting out in the sunroom. It was towards the end of the afternoon and the sun was suffusing the willows down along the creek with a refulgent green-yellow gauze, glinting off the blue-white insulators of the lightning rods on the barn and turning the little windows of the pig-pen into blood-red rectangles.

They had finished reading the two sections of the Mapleville *Banner* which had come that afternoon. Now they were slouched back lazily, saying little, musing.

"What are you thinking, Millie?" Charles finally murmured.

"What am I thinking? I'm just wondering what this old house would say if it could talk."

"It'd have some great stories to tell, that's for sure — about all the things that happened here for well over a hundred years. Jim Duncan and I were talking about that when we had a chin-wag in the tree house. Look at those old bricks on the north wall there — built with the blue clay out behind our barn. Before the summer kitchen was built — which we turned into this sunroom — the elements weathered them for years. And look at them now. I'd defy an artist to exactly describe these colours. They're half a dozen rich, warm colours blended together. And how about that threshold leading up from the sunroom into the living room there — made with a beautiful two-inch plank. Look at that scoop effect across the centre of it where it's been worn down to about half the thickness by all the traffic over it — heavy hob-nailed boots, dress shoes, rubber boots, slippers, moccasins, the Lord knows what. It's taken tens of thousands of feet stepping on it to do all that — tens of thousands of feet and more than a hundred years."

"This house has seen a lot of living. It could tell stories about men and women and children and happiness and sorrow and quarrels and remorse and laughter and marriages and deaths and a hundred other things."

"Oh, to have a diary of every day's happenings since this house was built, eh? Wouldn't that be wonderful, Millie?"

"Of course, the day's events don't mean much as you experience them. The person who could write it doesn't realize that it could have so much meaning to people a century and more later. That's the way life is. Each day has its little set of problems and we're too busy settling them to think about the remote future."

"And to think of all the harvests and hayings they've had on this farm, eh? — right from the time it was carved out of the white pine forest that covered all this farm. I guess they had their drought years and their wet years and the good years in between, the same as they do now. And they were probably just as happy and maybe happier than people are these days."

"Life was hard but it was also simpler, Charles. Nowadays things are so complicated and complex. Because of rapid communications and the increase in population more problems are created. I heard someone say the other day that when the very first census was taken in New France, as it then was in Ontario here, in the 1660's, there were only 3,003 inhabitants. Three hundred years later we have about twenty-two million. And I also think . . . oh, dear, here's Walter coming in. He saw us out here — and just when I felt like doing a little reminiscing."

"He's bringing in some strawberries so you can't argue against that."

Walter saw them through the screen door facing the stone patio and held up the strawberries. Millie asked him to come in.

"This'll be about the last quart of the 'Lathams', Mrs. Brewster. I had to do a lot of lookin' to get this many."

"They're lovely looking berries. I think the last of the crop is always sweeter. Thank you, Walter."

"Next year you'll have them 'Everbearing' kind as well as the new plantin' of 'Lathams'. That should be enough, eh?"

"Yes, more than I need. Oh, your fingers are all stained. Do you want to wash them?"

"Nah, I'll scrub 'em later on when I go out tonight."

Charles looked up at him and smiled. "You're getting to be quite a night-owl, Walter."

"You figure I'm usin' your truck too much?"

"No, I didn't mean that. I don't mind you using the truck."

"Well, I might just drive down to the village for a while, just to see who's there. There's always somebody down there I can yarn with."

"There should be some pretty girls down there wandering around with nothing to do, Walter."

"Oh, I ain't much on girls. Besides, who'd have me at my age, seein' I turned sixty just lately?"

"Oh, you're a good looking man yet, Walter — full head of hair, not many lines, healthy. You don't look sixty."

"Well, I dunno about that." Walter was obviously a little pleased but he was also ill at ease. He wasn't used to compliments. "Of course I got took for bein' just over fifty a week or so ago."

"Well, there you are."

"Yeah, just when I was beginnin' to think it was about time somebody shot me like I did the old cat." Then Walter looked apprehensively at Charles. "I guess I shouldn't have come out with that, Mr. Brewster."

"It's all right, Walter. I told Millie the day after we shot old Tabby."

"It had to be done, Walter. I realize that. Charles buried her down under the mountain ash in the meadow, as you likely know."

"I guess we don't none of us last forever, eh? Well, I better get along. Say, it'll be time pretty soon to start pickin' the raspberries. I was lookin' at 'em. They're startin' to turn." And with that Walter departed to finish off the grass-cutting down by the pond that he had started earlier that day.

"What have we in the freezer so far, Mill?"

"Oh, strawberries, green beans and peas. Oh, don't forget all the fiddleheads I put into the freezer earlier. And do you know what they cost to buy in the city? When Martha Humphrey phoned me from the city the other day she said she paid 98 cents for just a small package of fiddleheads. At that rate we have about $25 worth in the freezer."

"Good for you."

"And we'll have raspberries soon and then the harvest apples in August — the Duchess and Transparent — and all the later vegetables and the early potatoes and the late potatoes and . . . what else? . . . oh, the winter apples and the apple butter towards the end of October and I think that's about all."

"That big freezer is going to bulge right out, eh, Millie? And we're going to have a quarter or maybe a half of beef to put in about the end of October."

"And we should have our own eggs in September. The pullets are really growing now. And of course we'll be killing the cockerels at whatever age we want to."

"Millie, you forgot all the little banties we'll be eating, eh?"

"Oh, dear. I don't know what we're going to do with them. I don't think there's much sale for them as pets. Bobby had trouble getting rid of his. I'm afraid we're going to be stuck with them."

"Here's something else we're stuck with — this here Laddie-dog."

"Oh, now. What's he saying, Laddie? Look, he's wagging his tail as if he's trying to shake it off. He wouldn't do that a few weeks ago."

"No, I guess that's right, Mill. So you're improving, eh, boy?"

"He's licking your hand, Charles. And look at that tail wag."

"When are you going to start barking? We want you to sit here at the window and bark when a strange car drives in."

"I think he's getting ready for it. The other day he growled when Jim Duncan's car drove in. I thought he was going to bark. He even gave a sort of a 'whoof' sound. Oh, he'll make it one of these days."

And with that Millie stood up, remarked that she had to start supper and left Charles to look out the big picture window that framed the view to the south — out beyond the red pig-pen to the meadow and the grandfather willows. The ten Holstein feeder cattle were mooching slowly along with their heads down at grass level and to the left a little he could catch a glimpse of the ten ewes, the ram and the fourteen lambs in the paddock into which Walter had just turned them that morning from the orchard where they had grazed the grass down as closely as it should be for good husbandry. There were nine ewe lambs and five "buck" lambs, as Walter called them and Charles' taste buds jumped ahead about four months as he conjured up the thoughts of some good lamb chops through the winter ahead of them. The ewe lambs he would keep through the winter but sell as "bred" ewes the ones that were growthy enough to be bred late in the fall — although Walter maintained a ewe shouldn't be bred until the second autumn after it was born.

Charles had decided that he should do as most of the other farmers who kept sheep were doing — breed the ewes early in the fall so they would lamb in January. Then the lambs could be sold when they were only a few weeks old to the increasing market for young lambs among the Greeks and Italians. Although they didn't weigh much the demand for them prior to and at Thanksgiving time was very great. The new Canadians would pay almost any price to be able to observe the traditional custom of their homeland of roasting an entire lamb for a great banquet and celebration. Charles decided they should be bred about the beginning of September.

"Charles, come here! Quickly!"

Millie's voice sounded sufficiently imperious that it brought an instant reflex action to Charles' locomotive parts. He was out in the kitchen in almost no time at all.

"See? I turn the tap. No water."

"Oh, hell," said Charles. "No water." He rubbed his right cheek in the manner of a genie rubbing the lamp as if expecting that might cause the water to gush out of the tap. Still no water. "Well, I'll just have to get down to where they're drilling in Mygrange again. I guess they're testing those big wells or something. Be back as soon as I can, Mill."

Charles collected Walter from the seat of the riding mower down by the pond and five minutes later they were standing beside the four ten-inch pipes that had been sunk on the former Stockley farm adjoining Mapleville to the west.

"No water comin' out of 'em, Mr. Brewster."

"That's funny. They can't be testing. So these wells aren't taking our water."

"Hey, you know somethin'?"

"Right now I don't know what I'd like to know."

"I seen some men drilling on Jim Duncan's farm lately — back where we can't see 'em from the road. Now our crik is the same one that runs through his farm, before he sold it, I mean. And like as not the underground river that we get our water from is the same one that runs through his farm, too."

"Which might mean that they've tapped the same river with these wells they've been drilling."

"Yeah, so they're grabbin' off the water before it gets down to the well at your place."

"Maybe you've got the answer, Walter. We better go up and have a look at those wells."

Ten minutes later Charles and Walter were standing beside two drill-pipes on the golf course property. The water wasn't coming out. Charles scratched his wisps of rufous hair. "If it isn't coming out that means it should be flowing on towards our well, Walter. We should be getting water as usual."

"What's them there two valves there for, half way down the pipe? Looks to me like when you turn them they can shut the water off or on."

"Yes, I wonder. If that's true the valves might be turned right now so that the water could be flowing underground and coming out somewhere else on the golf course — through metal pipes that are buried. I think you've got a point there, Walter."

Walter puffed up appreciably at this estimation of his deductions. "These golf course fellows are swipin' our water. They're grabbin' it off so there's none left to keep on goin' down to our well."

"But what use would they have for water right now? The club house isn't built, and the fairways and greens are just being constructed now. They'll be needing water to keep the grass growing later on but not yet."

"Maybe they're just tryin' it out to make sure they got plenty of water, eh?"

"I suppose it could be that. Well, we'd better find somebody in charge."

They drove through the golf course on a maze of temporary roads but couldn't discover anyone. Even the labourers who were working at the landscaping had gone home for the day. So Charles decided that all he could do was to telephone to the city and try to locate someone who was on the board of the golf club and find out what was going on. But before Charles left they drove back to where the drill-pipes were located, with the idea of turning them off. But when they examined them they found a lock on each one that prevented it from being turned. With a smouldering fire in each of his blue eyes Charles got behind the wheel of his car and they drove back home. Walter was curious as to the ending to all this so he went into the house with Charles, who extracted the city telephone directory from a pile of outdated newspapers and women's magazines and proceeded to look up the number of the Rockside Golf Club. This was the club that had sold out and then purchased Jim Duncan's farm. Apparently the name was to be changed, when the golf course was opened for play, to the Sunny Valley Golf and Country Club. He was fortunate to get one of the board members of the club on the line and explained the situation to him concerning the water supply. Millie and Walter were standing a few feet away and they heard Charles' tone change from a loud bellicose to a composed pacifism, which included a couple of chuckles. And he hung up with a "Thank you, Mr. Graham, thank you very much."

"Well, Charles, for a man who hasn't enough water in the house to make a cup of tea that was certainly quite a switch."

"My dear, Mr. Graham had the soft answer that turneth off wrath."

"It may turn off wrath but does it turn on water?"

"As soon as Mr. Graham can get a man out here to change the flow of water. And if he can't get hold of his man he'll drive out himself."

"Well, I'm sure I don't know what I'm going to get you and Walter to drink tonight. There's only a little milk."

"I can't understand why there wouldn't still be water in the tank in the cellar. Apparently that's been exhausted, too."

Before Millie could comment on this Walter came up with quite a suggestion. "I was just thinkin', Mrs. Brewster. In a pinch Mr. Brewster and me we might be able to choke down a little hooch — just to wet our whistle, you know."

Charles caught up the suggestion. "Yes, that goes under the heading of liquid, Millie. It would help to get our food down."

"The food you have to get down, if we don't have anything else happen to hold us up again, is macaroni and meatballs. And they're all ready so you two just sit right down."

Charles and Walter sat right down.

About two hours later, after Walter had gone back to his cottage, there was a knock at the door as Charles and Millie sat reading.

Millie opened the door to a man who introduced himself as Hal Graham and took the chair offered him after he had shaken hands. He was a man of about fifty, well-dressed in a brown Norfolk jacket and gray flannels that matched the gray of his eyes and hair as Millie mentioned after he had gone. He had a ready smile and started off by commenting on the warm, inviting atmosphere of the living room."

"It used to be the farm kitchen, Mr. Graham. It was larger than we needed so we made it into the living room."

"Great idea. Well, I'd better tell you about the water." Mr. Graham asked if he might smoke and took out a Meerschaum pipe which Charles recognized to be expensive briar and lit up. "I couldn't get hold of a maintenance man tonight so I've been over to the club and turned off the valve controlling the water. You may wonder why we have the water on now but we're drilling ten wells in all over there so as to be ready when the club opens and we test each one for volume and chemical content when we drill it."

"You're drilling ten wells, Mr. Graham?" asked Millie.

"Yes, at various parts of the course. The only wells that will be sunk to the stream that feeds your well will be the two Mr. Brewster saw today. And I'm sure we can come to some agreement about that. As part of our goodwill we want to keep on friendly terms with everybody in this area. So any time you're having trouble I want you to get in touch with me right away — any time of the day or night. Here's my card with the office and home phone numbers on it."

"When will the course be open for playing, Mr. Graham?"

"Oh, the nine-hole course may be open by the middle of next summer — the eighteen-hole later than that. You see we have access to our course in the city for this year and next so we're in no hurry. We're starting to build the club house next spring."

"What part of the course will it be on?"

"The entrance to the course, Mrs. Brewster, will be almost across the road from your gate. It will have stone pillars at the entrance, according to the architect's drawing, and the driveway will be paved right back to the clubhouse which will be about a half-mile back from the road."

Mrs. Brewster stood up suddenly. "Mr. Graham, forgive me, I should have asked you if you'd like a cup of coffee."

"No, thanks, I want to get back, thanks all the same. By the way, I understand they may be paving your sideroad here next spring or summer."

"Well, they've been saying that for quite a while," Charles replied with a little knowing smile. "We'll believe it when we see it. Of course, the fact that we're going to have all you rich fellows coming along our road here may have influenced it, too."

Mr. Graham laughed. "Well, I don't know. We had no assurance of that in the agreement when we were examining the rezoning for the golf course. By the way, do you play golf?"

"Oh, I used to many years ago. I got so I could shoot in the middle eighties but I'm afraid I couldn't break a hundred right now."

"Well, I'm sure I can see that you get a guest pass or come in as my guest whenever you feel that you might like to have a game."

"Thanks very much."

"By the way, I've often admired your place here. It's very attractive — with the pond and creek and all the rest of it. Have you ever thought of selling?"

Charles looked at Millie who gave a tiny, surreptitious shake of her head. And Charles got the message fast. "No, I don't think so, Mr. Graham. We sold 94 acres of Briarwood Farm last year and I think we'll keep our present six acres for a long time."

"I don't blame you. The reason I ask is that a number of the members of what is going to be named the Sunny Valley Golf and Country Club are interested in moving out this way."

"I heard that some of the land is earmarked for houses."

"Yes, that's true. But the acreage won't be large. You could likely get a very good price for your estate here."

"Well, maybe fifty years from now when we get old we might consider it."

This extravagant statement inspired general laughter and acted as the signal for Mr. Graham to rise to his feet. Everyone shook hands again and the farewells were made.

"Now you know, Mr. Brewster, how to describe our six acres. We have an estate. And don't you get any ideas about selling it right away, either."

"No, I haven't, Millie. Cross my heart. No, this suits me fine, just as it is. We're part of the neighbourhood around here now and I don't think I'd want to move. No, I think we'll be sitting right here for a long time."

"It seems we'll be sitting right here at the mercy of the Sunny Valley Golf and Country Club and the Mygrange Development Company. The golf club can cut off our water before it reaches us and Mygrange can drain our water away on the other side of us so it can't come up in the well."

"Yes, I'm not sure where that leaves us, Millie. Or wait a minute. We have forty-five old apple trees in the orchard. Instead of depending on water to drink we can make barrelfuls of apple cider to drink and cook with. And we can pipe up water from the creek for the bathroom and washing dishes. So, you see, the problem is solved."

19

The Brewsters Hold a City-Country Corn Roast

Charles and Millie had been planning the big corn roast for over two weeks. They had sent out neat, little, informally-worded invitations to some of their friends in the city — their real friends, as Millie termed them — and to a number of their neighbours. No R.S.V.P. was asked for. Those who really wanted to be with them would be there. And following the invitations Charles set to work to get the site ready.

The spot he chose was in the meadow down on the banks of the creek. Here the late afternoon sun would still fall warmly and anyone who preferred to find the shade could move into the shadows of the huge old gnarled willows that stood sentinel along the banks of the creek. It was on Mygrange Development Company property but Charles had checked with Frank Myers who said, "Yes, you bet, Mr. Brewster. Quite all right. You just go right ahead and enjoy yourself now." Then he had added that he would be dropping in about something one of these days. Charles had no idea what the something was and let it go at that.

In planning the entertainment part of the program Charles had a lot of fun. He decided to take the dart board and hang it to the butt of a big willow, about eye level above the ground. He and Walter set up a horseshoe-pitching game, too. They dug up the ground and loosened the soil at two spots where the shoes would land, drove in an iron peg at each end and chose four heavy horseshoes from the collection of the years that hung on pegs in the horse-barn. As an afterthought Charles also picked four light shoes worn by driving-horses in case the ladies might want to take a turn at pitching. Then he had Walter bring down the power mower, set the knives down low and mow an area about a hundred feet square. In this area he dug six holes in calculated positions. When it was finished he termed it a putting green and jocularly christened it "The Sunny Valley Golf and Country Club Duffers Putting Green."

"Well, what else can we do to let them have a little fun, Walter?"

"We could let them have a log-sawin' contest, I s'pose."

"Oh, I'd rather see them relax."

"You got two hammocks up at the house for relaxin'."

"Good idea. We can swing them between two branches of these willows, Walter."

"We could cut a few fishin' poles and let 'em do some fishin' in the crik here."

"I'm afraid they wouldn't have much luck. We've asked them to bring their kids, too, so I suppose we could have two or three potato-bag races or something like that."

"If'n you keep on you ain't goin' to have much time left to eat the corn and hot dogs, Mr. Brewster."

"Oh, we'll find time for that. By the way, we'll have to get the trailer out and bring down a lot of wood for the bonfire. We can use some of that wood from the old pea-barn we took down. There's a lot of it that's of no use. And there's some old wood in the barnyard that's only good for a bonfire. By the way, did you know that bonfire used to mean a fire of bones — for burning up corpses?"

"Can't say I did. Fire for burnin' up dead people, eh? You figure on burnin' anybody up the night of the corn roast?"

"No, I haven't. Is there anyone you'd like to roast, Walter?"

"Yeah, but I better not. I might go to the hoosegow the rest of my life, eh?"

"Yes, you might. Well, now, what else? Oh, we'll have to bring down that big iron kettle and the two smaller iron kettles. And we'll have to build some kind of an iron tripod to hang the kettle from to hold the corn over the fire."

"Looks like we're goin' to have quite a circus."

"Oh, we're inviting quite a few, Walter. We like the idea of having our friends we used to know in the city meet some of the nice people around here."

"You're invitin' just the folks you know best around here, eh?"

"Oh, well, I wouldn't say that. We'll probably forget to invite some neighbours we should have invited. Why?"

"Nothin, Mr. Brewster, nothin'."

"Now is there something we're forgetting?"

"The eats, eh?"

"The eats? Well, Millie is looking after that — wieners and corn, mostly, rolls, butter, coffee, tea, soft drinks for the kids, plenty of Millie's homemade butter tarts for dessert. That's about all."

"No beer or hooch? Not even a punch bowl?"

"Not even a punch bowl, Walter. This is going to be a nice friend-ly, sober party."

"Sounds that way, yeah. Yeah, I s'pose that's best. And this is all goin' to happen on Saturday, eh?"

"Yes, the first day of September. It's still nice and warm and all we have to worry about is rain."

"Nah, it ain't goin' to rain. We're in for a dry spell. Well, we better get busy I guess."

"Yeah, I guess." But Walter didn't get busy too fast. He stood around, looking down at the grass. He dug the toe of his farm boot into the ground. Then he said, "Well, I just wondered," in a flat voice.

"What's on your mind, Walter?" Charles could see that he wanted to talk to him about something but seemed shy.

Walter did some more standing on one foot and digging into the ground. "Well, there's a woman that I figure might like to come to this corn roast thing but she'd never go out of her way to ask you. So I says to her, well I'll ask you, see, so she says no you better not so I says I don't mind askin' you so I'm askin' you, Mr. Brewster."

"Do we know her, Walter?"

"I dunno. Her name is Barton."

"Barton, Barton. I don't think I . . . no, wait a minute. There's a Barton lives up on the 18th sideroad."

"Yeah, that's her. Leastways, that's the daughter. She ain't married but she lives with the old folks."

"Oh, I see. Well, I don't know why she shouldn't come. Does she drive?"

"Yeah, she can drive a car but . . . well, I s'pose I might as well pick her up while I'm at it. She might be kind of shy about just walkin' in here all alone like."

"Yes, sure, Walter. You bring her down. By the way, what's her first name?"

"She's got kind of a funny name — on account of when she was born her folks were wantin' a boy. And on account of that and her bein' a girl they called her Sonny. Funny name for a girl, eh?"

"Sonny? That's kind of a nice name. Well, you bring Sonny down to the corn roast."

"Thanks, Mr. Brewster."

And with that Walter strode off back towards the barn and left Charles muttering to himself down by the creek.

"Sonny? Sonny? . . . Bunny? . . . Sonny Barton? . . . Bunny Barton?" Charles rubbed his nose. That had to be it. That just had to be the answer.

They came in couples, mostly, except certain friends from the city who doubled up to make four in a car. The ones from the city wore informal slacks, the women as well as the men, and they brought along a sweater or jacket in case the evening turned cool. The neighbouring farmers were dressed similarly.

The cars started arriving about half past four and, directed by arrows printed on cardboard and nailed in helpful places in the area of the barn, followed a route that let them drive across the pasture and park in a row not far from the corn roast site. Charles and Millie were on hand to greet them and as each car eliminated its occupants there were little feminine soprano shrieks of familiarity and a more subdued masculine interchange of jollity. The neighbours were a little diffident at first about meeting the city folks. They shook hands limply and had trouble smiling confidently. But later intermingling soon healed this gap. As for the children, of whom there were not a great number because it seemed that many of the city children, especially, had Saturday night dates, they flowed together with little reticence and soon acted as if they had known one another for a long time.

The guests took turns, while Charles and Millie continued to welcome the arrivals, strolling along the edge of the river, wandering about the meadow or sitting on the bales of straw that Charles and Walter placed both in the shade and out where it was sunny. Around the entire area Charles and Walter had driven in a number of steel posts and strung up a temporary two-wire fence. This was to keep the inquisitive cows from trying to discover what manner of animal had invaded their meadow. It was also, as Charles laughingly told Walter, to keep the ladies from feeling that they might be subjected to a mad charge of four-legged bovines at any moment. And it worked very well. The cows had as good a time as the human beings. They stood looking across the wire barrier, stared for a while and then began bawling in appreciation of the spectacle they apparently decided was being staged on their behalf.

There was constant movement beside the creek. Men and women, country neighbours and urban friends, criss-crossed in an interesting intermingling pattern that would have excited an artist, if he had been present, into grabbing colours, a palette and a paint brush and recording it on canvas. Big, small, fat, lean, young, old, farmer, accountant, smiling, grave, store-keeper, city clerk, dull, bright, talkative, quiet. To one degree or another and with their numberless combinations of attributes they were all there beneath the old willows and in the sunlight.

From the uncrowded edge of the assembly Charles beckoned Millie to come over. "Walter hasn't turned up yet," he said quietly. "Maybe he's decided not to bring this girl Sonny."

"I hope he does. Now that he's broken down and decided to let us know he has a lady friend he might as well go through with it. There's time yet."

"I think everybody is enjoying themselves, eh, Mill?"

"Are they ever. Look at them — playing darts over there, three of them fishing, including some of the youngsters, strolling around, arguing in a good-natured way about politics. Oh, they're enjoying it. And after organizing the races for the children I put Sandy Mac-Donald's wife in charge of the sports. By the way, Horace Greene and his wife aren't here."

"I doubt if they will be. Since I resigned from his advertising agency at the end of July I haven't even heard from him. Yes, Barbara?"

"Do you think we could wade right across the river, Mr. Brewster? Is it too deep?"

"No, it isn't too deep but you'd better ask your mother."

The petite seven-year-old blonde child ran squealing away. Her place was taken by the overpowering figure of "Fats" Little, who had helped scoop out the hole for the Brewsters' pond.

"Well sir, she's a humdinger of a corn roast, eh? Never had so much fun. I see the old pond is still doin' business, eh?"

"Yes, you did a good job digging that, 'Fats'— even if you did get stuck a few times in the mud."

"Fats" boomed out a great laugh and slapped Charles so hard on the back that he was pushed over against Millie.

"Hey, you want some help gettin' all that stack of wood burnin'? I got a can of gas in the car. I can throw some on."

Charles held up both hands. "No thanks, 'Fats'. Let's not have an explosion. I've got four little piles of kindling wood at places around the edge of it, though. I think if you want to help me get those lit we might as well start it, eh?"

Although it was still light Charles had decided it would take quite a while to get the big timbers burning and that it would be dark before the water in the huge iron cauldron on the tripod was boiling and ready for the corn. And Millie had reminded him that some of the people from the city had said they didn't want to be too late leaving.

When Charles and "Fats" had left Millie stood alone for a few moments. They were all there — her friends, neighbours and some of their city relatives and their children. The Hazeltons from the seventh concession were there; the Bromleys from the third; the Johnstons from the ninth; the Dirks from two farms east; the Watts from the next farm; Jim Limbarger, the ag. rep. and his lovely wife, Denise; Philip Cranbrook, the lawyer in Mapleville and his quiet wife, Mary; Len Harding, from the hardware store and his very shy wife, Edna. From the city the Humphreys were there; the Beatons, their old friends of many years; Millie's sister, Dorothy, and her always-giggling husband, Tom; Millie's young nieces and nephews, Hildegard and Dean and their parents, the Jenners; Charles' aged father and mother; the Forsythes, a youngish couple who had the apartment next to them in the city; and Harry Drake, a man with whom Charles had often lawn-bowled in the city and liked, with his very talkative but likeable wife, Nora. As far as Millie could remember all but two couples who were invited were present. And with that she left to join her sister, Dorothy, and Tom, who were giggling over a joke Tom had just told.

The fire spread from the kindling wood that Charles and Walter had ingeniously placed beneath the old, dry timbers and branches and finally the entire pile was alight. It was not until then that Charles decided it was time the corn was shucked. He had purposely waited until the last moment, almost, to do this so the corn would be sweet and tender when eaten. Now the moment had arrived. He walked over to the trailer which held a great pyramid of corn that Walter had picked that same afternoon and stood up on it ready to declaim.

"Ladies and gentlemen . . . neighbours . . . friends . . . children." As he waited for the voices to die down he began to feel as if he were Mark Antony, delivering Shakespeare's speech on the death of Julius Caesar in the Roman Forum. "We need some able-bodied men to make a bee to shuck some corn." There was a mock cheer at this and at once the men rushed forward.

"All you have to do is strip off the husk and lay the ears of corn on this plank. Throw the husks in a pile and the cattle may eat them up tomorrow. Okay."

"You've got enough corn here to feed all Mapleville for a week, Charles," commented Tom Dirks.

"I dunno, Tom. Everybody is starting to look pretty hungry. And don't let me see you stashing away a few cobs in your pocket to take home to your pigs, either."

Charles left to check the wieners but found Millie already beside the boiler which had been set up at the edge of the fire to hold the hot dogs. "Guess we don't need these for quite a while yet, Millie?"

"No, I just want to have them ready. I'd better keep this cover over them, though. I just saw Jim Duncan's dog slinking around."

"Where are the Duncans? They're supposed to be here."

"Oh, I forgot to tell you. Her aunt died and they've gone to Orangeville for the week-end. She phoned me just before noon."

While the fire roared and the shucking bee progressed the guests settled down and were content to be spectators and just talk to whoever was beside them. Farmers told city folk about the routine of life on the farm and the urban guests described things that were happening in the city — many of them adding that they would give a lot to be able to buy a nice place in the country and how lucky farmers were if they only realized it. Then the farmers told the urbanites about their bad crops and their hogs getting rhinitis and their cows contracting Bang's Disease. It made an interesting and, possibly, educative interchange of conversation. The main thing was, as the Brewsters could see, that everybody seemed to be enjoying themselves.

It was after dark when two figures moved quietly into the area of the firelight. Charles saw them first as he stood beside Millie.

"Look, it's Walter. They've decided to come."

"And that is Bunny — pardon me, Sonny."

"I guess it is. We'd better make them welcome." They went over and Charles tapped Walter on the shoulder. "We thought you weren't going to come, Walter. We're glad you did."

"Yeah, well . . . I guess we're kind of late, Mr. Brewster." Walter was never more awkward in his life than he was at that moment. He put his hands in his pockets and took them out again. He shifted from one foot to the other as if he were rehearsing a dance step. And there wasn't a smile on his face. He was scared stiff. That was when Charles took over.

"We're Charles and Millie Brewster and I guess this is Sonny."

"Yes, I'm Sonny. It was nice of you to ask us."

She was about fifty, not too plumpish, dark-haired and with a smile that showed her to be more at ease than Walter was.

"Well, now, we'll just walk around slowly and introduce you," suggested Millie. "You'd know many of the people here anyway, Sonny."

"From around these parts I s'pose I would." Sonny glanced around at the people and waved at two or three of the neighbouring farmers. "Maybe we could just make ourselves known as we go along."

"Yes, of course."

"Hey, that's some rip-roarin' fire you got there, eh?" said Walter. "That old wood from the pea-barn sure burns good."

"It should, Walter. It's been seasoning for a hundred years and more. But these were pieces that were split and no use for anything else. Well, look, you and Sonny find a place to sit. There's a bale of straw over there with no one on it and it's right beside the MacNabs. You'd know them, Sonny."

"Oh, sure. Come on, Walter. We'll sit there." Sonny led the way and Walter followed docilely as Charles went over to give orders to heave the husked corn into the iron kettle where the water was boiling. This was the signal for the ladies to check the table on which had been placed the condiments. Set out for use as soon as the corn and wieners were ready were mustard relish, hot mustard and French mustard, pickled beets, catsup, salt and pepper, three half-pound sections of butter and a pile of paper plates and extra-large serviettes to help blot up the vari-coloured remnants of food and trimmings that might stubbornly cling outside the mouth.

But finally it was ready. Charles yelled "Come and get it!" and his call was passed on as if by echo until there was no doubt that the corn was ready. By this time the fire had died down sufficiently so that Charles and three other farmers were able to get close enough to the iron pot to reach into it with silage forks and lift out half a dozen ears at a time. These were distributed among the crowd who proceeded to slide them back and forth across the half-pounds of butter, add salt or pepper as wished and then start using their rows of white teeth against the rows of yellow corn. As the serving continued exclamations of delight were heard as to the tenderness and goodness of the corn. When everyone was busy eating the remainder of the corn was taken out so it wouldn't cook too much that it would be tough and placed in a pile where everyone could reach it.

Millie saw Walter and Sonny standing over at the edge of the crowd and went over to try and make them feel at home. "How's the corn, Sonny?"

"Oh, lovely. Isn't it, Walter?" Millie again noticed her pleasant smile. She was quick-thinking, too — quite a different personality from Walter. And she wore her informal well-tailored slacks and blouse well, too. It could be said that she seemed a cut above Walter in her general bearing and outgoing personality. But she seemed pleasantly at home with him, gave the impression that she liked him, and Millie was glad.

"Sonny, there's wieners, too, you know over at the table — when you've had enough corn, I mean."

"Oh, I'll make out, Mrs. Brewster. By the way, I've been talking to some of your friends from the city. They're real nice. I like them."

"Well, I'm sure they like you, too. Walter, you'll have to bring Sonny down sometime when we can talk without having so many people around."

"Yeah, that'd be fine. That'd be just fine, eh, Sonny?"

"I'd like that. Now you go along, Mrs. Brewster. I know you have a lot of guests to look after. I'll see that Walter gets enough to eat."

Millie left to join two of her nieces who were giggling with butter and corn all over their faces and having a wonderful time. She then chose a small ear of corn, prepared it with butter and joined Charles' father and mother who were doing their best to make their second set of teeth cope with the corn. She offered to slice off the kernels but they protested they'd handle things in their own way, thank you.

And so the pile of corn was lowered so effectively that it appeared there wouldn't be many left for Tom Dirks' pigs. Everybody was groaning to indicate they were filled but after a brief rest the wieners started disappearing, although there were many left at the end of the evening.

The fire slowly died down and the figures around it became more shadowy, until it was hard to tell who people were until you saw them close beside you. It was decided that while some light from the fire still lasted the guests should find the way to their cars across the rough pasture. Then the farewells started and the expressions of thanks as the party broke up. Standing with Walter and Sonny as they watched them go Charles and Millie listened to the ejaculations and laughter as their guests found their cars. Charles' father and mother had already been helped into the Beatons' car because the Beatons lived a block away from them and were driving them home. Soon there was the sound of motors starting and the cars moving away, with a few final shouts of farewell as they left. Then the sounds became less and less until there was only silence across the meadow.

"Well, Walter?" said Charles questioningly. "I think we'd better throw a few pails of water on this fire. You never know."

"Yeah, we best do that. You never know what might happen."

They used the pails they had brought down for this purpose, scooping up water from the creek and spreading it back and forth across the fire, thereby causing a great hissing and clouds of steam until the last spark appeared to be safely out. Then the four of them made their way back towards the house and Walter helped Sonny into the pickup truck.

"Well, Sonny," said Millie, "we'll see you again and fairly soon I hope."

"That would be nice, yes. I have to stay pretty close to home because my parents are nearly eighty and they take a lot of looking after. But my sister-in-law comes in sometimes if I need to go out. And thank you ever so much for letting me come."

The Brewsters assured her that they had been glad to have her and Walter drove away.

"Well!" said Charles, as the truck moved down the driveway.

"Well, what?"

"I dunno. Just 'Well'."

"She seems like a very, very nice person."

"How the devil did Walter hook onto her? That's what I'd like to know."

"Oh, it all started with that silly April Fools' Day note you put in the mailbox. You signed it 'Bunny'."

"Sure I did but this woman's name is 'Sonny'."

"You know what I think happened, Charles? I know that Walter pretended not to be the least bit interested but I think he got curious and started inquiring along 18th Avenue for a woman with the first name of 'Bunny'."

"That doesn't sound like Walter. He couldn't just knock on doors and ask if there's somebody there named 'Bunny'."

"Maybe he asked around the village. So when whoever it was mentioned the name 'Sonny' instead of 'Bunny' it got Walter thinking. And he just followed it up in some way we may never know until he got to meet 'Sonny' Barton."

"I dunno, Millie. Maybe Walter will come out with it one of these days. Anyway, it was sure a great evening, eh?"

"Yes, everything went just right. So different from that party we had one year when we invited all the people out from the city — when I made my famous macaroni dish and everybody got so tight they hardly touched it."

"No more of that, Millie. That was just nonsense. Yes, we'll have to do this again. I think it's good, too, to encourage rural-urban relations. There should be more of this thing — getting city and country people together and letting them discuss their problems."

With that the Brewsters went into the house. And they were very happy people.

20

The Strange Story of "Cariboo" Cameron

About the middle of September Charles realized that he was running out of material for his column in the *News*. He had had a tip from Larry Dinsmore, managing editor of the paper, that Glengarry County was filled with human interest stories and anecdotes and that he might do well to take a trip down that way.

"While you're there you might look into the French-English situation," Larry had added. "I hear they get along together just fine — go to one another's weddings, farm suppers, fall fairs and all that. You might come up with a good bi-cultural story."

And that was why Charles embraced Millie in farewell one morning as she was busy effecting the transformation of some wild carrot into a Ming tree as part of her efforts to "turn lowly weeds into gorgeous gimmicks" as she had laughingly said. "Some people call wild carrot by the name of common yarrow. And I make this Ming by simply taking yarrow, painting it and twisting the leaves and stems with wire and wrapping the stems with paper." With a pat of approval Charles drove away.

Glengarry County was a fairly long drive from Briarwood Farm but Charles made good time by taking the 401 Highway through Belleville, Kingston, Brockville and Ogdensburg. Then on to Cornwall and Lancaster where he turned north on Highway 34 to Alexandria. Here he went into a store to buy some pipe tobacco and soon found himself talking to the genial ruddy-faced proprietor. And Charles asked his stock question.

"Yes, I'm Charlie Brewster and I'm chasing around looking for anything of human interest . . . stories . . . tall tales of the area . . . success stories. I write a column for the Toronto *News*."

Harry Simms stroked his chin, hoisted one of his buttocks up on the edge of the counter and smiled. "I can tell you where you'll get a story you probably won't believe. You'll think it's just a yarn."

"Well, I'll take a chance on it."

"Okay, go on from here to Lochiel, not far away. Then you turn to the . . . wait, I better draw you a map or you'll get lost." Mr. Simms zipped off a piece of wrapping paper and started making a road map. It seemed to consist mostly of "Z's" and "S's" but he declared, as he sketched it, that it would get Mr. Brewster to the farmhouse where he had put an "X" mark, where D'Arcy MacCallum lived.

"I understand the French and English in Glengarry live very happily together, Mr. Simms."

"We'd better, Mr. Brewster. The Quebec border is only ten miles away. But joking aside, the answer to your question is that we do get along well together. But it would be more correct to say that the Scot, the Englishman and the Irishman, who are mostly of United Empire Loyalist stock, get along well with the French people at the eastern end of the county. Cornwall, for instance, is a melting pot for all the races that have been the makers of Canada, I would say, as my own opinion."

"Well, thanks very much, Mr. Simms. Oh, by the way, have you a good hotel here?"

"Right across the road there. Good rooms, good meals."

"I'll be back here tonight I think, so I may see you again."

"Good luck to you. And, as I said, you might not believe the story you're going to hear but it's supposed to be true."

Charles smiled, went out to his car and by driving slowly he managed to follow the conundrum of roads that finally took him to the farm of D'Arcy MacCallum, where he found his man fitting a new share on his three-furrow plow.

"I'm Charles Brewster from up near Toronto, Mr. MacCallum. I was talking to Harry Simms in Alexandria."

"Oh, Harry, yeah. He's quite a fellow." Mr. MacCallum put his foot up on the draw-bar of his tractor and smiled. He was about fifty, had a nice head of grey, curly hair and had honest-looking brown eyes. "Where you from?"

"Mapleville, near Toronto." Charles explained his mission.

"You sure drove a long way to listen to a story. Nobody up your way got any stories?"

"Oh, they have but down here you're supposed to have some yarns that I'd like to hear. Mr. Simms said you had one that I might not believe."

"I guess that's the one about the grave in Summerstown — the grave where the wife of 'Cariboo' Cameron is buried."

" 'Cariboo' Cameron? Who was he?"

"Well, I better start at the beginning. It all began February 22, 1862. That was the date that John Angus Cameron disembarked at Victoria, B.C. on the first step of an adventure to lead to fortune and then to tragedy. He had his wife with him and she was a mighty attractive woman, so they say. Anyway, they went into the Cariboo country in search of gold but his wife got typhoid fever the first winter they were there and she died. Well, her body was put in a tin coffin that was put inside a wooden coffin. Then kind of a crude funeral service was held for her and the double coffin was put into an empty shack to keep until the spring."

"That was a pretty sad start on finding gold, eh?"

"Yes, it was, Mr. Brewster, it was. Well, Cameron had promised his wife on her death-bed that she would be buried in Ontario. The trouble was, though, that he didn't have the money to bring her back here to Ontario. So he hiked it out to the diggings to start looking for gold. And, by golly, he found it, two days after he got there — found it only 22 feet down, stickin' out of the rock everywhere. He had money. So he lashed his toboggan to a sleigh and put the coffin on it and started off on the 400-mile trip to Victoria. Yes sir, 400 miles away that trip was. Say, I see you smoke a pipe. I wonder if I could bum a bit of tobacco. I left my pouch on the kitchen table."

"Sure can. I bought this in Alexandria." D'Arcy MacCallum filled his pipe, got it drawing well and continued his story. "Well, now, on top of the coffin he had on the toboggan he tied a supply of food, a keg of rum and 50 pounds of gold. And so he reached Port Douglas and there he took a side-wheeler to Victoria. Well, it was coming along spring by then and the days were getting hotter and Cameron knew the body would start unfreezin' so he knew he had to do somethin'. So what did he do? He filled the tin casket full of alcohol and sealed it up good and tight so it wouldn't leak and there was a second funeral for Mrs. Cameron — but her first burial, y'understand?"

Charles nodded. "What did Cameron do then?" he asked, getting more and more excited by the strange story.

"What did he do then? 'Cariboo' Cameron went back to look for more gold. And in a few months he had it. In fact he had $350,000 worth of gold. So he had his wife's body in the tin coffin dug up and he started the trip back east — and that was a 12,000-mile journey in those days, 1862 or '63, by way of Cape Horn to New York and then on to Glengarry County here."

"Where she rests today," Charles added.

"Yes, but a lot happened before that. On the way across the border into Canada the customs men questioned the 450-pound weight of the alcohol-filled casket. They thought it was filled with gold. But Cameron finally managed to get it through without having to open it. He got here to Glengarry County and a third funeral was held. Then he bought a big farm and built a huge mansion of a house. It still stands if you want to drive over and see it today."

"Yes, I will, Mr. MacCallum."

"Well, several years went by. 'Cariboo' Cameron married again. But then suspicions and rumours started up about the mystery of the coffin. And to try to put an end to these rumours Cameron announced that on a certain day he would have the body of his wife exhumed. And this was done, by golly. There was a huge crowd, too. A tinsmith punctured the metal casket and the alcohol gurgled out. And members of his first wife's family saw the face of their long-dead daughter."

"That must have been a trying experience for Cameron," commented Charles.

"Yes, I guess it must have been because he removed the coffin to a country cemetery and a fourth funeral was held. And there she sleeps to this day, Mr. Brewster."

"What happened to all this gold that Cameron had?"

"Oh, 'Cariboo' Cameron's wealth disappeared. He went back to the gold fields but the boom was over. So he came back here to Glengarry County completely dejected. And he died on November 7, 1888."

"And his big house is still there."

"Yes, the last time I heard it was a training school for boys who want to be priests."

"Well, that sure is quite a story — and it all happened because of a man's thirst for gold."

"Yes, that's right — Cariboo gold."

"Mr. MacCallum, this is a pretty old section of Ontario," Charles said, changing the subject.

"Yes, Cornwall, for instance was settled in 1783 by people coming over from the United States after the war to build their homes on British territory. I'd say that Cornwall is about the most Canadian of all the cities in Ontario, with the possible exception of Ottawa itself."

"Well, Glengarry County is known for its writers, that's for sure. Ralph Connor for one. He wrote *The Sky Pilot* and *The Man from Glengarry*."

"Yes, I have a copy of Ralph Connor's book *Black Rock* in the house, autographed by him."

"Alexandria is quite a mixture of nationalities, eh?"

"Yes, you can almost fancy you hear the sound of bagpipes there. And you're just as likely as not to hear 'Bon jour, comment ça va.' Oh, it's quite a county this Glengarry is, in spite of the fact that its per capita income is so low on the list of Ontario counties — down at the bottom, I heard at one time. I guess maybe it still is. But we're pretty nice people down here if I do say so myself."

"I'm finding that, Mr. MacCallum. What about another story before I go?"

"Oh, I just have the one story, Mr. Brewster, I'm afraid. But my brother might have one. He lives near Napanee. You go through there on your way back."

"Yes, I was near there a month or so ago."

"Well, you look up Hughie MacCallum back near a village about ten miles north of Napanee — Roblin. He's near there so just ask anybody in Roblin. He'll have a story or two for you."

"Well, thanks very much, Mr. MacCallum, for the story. That was a very good one."

D'Arcy MacCallum smiled his engaging smile as Charles climbed into his station wagon and started back for Alexandria where he had decided to spend the night. But before he did that he detoured enough to see the mansion where "Cariboo" Cameron had lived so long ago. It was an immense building and interesting in many ways but Charles couldn't help but associate it with the tragedy and dejection of Cameron's life.

That evening he had a very good roast beef dinner at the dining room at his hotel, went for half an hour's walk around the town, read the Alexandria Glengarry *News* in bed until he began to yawn and drifted off on clouds of dreamless slumber. The next morning, following a shower and a delicious breakfast of poached eggs, whole wheat toast and two cups of extra good black coffee he set out for Napanee. There he turned north on Highway 41, drove through the hamlet of Selby and on to his destination at the village of Roblin. He went into the general store there and inquired where Hughie MacCallum lived.

"Well, you go out to the north edge of the village here, just beyond the United Church and the school, and turn left for about half a mile or less. Hughie lives on the north side of the road in an old brick farmhouse — the old Hughes farm, we call it sometimes."

Charles thanked him and had no trouble finding the farmhouse he was looking for. It sat back about a hundred feet from the road and there was a two-level lawn in front of it. The aged bricks gave a good clue as to its age — at least a century, Charles decided as he knocked lightly at the side-door at the west. A pleasant-faced lady opened it after a short delay.

"I'm looking for Hughie MacCallum. Judging by the mail-box I should be in the right place."

"You certainly are. And you've found him in the house, too, which is unusual." The lady stepped aside and let him come in. "Hughie sprained his ankle a few days ago and he still has trouble getting around so our son is out plowing." And with that a man of about 45 came in from another room, limping a little. "Somebody taking my name in vain?"

Charles introduced himself to the MacCallums and told them

he had seen D'Arcy MacCallum the afternoon before.

"How is his fall plowing coming along?"

"I don't really know. He spent most of the time telling me a very strange story."

"About 'Cariboo' Cameron, I'll bet," commented Hughie's wife.

"Yes, it was. And he said that you would probably know a story or two I can use in the column I write for the Toronto *News*."

"You're a newspaperman, eh?" asked Hughie.

"I just write this weekly column."

"Well, I dunno about a story. Janie, do I know a story?"

"Oh, you could always tell him about that eagle up north last year. And I wish you two would sit down. Hughie, get that foot up on a chair."

"Yes, ma'am." And with that Hughie flopped awkwardly into a rocking chair and put his foot on another one, while Charles took a seat nearby. "About that eagle, eh? Well, that's one thing I'll never see again if I live to be 120 years old."

"Which you won't," laughingly observed Mrs. MacCallum.

"I might fool you, woman. Go on, get us a coffee, eh? Mr. Brewster has been doing some travelling."

"Would you like tea or coffee, Mr. Brewster?"

"Coffee, thanks. Black."

"Well now, so you want a story. Well, I'll tell you about this eagle up at Lake Huron. I don't know whether you know the Saugeen Fishing Islands that spread out around the little summer resort place of Oliphant or not."

"Strangely enough I was up there not too long ago. It's a wonder I didn't hear this story, Mr. MacCallum."

"Not so strange. I was up there staying in a cottage on Sunset Island with a friend and I wasn't talking to anyone up there about it. Want to hear it?"

"I certainly would."

"Well, I was standing one day on Sunset Island with Frank, this friend of mine, when I saw an eagle — a bald eagle — flying over Little Wildman's Island, as they call it. It flew across the channel about 200 yards away. But it seemed to be flying very queerly — without much sense of direction. Then as it flew close we saw there was a smaller bird above it, pestering it — you know the way small birds get after crows when the crows steal their eggs? This small bird would dip down towards the eagle from above and peck away at it, then veer off, then come back at it again. So these dive-bombing attacks kept on going and the eagle might have been looking for some kind of shelter but it was sort of travelling in a circle, almost. But it was a fair distance away so Frank told me to jump in his motor boat — he's got an aluminum 15-foot boat with a twenty-horse on it

— and we'd get closer. So that's what we did and in a couple of minutes we were right underneath the two birds."

"How high above you were they?"

"Oh, a couple of hundred feet, maybe. So then we saw that the small bird was a kingbird. You've seen them around — a little smaller than a robin with a fan tail and a broad white band across its tail. Black and white. It makes kind of a *dzeeb* sound."

"Yes, we have them around our farm."

"Well, anyway, this kingbird was aiming its attack at the eyes of the eagle. And since the kingbird was above it the eagle couldn't get at it with its talons."

"Gosh, I never heard of a scrap like this."

"It wasn't an even scrap, either. The eagle couldn't seem to get at the kingbird. Anyway, there are shoals between Little Wildman's Island and Big Wildman's and Rowdy Island so we had to take the boat pretty slow through there and the birds got ahead of us. But when we did catch up closer to them we saw the eagle starting to weave from one side to the other in a very funny way and then it headed down towards the water not too far up ahead of us — trying to get away from this sharp beak of the kingbird. Down came the eagle, kind of rolling from side to side, then it'd drop like a lead weight for a few feet and climb up a few feet into the air and keep flopping its wings as if it was really in trouble. And it sure was because, after a couple of minutes down it went — kerplunk — and landed in the water."

"It was just about done for."

"Well, we didn't know just what was happening because by that time we were out near what they call the Outer Rowdies — right out facing the open lake — and the waves were pretty high. They were dashing up against the limestone cliffs of Main Station Island pretty hard. But we wanted to see the end of all this, naturally, so we turned off the motor and poled along over the shoals. Well, by this time the kingbird had disappeared. Its work was done."

"Oh, dear," murmured Charles, moved by this sad story. He turned to thank Mrs. MacCallum who had just set a cup of coffee and a bran muffin on a side table near his chair and prepared to hear the rest of the story.

"Well, poling along a few more feet we could see the eagle in the water. And it was completely helpless. I don't know whether an eagle can swim or not. That I can't say. But this one was sure helpless. Its wings were spread out and it was rocking back and forth on these fairly high waves. As a matter of fact they were so high that an especially big wave caught our boat and rolled us to shore and beached us. Well, we didn't try to get off again. We just pulled the boat up a bit higher and stayed there. Then we turned and looked at the eagle. And the kingbird had sure done its work. It was really sad. Here was this eagle with its sharp eyes that could spot even a tiny little thing on the ground from away up in the air — and its eyes had been pecked so much they were useless. The eagle was blind."

"My God!" Charles felt a lump in his throat. It was a tragic story.

"Well, without its eyes," concluded Mr. MacCallum, "it was doomed, of course. The waves kept rolling it around, closer and closer to the limestone cliffs and finally started banging it right up against the cliff. Well, we wanted to get away from it all so we poled the boat back to where we could use the motor again. And then we spotted the kingbird. It was on the branch of a little aspen growing up against the side of the cliff. And it sat there twitching its tail, the way kingbirds do, watching the death of the great old bald eagle. Then it flew away, the white band on its tail showing up so that it sort of looked like a sign of victory, you know. And we got out of there as fast as we could and back to the cottage."

Charles was profoundly moved. He finally took up his cup of coffee and sipped it, put it down and shook his head, in lieu of saying anything. Mrs. MacCallum broke the silence by asking Charles if he would like more coffee.

"No thanks, Mrs. MacCallum. I just can't get over that story. To think of a fairly small bird being able to do that to an eagle."

"If I hadn't seen it with my own eyes I wouldn't have believed it either," commented Mr. MacCallum. "However, that's what happened. Now, Mr. Brewster, how long are you staying around here?"

"Oh, I'll be going back today."

"Well, you should stay a little longer — get more acquainted with the counties of Lennox and Addington."

"Yes, I don't even know who they were named after."

"Well, Lennox was named after Charles Lennox, the Duke of Richmond and Addington was named after Henry Addington who was Viscount Sidmouth."

"Isn't there a very old pioneer church south of here someplace?"

"An old church?"

"I think Mr. Brewster means the old loyalist church in the Quinte district, Hughie," suggested Mrs. MacCallum.

"Oh, yes, sure, the original loyalist church of the Quinte district on the shores of Hay Bay. It's a small frame building that was built about 150 years ago or some such date. We should take you for a drive around. Why not stay over here with us tonight?"

"Well, I'd like to but we're pretty busy at home right now, Mr. MacCallum. But I appreciate the invitation. I guess there are some families right here in Roblin whose ancestors go back quite a few years."

"Yes, the Pauls and people like that. Some of the people go back to at least 1800. That's a century and three-quarters. This old Hughes house you're in is pretty old. I'm not sure exactly when it was built. I know the farm was originally a very stony 150 acres. We have a lot of stone fences on it as evidence of that."

"We have a lot of good neighbours, Mr. Brewster," commented Mrs. MacCallum. "The very best."

"I don't imagine you'd want to move to the city, eh?"

"Move to the city?" Hughie MacCallum smote his brow in a mock dramatic gesture. "I wouldn't move to the city if you gave me that new city hall in Toronto to live in."

This provoked an agreeing nod of the head from Mrs. MacCallum as Charles rose from the chair and motioned to Hughie MacCallum to stay where he was because of his foot. With a warm farewell and a "safe journey home" from his hosts Charles drove down to the sideroad and headed back for Roblin. He drove past the little brick United Church at the north end, on past the houses and stores, across the Salmon River farther down and headed for the highway at Napanee that would take him west to Briarwood Farm.

At Belleville it began to rain and didn't stop during Charles' entire trip. He stopped to have a western sandwich and a cup of tea at a small restaurant on the outskirts of Port Hope and reached home about the middle of the afternoon. Walking back towards the house with his travelling bag after putting the station-wagon in the drive-shed he heard a sound that made him come to a sudden stop. He listened intently. And he heard what he thought he had heard — the sound of a dog barking. Not continuous barking. Just three or four sounds that came between intervals of silence. He walked on towards the house. And he was smiling. Laddie had learned to bark.

21

A Winter's Store of Preserves

It was very quiet in the tree-house where Charles and Millie sat looking out the south window. The rain had stopped during the night but the leaves that dressed the willows overhanging the creek still dripped water. The drips fell on the quiet flowing creek like little bauble-boats which shattered their prisms in the slope of forenoon sunlight. The sunlight fell also like a filigree over Millie's head and face, which occasioned a remark from Charles.

"We should have that artist chap we used to know in the city up here now, Mill. He could make a real head and shoulders picture of you with that sun on you."

"Thank you, Charles, my boy. That's the nicest thing I've heard today. Now tell me why you wanted me to come over to see you."

"Yes, I'll come right to the point. I've been keeping my light under a bushel, so to speak, for some weeks now — for months, really. And I've written quite a few pieces which I ambitiously call poetry."

"Oh, I knew you were. One fell out of your pocket during the winter. I found it in a snowbank and put it there in your desk drawer."

"I'll be darned. Well, I don't rate most of them with the poets of the ages, by any means, but half a dozen or so I think are fairly good. And I'd like to read you just one."

"I'd love to hear it. I'll just face out the window and listen to it."

"Well, it goes like this and the title is 'The Last Crop'. Oh, I should say first that what inspired it was the fact that all around us, and especially to the south of us, many farmers are harvesting their last crop because by next year or very soon their farms will be built up into subdivisions — with houses and stores and all that on the land that was formerly in grass and crops."

"Yes, that's true."

With this prologue Charles cleared his throat and started to read:

> "I cannot believe
> That I am harvesting the last fine crop
> This field will ever know; that not again
> Will plow turn over this black, fertile earth

To grow plump kernels of Canadian grain;
That not again
Upon these grassy hills will graze my cows
As they have done so many happy years;
This June-time sun
Will not another summer heat this soil
And make it blossom into life again.

These acres I have known so long will be
The burial ground of grass and shrub and tree —
Their only dreadful monument
A wasteland plain of corporate cement.

There in that spot where I have mired the discs
In a wet spring will rise a tower of steel;
Upon that slope where once I stooked my grain
Will be a shopping plaza; farther down
Where those gnarled willows lean across my creek
Will stand a metropolitan motel.
(So reads the blueprint of the time to come.)

Streets there will be and crescents, malls, arcades,
Webbing my farm from road to boundary fence;
A thousand houses, so they say, will hold
Five thousand folk where once a family
Lived here alone and walked across these fields,
Nor did foresee the city's greed for space,
And did not know the city would reach out
And slowly claw the little, fringing farms
With claws that sink into the joyless hearts
Of men and women who have loved and worked
These lands since they became their legacy.

I stand and look and weep and feel that God
Grieves for the vicious raping of this sod;
These time-old hills where grass and grain have grown
Will grow no crop but glass and steel and stone."

Charles read it quite well and when he had finished Millie's eyes
were moist. She continued to look out the window in silence. Then
she turned to him and said quietly, "I think it's an excellent poem,
Charles. I really do. I don't know that much about poetry but it
moved me. They say poetry is supposed to be evocative and to me
that poem certainly is. It says what you wanted to say beautifully,
I think."

"I think you really mean that, Mill."

"I wouldn't say that just to flatter you."

"I know. Well, it's hard to judge one's own stuff. One minute I thought it was pretty good. The next minute I just didn't know."

"I think you should do more of it, Charles."

"Yes, I am now, as a matter of fact. I'm collecting a little sheaf of them."

"If they're as good as that I think a publisher might be interested. At least you can . . .". Millie stopped and turned to the door in a listening attitude. "What's that? I thought it sounded like a whimper."

"I heard it. And we'll soon find out." With that Charles opened the door of the tree-house. And there was Laddie, squatting on the topmost step. Millie reached down towards him. "Laddie, you imp. How did you get out?"

"He's getting real smart," commented Charles, laughing. "He can not only bark now. He can escape from houses."

"I must have left the door ajar. Oh, it's all right. I'm not scolding you."

"Isn't it amazing how fond of a dog a person can become, eh?"

"Of course it is. And it's amazing how fond of people a dog can become — if they have half a chance, eh, Laddie?"

"Even between a murderer and a dog there can be a real love — assuming that the murderer treats the dog with compassion. And that often happens, too, because the murderer needs the dog as a sort of confessor — maybe in hopes of getting a kind of silent absolution. Oh, I'm just ranting away, Lad. You don't know what I'm saying."

"Don't be too sure. Anyway, I'd better get back to the house. Oh, when you get next week's column written you might come down to my cellar, sir, if you will."

"I certainly will. In another hour or so."

"I have some poetry to show you, too, Mr. Brewster — or at least I like to think it's poetry. I'd like your opinion of it."

Millie lifted Laddie down to the ground as he appeared to be afraid to descend the wet steps. Then she let him loose. It was something she hadn't done before, for fear he would run away or go out on the road. And he seemed to enjoy this new freedom. He scampered back and forth across the lawn, criss-crossing in front of her in complete abandon. Once or twice he barked his delight. He was still doing his acrobatics when they reached the station-wagon which was parked out on the driveway. Here Peter the Bantam stood in front of the shiny hub cap of the vehicle. Laddie took one look at him and decided it was something to be chased. And Peter was so surprised at this new thing that had appeared that he stopped preening himself as he observed his reflection and flew straight up into the air, over the station-wagon and down in the general direction of the barn. Millie called Laddie and kept him under control until they reached the house.

An hour later Charles was on his way back to the house to see Millie's "poetry" when Walter called to him from where he stood beside the chicken coop where the bantam hen and her chickens had been housed.

"Yes, Walter, what seems to be the trouble?" Charles inquired as he walked over.

"Damn hawks, that's what. They been gettin' the banty chicks."

"Just lately, you mean?"

"Oh, they got three a month or so ago. I didn't say anything. I thought your missus would only worry about it. Just now they got two more."

"You're sure it was a hawk?"

"I know a hawk when I see it. Chicken hawk. Kind of blue or gray like."

"Maybe they should have been shut up in the coop, eh?"

"I kept 'em shut up a lot of the time while they were little. I let 'em out about two-three weeks ago. You can't keep 'em shut up till they're dead."

"Well, I guess five are dead now. How many are there left?"

"I guess that leaves six if I can subtract straight."

"Yes, I guess it does. Too bad. They've grown pretty fast, Walter."

"Yeah, they were late hatchin' out, you remember. Well, I better shut them all up in the old goose-shed and keep 'em there for the winter. We better put the ten pullets in there, too, separate from the banties. And I better put some insulation on that goose-shed better'n what there is now. If you're goin' to have 'em lay decent all winter we got to keep 'em warm in cold weather — warm as we can anyway. And they're layin' pullet-sized eggs now so I better get 'em moved."

"Well, if you need some help let me know, Walter."

"No, I'm not askin' for any help. A hammer don't need two hands on it to drive in nails."

"No, I guess not. Well, it's too bad about the banty chicks. I'd better tell Millie, though she likely knows and isn't saying anything. After all, she feeds them every day."

Millie did know. And Millie hadn't said anything, as Charles found out when he went down to the cellar to see what she had to show him.

"Yes, I didn't see any point in telling Walter about it. It might have sent him into a huff again the way he was once before."

"Well, there are still six left. Oh, by the way, Walter is going to make the goose-shed warmer with some better insulation and you'll be moving your pullets in there to lay from now on — instead of keeping them over the pig-pen."

"Yes, I was wondering about that. That area over the pig-pen is too big for just a few pullets. We'll be killing the cockerels before very long to put into the freezer and it's going to be far too cold with just the few pullets in the pig-pen."

"You could knit a little coat on each one, Millie. In different colours."

"Now wouldn't that look real cute. Well, would you like to see that 'poetry' I told you about?"

"Sure would. I haven't been down cellar here for a while. What's up?"

"Turn around."

Charles obeyed. He twisted his head around inquisitively. Then his eyes centred in the right direction. Ranged on the shelves which hung from the ceiling by a series of straps he saw the results of Millie's preserving.

"I wanted you to see them with that shaft of sunlight on them and it's only this time of day that the sun gets in through that low cellar window."

"Millie, it's terrific. Holy Susie! There must be hundreds of sealers."

"About two hundred, I think. I haven't counted them lately."

The sun bathed them in a refulgence that brought out the polychromy of their contents. There were variegations of cerise, cherry, crimson, dappled russet, tawny cinnamon shades, splendours in malachite beauty, sea-green and leaf-green, yellowish ochre, saffron loveliness, cobalt blues, warm apricots and glowing yellows. It was a Louvre of colours, subtle mosaics, bold graphics, classical blendings of light and shade, rich Rembrandtian tones that merged into the dark background of the cellar wall.

Charles looked at it with admiration for the colours at first, the overall impression. Then he began to realize the amount of work that had gone into the processing of all these shelves of fruit, chili sauce, and pickles of various kinds. He slipped his arm around her waist and kissed her lightly. "It's terrific, Mill. It really is."

"Not bad for an old lady, eh?"

"Well, I've seen all this ever since we moved to the farm — every fall. But I never cease to be amazed. In this day of supermarkets and shelves filled with canned goods you still like to do down your own, Millie."

"Oh, sometimes I don't like doing them down. I get a little weary and bored. But I like eating them. And you like eating them. And Walter likes eating them. So what is a lady to do? Besides, I'm not the only woman who preserves a lot of fruit. Thousands of women do — especially rural women, of course."

"And we have a lot of home-grown food in the freezer. Hey, that's great, eh?"

"And we have beets, squash, apples and so on in the outdoor entrance to the cellarway. They'll keep for quite a while yet before they start to rot — until Christmas, probably."

"I guess this preserving business has been going on for hundreds of years, eh?"

"Not quite in the form it is now. I was reading in a cook-book the other day. Sterilization by heat only goes back a little over a hundred years. But long before that nature did her own preserving — by desiccation or drying. Nature preserves her cereals by simply removing the water. Bacteria can't grow on dry materials where the water content is lower than 10 per cent, I think it is — except a bit of mould which isn't harmful. And salt is another preservative, that's for sure."

"The old pork barrel with the meat surrounded by salt."

"Smoking is another way of keeping foods — usually ham and fish. And freezing, of course — though freezing doesn't kill bacteria. It just reduces their activity. But it's been used for a long time — especially in the Arctic."

"Well, this is very interesting. Now we just chuck our meat and a lot of our vegetables in a home freezer."

"Plus what Millie Brewster preserves in sealers."

"Oh, I'm not forgetting that. Well, all this sure comes under the heading of poetry, that's for sure. We'll think so when we're enjoying it this winter."

"While you're down cellar here you might as well see some more poetry. Come this way, sir."

"Now what, eh?"

"Over here to the other part of the cellar that I'm using for my workshop. Watch you don't hit your head."

"Yes, these old, low farmhouse ceilings were built for very short people. Such as Charles Brewster."

"Oh, you're not that short, Charles."

"Five-feet-seven-and-one-eighth. I've grown an eighth since we moved out to the farm. Ah, what have we here?"

"We have some of that furniture we bought at the Duncans' sale."

"Hey, it's beautiful. You've put a lot of work on all this."

"I certainly have. And I haven't done all the pieces yet. But this pine kitchen cupboard I'm very proud of. Doesn't it look beautiful?"

"Sure does. What'd you pay for that?"

"$50. And I'd say I could sell it for a hundred. And how do you like this wash-stand or commode as it was sometimes called?"

"Ah, this is the one that was often used to hold chamber pots, to put it delicately — in the old days when a privy seemed a long way away on a cold, dark night. How much did you pay for this?"

"$38. It's veneered mahogany with a touch of trim around the base. There's the gunstock chair I paid $45 for but I haven't touched it yet. And of course I won't be doing anything to the butter mold and paddle and this burl bowl."

"And there's my tin lantern that cost me the ungodly sum of $34."

"Yes, what on earth are you going to do with it, Charles?"

"Well, I had in mind mounting it down at the gate but I guess that's a little impractical."

"Oh, you men. Now what use would a tin lantern be at the gate with one little candle burning in it?"

"Not a darn bit of use—except to look at in the daytime. I completely agree, Millie. I guess all it needs is the rust sand-papered off it. And one of the little windows or glasses or whatever you call them is a bit loose. And when that's done I think I'll just hang it up above my desk in the tree-house. And when I decide I'd like to go out at night and look for an honest man like Diogenes the Greek cynic did I'll light my lantern and go sallying forth."

"My, what a strange sight you'd be, Charles. I can just see you walking along the sideroad looking for an honest man with that little candle in the lantern flickering away and then blowing out in the wind. I think you'd better take plenty of matches with you."

"Or a flashlight, eh? Well, seriously, I'll look after my lantern. I'll get the rust off and fix it. You have enough to do."

"What are you doing today, Charles?"

"I have to consult my boss, Mr. Walter Purdy. I think the fall work is coming along pretty well. Walter has dug out the tile drains leading away from the barnyard down into the meadow. So they're in good shape for the spring run-off. And he's brought up plenty of wood from the barn for the fireplace to last the winter. The ewes have been bred in time for them to have late-January lambs in time for the Greek and Italian buyers. We're through cutting lawns for the season. What else?"

"The late potatoes have been dug and the pullets are laying. And Walter will likely have the goose-shed insulated for the pullets any day now."

"And the snow-fence is ready to put up to the west of the driveway to keep it clear this winter. I think we're in pretty good shape."

"We still have the ten feeders to sell, Charles."

"Yes, when Mel Kirby delivered them in the spring he said he'd phone about the end of October or early November to see when we wanted him to pick them up to go to the stockyards — except the one we'll be killing for our freezer."

"We'll only be keeping one quarter of that and selling the other three quarters. A hind quarter is all the beef we'll need, what with the old laying hens and the cockerels."

"By the way, a couple of weeks ago you showed me some of your weeds you were turning into gimmicks, I think you called them."

"Charles, you're not very observant. I'm using one of them for a centre-piece on the dining room table. The wild carrot, or yarrow as some people call it, that I made into a Ming tree."

"Yeah, I guess I did see that. That looks pretty good."

"While you're down cellar you might as well look at some others I did. Over here in the corner." Millie led the way, looking quite proud to be showing off all her accomplishments. "Now here you see a miniature country garden, growing out of a cedar root that you brought down when we sold the farm. The root came from that stump fence up near the fifth concession."

"We made a table lamp with part of that root."

"There were plenty of nice gnarled pieces left and this is one of them. In the little hollows where the roots grow out I put soil and then put decorated grasses and weeds in them — swamp grass there and this is Scotch thistle I got out in the pasture and another weed. I don't even know the name. And look at the weeds and collection of this and that I have in this tropical garden — artichokes, broad bean pods, common gourds, dried grapefruit skins and this thing is a burnt banana — all of them painted in tropical colours."

"What a weird assortment of things."

"Oh, you can use anything — if you use your imagination along with it about what to do with them, Charles."

"I can see that. Gosh, look at this collection of grains and grasses, eh?"

"Yes, stalks of wheat and oats and grasses and these right here, believe it or not, are the shredded leaves of bullrushes."

"I'd never know it the way you've dyed them all in those beautiful colours — pink and blue and rose and the works. How'd you do it?"

"Oh, I just shook a bag of powdered chalk over them."

"Just like that. Nothing at all."

"Well, a bit more. The arranging of them in an attractive way is what helps too, of course."

"Golly, this 'weeds for decoration' or whatever you want to call it can be quite a thing. And you can sell these, eh? . . . if you want to?"

"Yes, of course, if I want to. I've seen a table-top arrangement of weeds selling for as high as $25 in the city stores."

"You've just given me an idea, Millie."

"I'll bet."

"If you just developed this 'weeds for decoration' into something really big I can see great possibilities in it. You'd always have a source of supply — from this farm and from other farms. Weeds are always with us."

"But what are the great possibilities you see in it, aside from the millions of dollars I might make?"

"Why, you'd be considered a great environmentalist. You'd be doing something that good husbandry hasn't been able to do for years. You'd be pulling out the weeds by the roots and getting rid of them for good. You'd take the place of weed-killers. Why, you'd be . . ." It was about here that Millie held up her hand.

"Charles, my boy, do you mind going and writing one of your bright little limericks. I have work to do."

And Charles did just that. Later that day he climbed into his tree-house and quite aware that he was descending into bathos, compared with his serious poem he had read to Millie, wrote a limerick.

> "There once was a lady called Millie,
> Who preserved ambrosial chili;
> Till one day she found
> That the weeds in the ground
> Would make gems that would turn out quite thrilly."

22

The Massacre of the Sheep Flock

The Brewsters would never forget the date of the tragedy!

Charles woke early that morning of November 3rd. As he yawned, stretched and looked at the alarm clock he began to think that something had awakened him. He raised himself on an elbow, wondering whether to get up or not. Then he heard an unusual sound that caused him to throw back the covers and sit up in bed, listening. There was a very strong northeast wind that surged into excessive gusts and made it difficult to identify the sound. But finally he decided it seemed like a dog barking in the distance. The sound was almost continuous and perhaps, he thought, it was more than one dog.

"Millie?" From the other twin bed Millie made a half-asleep answer.

"That sound like dogs to you — barking?"

Millie sat up and listened. "I think so. Over to the west."

"Yes, the wind is blowing the sound away. I wonder if it's dogs bothering the sheep."

"Walter should hear it if it's to the west. His cottage should be closer to it."

They both rose and started dressing. Five minutes later Charles ran out the side door with Millie close behind. They could hear the sound more plainly now. At least two dogs were barking somewhere over by the creek. Then they saw Walter running towards them shouting against the wind. They ran to meet him.

"Dogs! Killin' the sheep!"

The three of them ran towards the place towards which Walter led the way. They couldn't catch sight of the sheep and lambs until they were almost upon them because the dogs had them cornered in a lower level of ground on the creek bed. The rise of ground that blocked off the sight had also acted as a buffer that prevented the sound of the barking from reaching the house. Later, Walter said he couldn't understand why he hadn't heard the dogs as he was much closer to them than the Brewsters.

It was obvious at once that the dogs had been at the sheep for some time. Four sheep and two lambs lay stretched out, dead, on the gravel beside the water. A fifth ewe was floating in the creek, dead, caught on a projecting root. Two of the remaining ewes and two lambs were stumbling around with great gashes in their throats from which the blood was pouring through the matted fleece that hung down below their jaws. The other sheep and lambs were in a sort of pocket against the steep bank, facing the two black dogs with terror in their eyes. They were mute. There was no sound coming from them. They squeezed tightly together and faced the dogs, feeling that it was their only protection.

At first the big dogs didn't see the Brewsters and Walter because they were below the bank. They stood there barking continuously, their tails swinging from side to side. At intervals one or both dogs would spring forward, attempt to grab a sheep wherever they could get their teeth at it. Then they backed off with their jaws filled with fleece and chunks of flesh. On the far bank a small brown and white terrier kept up a never-stopping yapping sound, without taking part in the carnage. In the half-light the scene was a chiaroscuro of terror—the sheep mute, dumb with fright, the huge black dogs, high on the sport of killing.

Then the dogs saw that they were discovered. The barking stopped at once. The dogs turned, ran along the gravel edge of the creek, leaped up to the top of the other bank and loped away to the south.

"We ought to have your gun," yelled Charles. "We could shoot them. Where's your gun, Walter?"

In the excitement, not knowing exactly what was going on, Walter hadn't brought his gun.

"Too late, Walter. All we can do is follow them. But we wouldn't stand a chance walking over that rough ground."

"Nah, we couldn't keep up with them," agreed Walter.

"All right, they're headed roughly for Mapleville. Walter, you take the truck, I'll take the station wagon and you take the car, Millie. We'll all go by different ways. I'll go out to the road and come back into the farm by the track through the plowed ground over there. Millie, you go around to the village from the north and come out along the west side. You ought to be able to beat the dogs there, if they keep headed in that direction, and you might be able to catch sight of them coming towards you from the west."

"I better go up to the fifth and get onto that old road goin' down the hill from the west towards the dogs," shouted Walter. "I might be able to keep my eyes on them."

They ran towards the cars and set off on their routes. They had all been so shocked by what they had seen that they had hardly taken note of each other's reactions. Now, as she speeded towards the village, Millie saw again the packed bodies of the hypnotized sheep facing the slobbering jaws of the dogs; the still-in-death bodies of the dead, torn sheep; the staggering bodies of the sheep torn open at the throat but still alive. She was grim-faced, her teeth clenched to try and stifle, physically, the remembrance of mutilation. She had never seen anything like it before. It was death on the farm and in a brutal conflagration she would never have been able to imagine if she hadn't been an eye-witness. "My God!" she said quietly, and kept repeating it as if it was the only vocal reaction she could think of against the outrage. Thus she reached Mapleville, turned right at the rough, dirt road that ran past the old blacksmith shop and skating arena and finally reached the western perimeter of the village where the road ended not far from one side of the new Mygrange subdivision. Here she stopped the car, flung open the door and scrambled awkwardly up to the top of a small knoll from where she could look out across an area of rough grassland. She surveyed the open space for possible signs of the running black dogs. She saw nothing moving but decided she had a vantage point where she had better stay. What she would do if she did see them she didn't know. It would be impossible for her to run through the tangle of grass and shrub fast enough to keep up to them. But she might be able to see where they went.

Walter was leaning forward, both arms wrapped around the wheel, twisting his head from side to side as he tried to drive on the rough wagon-track without swerving off it with the truck, trying to catch a glimpse of the dogs as he looked towards the east. His lips were shaping a continuous flow of profanity against the fleeing dogs. "Damn gun . . . should have heard 'em barking . . . could've shot 'em . . . blown 'em to hell. . . ." And then, suddenly, he saw them. They were a quarter of a mile ahead. Two moving outlines, dark against the dead-grass gray of the field. Running towards the highway south of them and not directly for the village. Walter braked the truck to a stop, surveyed the chances of turning around by swinging out into the field, then twisted the wheel to the left. The car bumped over the rough terrain, narrowly missed a stump and then slithered back onto the lane road again. He would drive down the fifth concession to the highway, then travel east and see if he could cut them off when they reached there.

Charles could see the two dark figures running ahead of him but because he was driving the station-wagon through a rough field he couldn't keep up to them. He, too, saw that they were headed for the highway to the south of him. And he saw Walter's truck turn around and head back for the fifth concession. He guessed that he was headed for the highway with the idea of cutting them off. There was nothing he could do but go back to the sideroad and around by the same route Walter was on now, with the idea of heading off the dogs.

Walter reached the highway and drove along to a point where he reasoned the dogs would come out if they kept headed for the highway. A structural steel warehouse and sales office was located here and Walter pulled over onto the gravelled area that was used as a parking space. He got out and rushed along the side of the warehouse until he reached the back end of it, where he could see to the north across the area over which the dogs would be coming if they kept on their original course. Shading his eyes he looked back over the fields behind the warehouse. There was nothing in sight. The dogs must have changed course, perhaps headed east towards the outskirts of Mapleville. Maybe Millie might get sight of them but he wasn't sure just where she was. He was just about to get in the car to drive around and find her when he heard the sound of a dog yelp not far from him. It seemed to come from around the other end of the warehouse and Walter ran over. And there was one of the two black dogs.

It stood, sweating and panting from the exertion of the running across the fields. Its feet were muddy and in its open mouth, caught between the glaring teeth, remained the bloody fragments of torn fleece. Walter approached it and it kept wagging its tail, quite docile now that the sport of killing was over. It looked like a black Labrador but seemed bigger and with longer hair. But it wasn't loose. A chain was fastened to the collar on its neck. The other end of the chain was securely attached to a ring in the wall of the warehouse. Thus it looked as if the dog had been tied up for some time. Walter knew this wasn't so. It couldn't be so. Something was wrong. It was the same dog. He knew that. Somebody had grabbed him the minute he got back and put him on his chain. Walter started getting mad. He looked around for the second black dog but it was nowhere in sight. Then he started down the side of the warehouse to find the entrance. He swung the heavy door back and walked in, boiling mad. A fat man with black hair and horn-rimmed glasses was behind a sort of counter. Walter walked over to him.

"When'd you tie up your black dog?" he said, menacingly.

The man took off his glasses and squinted up his eyes. "What black dog?"

"Your black dog. Isn't that yours that's tied up at the back there?"

"Sure it's mine. And it's been tied up there all night. It's a watch-dog."

"How'd you like to come out and have a look at it?" Walter shouted.

"What the hell are you talking about? Why should I go out and have a look at it?"

"I want to show you somethin', that's why. Are you comin' or do I drag you out?"

The man behind the counter could see that Walter was mad enough to get him by the throat so after a moment's hesitation he came out through a low swinging door at one end of the counter. He led the way outdoors and back to the black dog.

"All right, so what?" he said. "This is my dog, so what?"

"And you're tellin' me he's been tied up all night?"

"That's what I said."

"How come he's pantin' and sweatin' like this?" shouted Walter, getting madder every moment.

"I dunno. I guess he's been jumpin' around on his chain?"

"I guess he got all that blood on him and that sheep's wool in his mouth by jumpin' around on a chain."

"Who says that's sheep's wool?" the black-haired man asked defiantly.

"I say it's sheep's wool. I been lookin' after sheep for forty-five years."

"So what? How do I know where he got it?"

"You dirty, rotten liar. That dog and another black dog almost like it just killed a bunch of sheep up at the Brewsters."

This news caused the warehouse man to lower his eyes and turn away. "I don't know a thing about any sheep being killed, mister."

"Is this your dog?"

"Sure it's my dog. I told you."

At that moment Charles and Millie appeared around the corner of the warehouse. Charles had seen Walter's parked truck. And Millie had also come past at that time.

When Walter saw them he pointed to the dog. "Well, we got one of the killers. Look at him — slobberin' and pantin' and with his mouth full of sheep's wool."

"The other one get away, Walter?" asked Charles.

"Yeah, but we'll get it. It'll come back here. It likely runs wild with this dog all the time. There was a little terrier, too, but it don't matter none about that one."

"Well, what do you say, Mr. . . . ?" asked Charles.

"Dineen's my name. And I've got nothing to say. This dog isn't a sheep killer. I've had him five years. I've never had any complaints."

"You've got one right now," said Charles. "I guess we better get the game warden or the Canine Control man or somebody to look into this."

Walter had the answer to that. "You phone Bill Sheardown at the Township Office, Mr. Brewster. He's the peace officer and stock valuator and the by-law officer."

"He'd have a copy of the by-law about licensing dogs and stopping them from running at large and all that, eh?"

"Sure, he'll tell you what to do. He's a pretty busy man but you might get him over here right now. Hey, it's early. He'll still be at home. Phone him there."

"What about phoning the Canine Control officer about it? Shouldn't he be in on it?" asked Millie.

"Yeah, you best phone him, too, like your wife says. Get 'em all over here."

"All right, I think I saw a telephone booth almost across the road from here. You and Millie better stay here — to make sure that dog doesn't lose the fleece from between his teeth. We need that for evidence, I'd think."

"Charles, if you find that Ace Restaurant in the village open you might bring Walter and me a cup of coffee. I think we can do with it. It's still early in the day but I feel we've done half a day's work."

Charles was gone about twenty minutes. In the meantime the owner of the black dog went back into the warehouse, knowing he wouldn't have a chance to clean the blood and wool from his animal. When Charles arrived back he reported that he'd caught Bill Sheardown at breakfast and he'd be right down. The Canine Control officer, Howard Varley, was out following up a complaint by an irate citizen whose child had been bitten by a nondescript dog belonging to his neighbour. As they waited for Sheardown they drank the coffee Charles had brought back in paper cups. By the time they had finished the by-law officer was there and the owner of the dog appeared.

"Well now, Mr. Dineen," said Bill Sheardown, "I don't have to look very hard to tell that this dog has been worrying sheep. And you know what I mean. And don't tell me he was tied up here all last night."

"Far as I know he was — unless somebody let him loose," Dineen replied, lamely.

"There was another black dog with this one. Do you know of another dog that runs loose with this one? Or does this dog usually go off alone?"

"He usually just goes off . . ." Dineen stopped, aware that he had already said too much.

"Usually runs loose alone, eh? Well, last night he didn't." Sheardown turned to Charles. "Why didn't you shoot this dog when you caught him killing the sheep earlier this morning?"

"I left the gun at the house," Walter explained, "when I went over to see what was goin' on. Then, as soon as the dogs saw us they ran off. I didn't have time to get the gun."

"You're allowed to shoot a dog, in this township, if you catch it in the act of killing sheep. Now I guess what you'll have to do is either for you, Dineen, to pay this man for his sheep and the damage your dog has done or you'll be faced with a court case."

"I'll take the court case. You can't prove a damned thing."

"There's pretty good circumstantial evidence to start with right there. And you'll be paying court costs, too, if you lose."

"I'll take my chances."

With that the strangely assorted group broke up. Bill Sheardown followed the Brewsters and Walter back to Briarwood Farm in order to assess the damage done to the sheep. When he walked over to the creek where the slaughter had taken place and looked down at the dead and mutilated sheep he shook his head.

"This is about the worst we've had around here for a while. Sometimes we get one or two killed and the rest of them worried and no good for breeding but this is pretty bad. How many did you have originally in the flock, Charles?"

"Well, there were 10 ewes and a ram and then the 14 lambs we had last spring — 9 ewe lambs and 5 ram lambs."

Sheardown was counting the dead ones and the others waited. Finally, he raised his head. "Five ewes dead and two lambs. Four other ewes and lambs we'll have to shoot right away — with their throats ripped open like that. That'll be eleven gone for sure . . . out of the original flock of 25 altogether. Just about half the flock."

"And them other ewes," commented Walter, "might not be much good for breedin'. They been worried quite a bit."

"Yes, that could be, Walter," said Sheardown. "Well, Mrs. Brewster, I think it would be best if you went back to the house. There's just no way out of it. Those sheep are suffering — the ones cut open, I mean. I'd better shoot them."

"Yes, I know," whispered Millie. "It's terrible, Charles — just when we thought we had a start on a nice flock of sheep."

"These things will happen, Mill. We've had pretty good luck on this farm. I guess it was too good to last."

"I'm wondering about the matter of this becoming a court case, Mr. Sheardown," Charles asked. "Do you think we should go through with that?"

"Your circumstantial evidence against the one dog is pretty good. I doubt if we'll be able to identify the other dog — though the Canine Control officer will be on the lookout for it. The case won't likely come up in court until sometime this winter. At that time you can plead for yourself or get a lawyer and Dineen has the choice of doing the same. It's up to you."

"What do you think, Charles?" Millie asked.

This was too much for Walter and he interrupted. "I'd say go after that skunk with both barrels, Mr. Brewster. He ain't even fit to own a tom-cat let alone a dog."

"Well, I don't know, Walter. I don't look forward to a court case.

I think we'd better just take time to think it over, Millie."

With that Millie walked sadly back to the house. A few minutes later she heard Sheardown's gun go off four times. The Brewsters' flock of sheep was now down to fourteen ewes and lambs. The ram was still alive. What she didn't realize was the effect of the worrying by the dogs.

Meanwhile, Sheardown, Charles and Walter discussed the aspects of the case as they looked down at the dead and living sheep.

'What we have to do now," Sheardown told Charles, "is get the vet and between him and me we'll try to value the dead sheep and get an idea, too, about the chances of the other ewes breeding properly. That's a tough thing to decide. They're all bred for lambing next spring, eh?"

"Yes, sometime around the beginning of February or a bit before, maybe."

Walter spoke up. "They'll likely be droppin' some dead lambs, too."

"It could be," Sheardown said. "Well, the next thing, Charles, is for you to get hold of somebody to take away these carcasses. I'll phone Bert Mallard in Markdale if it will help any. He looks after dead livestock."

"Could you do that, Bill? I'd appreciate it."

"I'll phone when I go back home. And I'll phone the vet and meet him here this afternoon sometime."

Charles had been looking at the remaining sheep. They stood huddled together in almost the same spot where they were during the killing. "Look at them, eh? It's a pitiful sight, Bill. They look as if they couldn't move."

"They won't be eating much today, either, I wouldn't think. They're scared stiff."

"It's too bad. They've just nicely been bred — not long ago — for early lambs."

"Too bad, Charles. By the way, these aren't registered sheep. They're just grades, eh?"

"Yeah, just grades."

"Damn good grades, though, Bill. Damn good grades," Walter commented.

"Yes, that doesn't matter on the form I have to fill out though, Walter. They're either grades or they aren't. If the municipality has to pay for them the highest they'll go is $100 a head — and that would be for valuable registered sheep. Anyway, I'll go back and make out my report for the Clerk and I'll give you a copy, Charles. I have ten days to do that and I'll have to get the Veterinarian's report on the flock damage — as nearly as he can arrive at something. So I'll be getting along now."

"Well, Walter," said Charles after the valuator had left, "we're having quite a forenoon."

"I know what I feel like doin' right now. I feel like goin' down to that dirty skunk of a Dineen and takin' hold of his head and twistin' it around six times, then throwin' him in the crik and holdin' him under for an hour — then stringin' him up on the nearest tree."

"There wouldn't be much left of Mr. Dineen after all that, Walter."

"Yeah, but, Holy Susie, he's just a bald-faced liar."

"Yes, I know, but there you are."

"Yeah, I know. There I am. But where was I when them dogs was barkin' this mornin' and I didn't hear them?"

"I think that strong wind had a lot to do with it. It's gone down some now but it was gusting up to forty miles an hour or so earlier this morning. And the sheep were down in the creek-bed, too, which cut off the sound to some extent."

"You seem to be takin' all this mighty quiet, Mr. Brewster."

"Well, it's done, Walter. We can't look back. We just have to accept it and decide whether we're going to build up another flock of sheep or not." And with that Charles left to go in and see Millie.

That afternoon the veterinarian, Dr. Waldron, and Bill Sheardown met at the Brewster place. Dr. Waldron examined the live sheep and lambs and gave his opinion as to the extent they had been damaged. In all the cases the mutilation was not severe enough to warrant destroying them. On the other hand the veterinarian admitted he could not tell whether or not their breeding capacity and lamb-carrying capacity was affected. But after Charles had talked over all the imponderables he decided that the live sheep and lambs might as well be sent to market.

"I don't know whether that's the right decision or not but I just don't like being left in a position where I'll be worrying between now and lambing time as to what will happen. I think I'd rather just wipe the slate and start off with a clean flock — unless I decide not to keep a flock of sheep. I'll have to think about that."

That afternoon the dead sheep were picked up by Bert Mallard of Markdale and early the following morning the drover came for the remaining sheep and took them to the livestock yards. As the truck rumbled off down the driveway Charles went into the house and found Millie sitting in the sunroom. She had been watching the truck leave. He put his hand on her shoulder sympathetically.

"Well, old girl, I guess that's that. We just have to face up to it."

"I made you a cup of coffee."

"Thinks, Mill." Charles sat down in his favorite corner chair. He realized that he smelled of sheep but it didn't seem to matter right then. But he felt he would like to say something to make Millie feel a little better.

"Maybe we're lucky. This is the first bad break we've had in our luck since we came out to the farm, Mill."

"Yes, I know. I realize that. I'm worrying much more about how those poor sheep died than any loss to us, I think. I'll never forget that horrible sight. And those black dogs. I'll never forget it."

"We will, Millie — slowly. Life is like that. And it's just as well that it is. So, chin up. Drink your coffee. You haven't touched it."

"Oh, I know I'm taking it a bit too hard. We did always have good luck before, didn't we?"

"Yes, no rhinitis in the pigs, no abortions in the cattle. Oh, your chickens didn't do so well that first year you had them. That coccidiosis disease."

"Coxidosis, as Mrs. Haggerty called it." Millie smiled in spite of herself. "Yes, but at that time I was so darned busy I didn't have time to worry about it. I just got busy and did something about it."

"And now you're going to get busy doing something about your antiques."

"You'll have to fix up the old pig-pen first."

"The what?"

"The old pig-pen. I've been holding it back from you."

"Yes, I remember you mentioning something about the old pig-pen weeks and weeks ago, Millie."

"I'm starting an antique business next spring — if you and Walter and probably a carpenter can get it ready."

"Well, I'll be darned. Hey, that might be a good idea. But you're not on a highway. Would customers be able to find it here on the sideroad?"

"Oh, I'll advertise it. They'll come to know where it is, Charles."

"You'll have to get a name for it if you're advertising it. How about 'Ye Olde Pig-Pen Antique Shoppe'?"

"I don't think we can mix pigs and antiques."

"How about 'Millie's Antiques'?"

"I thought of that. No, I think I'll simply call it 'Briarwood Farm Antique Shop'."

"Yes, maybe it's just as well. The name 'Briarwood' has come to mean quite a lot to us."

"So you're in favour of all this, are you, Charles?"

"Damn right I am. You go right ahead if it's what you want to do. You'll have to get busy this winter doing more buying than you have been so you'll have a good selection for the opening next spring."

"I think I'll enjoy that. You never know, if it proves a success I might have to take in a partner. I just might let you in for a full partnership, Charles — if you keep on being such a good boy."

23

Record Snowfall—but the Ambulance Gets Through

When the leaves of October fell they spangled the black furrows of the farmland with a gypsy blanket of crimson, gold, purple and orange. On the Brewsters' small farm the little yellow canoes of willow leaves fell into the stream and joined the gay regatta that was headed down-river toward the big lake many miles southward. The groups of white birches disrobed, quite unabashed, dropped their concealing yellow dress-leaves and proudly displayed the symmetry of their graceful lines. The Lombardy poplars beside the pond no longer lifted their green arms as if trying to reach ever closer to the sky. The green was gone and the arms they lifted now were black and scabrous and pleading. The maples staged a great fiesta and flung down showers of leaves of startling colours which frolicked together until they became paper-crisp and whispered in sibilants of coming death on the frosted grass. The apple leaves seemed loath to leave the parent trees. It wasn't until mid-November that they lay ankle-deep on the ground in the orchard.

To the Brewsters autumn was the time when the September-sown wheat showed green in the fields; when the neighbours' cows came to the barn sooner in the evening because the grass in the meadows had become short and they were hungry for the grain and hay they would find in their mangers; a time when there was a rush to get the fall plowing done before the land froze up, even after a light fall of snow had turned the ribbons of furrows into a field of alternate stripes of white and black; a time when the dead stalks in the flower beds were raked up and burned; a time, in later November, when a below-freezing overnight frost stiffened the grass-blades so that the marks of each outline of the Brewsters' steps were imprinted on the ground; a time when a gleaming skin of ice formed overnight on their pond but melted beneath the sun by noon of the next day.

It was early in December that the Brewsters first heard the old timbers of the verandah snapping. They were sitting in front of the fireplace at the time. The orange-blue flames rose up past the old crane and the iron pots strung along it and on up into the dark reaches of the flue. Millie was knitting and Charles sat smoking his pipe silently. Finally, he removed his pipe and gave a mysterious little grunt that made Millie look up.

"What's that for, Charles?"

"Do you realize that we're burning up a pig and a cow right now?"

"We are? Good heavens, Charles."

"Some of those sticks came from the elm planks that were once the floor of the horse-barn — and two or three of the sticks are from the trough in the old pig-pen."

"I should have saved them to sell as antiques."

Charles didn't hear her. "You see, what happens is, in time this wood gets old. Farm animals are hard on wood. So the planks and mangers and so on have to be replaced by new lumber. The horses' calks dig into the elm planks of the floor until they have to be renewed and we're burning up the old ones right now. And the acids from the animals rot them, too, and the wood finally gets thrown out onto the woodpile and gets sawn up."

"You know, Charles," commented Millie, smiling, "you've told me all this many times before. But I still like to hear it. It's quite a thing. We have a choice of pig-wood, cow-wood, horse-wood and sheep-wood. Now if I told that to some city people I know they'd turn up their nose, thinking that when it burned it would smell like the farm animals."

"No, the smell gets dried out of it, I guess. But, as you say, here we are burning up a lot of farm animals, you might say — because a part of them is right in the wood. That stick of wood right over there is a sheep. The other smaller ones to the right of it are little pigs. And that board from the manger is one of our Jersey cows we sold last year. Why, over the years we've been here we've burned up dozens of cows, pigs, sheep and horses."

"I think you'd better talk quietly or you're going to have the Humane Society after us." Millie was about to make another comment but she paused. "What was that, Charles?"

"Listen."

"It's the verandah snapping — the old timbers, speaking of old wood."

"Yes, that's what it is, Millie. This is the coldest night we've had so far this fall. And it's only the 10th of December."

"We might have a very early winter."

"Well, according to Martin Baldry we're going to have just that. He's supposed to be a sort of weather prophet. He says that if you want to find out what kind of a winter it's going to be all you have to do is catch yourself a muskrat and count the hairs. If the hairs are plentiful it means the winter is going to be real cold. If you can't catch a muskrat you're supposed to look at the breastbone on a goose. If it's thin the winter will be mild. If it's thick we'll have a cold winter."

"Isn't it too bad we haven't any geese," commented Millie, smiling.

"Another way to tell, according to Martin, is to look at the moss on a tree. If it's thick in the early fall the winter is going to be real bad."

Only a week later the Brewsters walked out of their house to find evidence that the winter was setting in early. The ground was hard under their feet, the smoke from the Watts' chimney was rising straight up into the air and an ominous stillness was over the land. About mid-forenoon it started to snow. All that day the huge flakes parachuted lazily down and silently found landing spots on meadows, trees, buildings and the heads and clothing of people. They profligately strewed their million-patterned, delicate needle-work across the dingy world and turned it into a flat dimension of whiteness only. The world became beautiful and when the Brewsters went down across the meadow for a walk in the afternoon it seemed as if they had suddenly gone on holiday to a white planet far removed from the black furrows of autumn and the red clovers of spring and summer. The white blanket was drawing tightly over the logs and branches and over the big bed where the fall wheat lay tucked in and sound asleep on Geordie Watts' farm. The topography of the land was being sculptured in drapes and folds that would sparkle like precious stones after the snow stopped falling and the sun came out.

During the following days the weather turned colder. The thermometer went down to 15 degrees below zero at night. The hairs in Charles Brewster's nose froze into silver wires (as he described it) when he walked as far as the barn and the wind shrieked and howled around the eaves and whistled through the interstices of the window sash as the Brewsters lay in bed. The following morning it started snowing again and, whipped by the strong winds, it began drifting. The snow kept falling all day and the snowplow didn't come through. It would have been a losing battle against the fast-drifting snow, driven by the violent winds. When Walter came over for supper he waded through knee-deep snow.

"Sure is somethin', all this damn snow. And them winds is the worst part of it."

"I think another worst part of it, Walter," commented Charles, "is that I have to get my column in the mail tomorrow to get it to the *News* in time."

"If it snows all night no mail won't be goin' anywhere tomorrow," explained Walter. "That mail woman, Della Brown, she'll be sittin' at home toastin' her shins."

"But the snowplow should be through if it stops snowing during the night."

"Don't look like to me as if it's goin' to. Good thing we ain't got no milk has to get to the dairy. We better stick to pasturin' ten steers every summer like we did this year."

"We likely will, Walter. We made a little money when we sold them three weeks ago."

"You likely made enough to pay for your own beef this winter anyway. What are we aimin' to do with them six banty chickens you've got left though? That's what I'd like to know. You goin' into the banty-raisin' business, Mr. Brewster?"

Charles laughed. "No, I don't think so, Walter. Are they old enough for you to tell whether they're male or female?"

"If it was a cow or a heifer I could tell but with banties I ain't sure. Three of 'em seems to have brighter coloured feathers than the others so I guess they're tryin' to be rooster banties." At that time Millie called them in to her beef stew supper and Walter lost no time getting to the table.

It snowed without letup all that night. When Charles tried to get out by way of the sunroom next morning he could hardly push the door open. A three-foot snowdrift was wedged against it. But by continuous shoving with his shoulder he finally managed to get it open about a foot and squeezed his rather portly figure through it and into the outside world. At each step he sank into the snow to his hips. His long rubber boots soon filled with snow. Then his thighs and posterior began to feel dampish and more than a little uncomfortable in the early morning cold. And with that he gave up and squeezed himself back into the house again, puffing like an antique locomotive. Over his three-minute eggs and toast he started worrying about getting his column to the *News* on time.

"I suppose, under the circumstances, they could leave it out of the paper for one week. Larry Dinsmore must know we're having a heck of a big snowfall out here and if he doesn't I can phone him."

"You can phone and tell him something else, too, Charles."

"What's that, Mill?" mumbled Charles, as he rubbed a bit of yolk off his lower lip.

"You can tell him to put a girl on the line who can take short-hand."

"Hey, that's an idea. She can darn-well take down my column. It's only eight hundred words or so. Why didn't I think of that?"

"Because I did. You would have, though."

"Yeah, maybe. Well, that's what I'll do after Larry gets to the office. That reminds me. I have to go out and get two or three more stories for future columns."

"Where are you going next?"

"I had a letter from a man in Gravenhurst. He says there's a gang of hillbillies a few miles from there, somewhere close to the Severn River. And he also suggests that I go to Hearst sometime and ask the man who owns a hotel there about a story."

"Hearst is a long way from here."

"Yes, west of Kapuskasing, I think — away up north of Sudbury. Yes, too far. I'll go there next spring. I'll have to wait until they get all the roads clear after this storm, too, and that may take awhile."

"I would think so. Look at it, the way the snow is coming down. I'll swear that some of those flakes are an inch in diameter."

Fortunately the wind dropped about the middle of the forenoon and the snow stopped at lunchtime. Charles had managed to phone in his column to a girl at the *News* who seemed to be a whizz at shorthand and he was much relieved.

"You know what we should do this afternoon, Charles? We should get out our snowshoes and walk down along the creek. We haven't had them out this winter."

Charles demurred. "You know I'm not much on snowshoes. Too much avoirdupois. But I'm willing to have a go at it."

And have a go at it Charles did and didn't fare too badly. The snow was powdery but the snowshoes held them up and they moved slowly down towards the creek. So thick was the depth of snow that it was like being wrapped in fold after snowy fold of delicate curtains, patterned in flakes of a thousand designs. Presently they came to the edge of the creek, at the spot where they had held the picnic weeks before. At a spot where the channel was narrower and the water flowed fast the ice hadn't frozen. Here the dark water ran with shivering eagerness between the jagged borders of ice jabbing at it from either side. It seemed to be hurrying along in an effort to find some place where it could slow down in the sun and warm up. But soon it was seen to dive suddenly into a frozen tunnel of ice, to spring out into the open again farther down the stream.

Along the banks the cedars were heavy with the newly-fallen snow and at intervals, when the boughs sagged beneath the weight, they curtsied to the stream and spilled their gift of snow, then sprang up again, ready to assume another burden. Here by the creek's edge the Brewsters were in an alabaster nave that curved and twisted through the white church of the pasture. The banks of snow rose high above the level of the creek on each side. And the strong winds had moulded the snow into graceful Gothic lines, sculpted many a beautifully fluted pillar and performed everywhere the most delicate of traceries. It was so still. The loudest sound was the shy shish of snow from the cedar boughs dropping upon the places of open water beneath. That shishing sound, barely heard every few minutes, was the only sound in the nave of snow. The Brewsters listened and didn't speak. And then they started back across the pasture.

At dusk Charles and Millie heard the familiar sound of the snow-plow. And from past experience they could tell by the sound what was happening. The plow was charging the drifts, trying to get a passage through. There would be a great, frenzied burst of sound as the powerful motor revved up, then another surge of the engine as it rammed into a ten-foot snowdrift. Then the sound would drop down to a fumble of noise as the operator backed up a few feet, followed by another attack on the wall of hard, wind-packed snow by the enormous V-shaped plow. The Brewsters could tell that the operator was getting almost nowhere.

The drifts weren't continuous. A mountain of snow covering a hundred-foot stretch of road would slope down to a bare expanse in which there was only a foot or so of snow and in places the road was completely bare for a few feet. But the drifts offered a resistance to man and machine that was hard to break through. The Brewsters could see the powerful light mounted at the front of the tractor and could see by watching it for a time that its progress was snail-like. Since there were only two plows in the township to clear the many concession roads and sideroads they began to realize how long it would be before normal transportation would be available. The tragedy of this uncertainty became apparent early the next morning.

The Brewsters' phone rang about 10 o'clock. It was Linda Martin on the seventh concession, up near the 18th sideroad. She just wondered if Millie had heard about old Mrs. Porter who lived on the next farm north of them on the seventh. Mrs. Porter had had a stroke during the night. It was a bad stroke, apparently, and her married daughter (with whom Mrs. Porter lived) had tried to get a Doctor MacKay from Mapleville. The telephone was in service and Dr. MacKay explained that he would try to get there but it would take a long time.

How agonizingly long it would take couldn't have been foreseen at that time. Since the road through Mapleville had blown fairly clear because of the direction of the wind Dr. MacKay started out in his car, minutes after he got the telephone call. But he had hardly reached the north end of the village before he ran into the wall of snow and abandoned the car. Knowing that Fred Brennan, who had a house and ten acres nearby, kept two teams of Clydesdales, mostly to show at rural fairs, he went over to see him, carrying his black doctor's satchel.

"I can have a try at it, Doc," Fred told him, "but I don't think we'll get through. The team'll get mired."

"I know your Clydesdales are show horses. If you think it'll do them any harm we'd better not try."

"That's all right, Doc. They've got good wind. But they can't walk on snow, that's for sure. They'll sink in to their belly and higher'n that. I'll hitch a team up to the sleigh I use for sleighin' parties and we'll try it."

The team got stopped when it was only a few feet into the first big drift. To make it worse the extra heavy duty strap breeching on one of the horses broke.

In the meantime, as the Brewsters heard it later, Mrs. Porter's daughter phoned Dr. MacKay again and said that her mother was sinking lower all the time. The message was relayed to him as he walked back to his house. Then he realized that an ambulance would be needed to get her to a hospital where she could have intensive attention. But it would be an impossibility to get an ambulance through until the snowplow cleared a track. And at that time the plow was half a mile away from where it could turn up the seventh concession and make its way for a mile and a half through the drifts to the Porter farmhouse.

Dr. MacKay realized there was only one way to do it. He phoned the township office and explained the emergency. Would it be possible to recruit a gang of men to work with snow-shovels to help the snowplow get through?

"Holy Cripes, do you know what you're asking?" said Mike Hannigan, the assistant road foreman, at the other end of the line.

"Sure I know what I'm asking. Do you know any other way to get that ambulance through?"

"Where the hell am I going to get enough men, Doc?"

"Tell every employee who managed to get to work this morning to phone every farmer within half a mile or so of where your snowplow sits now and tell them to grab a shovel and get over there, even if they have to wade in snow up to their necks."

"Okay, doc. We can have a try. Right now the plow should be somewhere along the 16th sideroad near the seventh concession. That means there's about a mile and a quarter, as a rough guess, to go before they'd reach the Porter place."

"That should give your employees plenty of exercise." And with that Dr. MacKay hung up.

As the story unfolded later it was only fifteen minutes after that that the first neighbour appeared at the location where the plow was busy butting against the snowdrifts on the 16th sideroad. One by one other farmers appeared and started digging. In an hour's time thirty men were working — farmers and any of their sons who were old enough to wield a shovel effectively. A hurried conference between the operator of the plow and the men ended with the decision that the most effective way to work would be for the men with the shovels to break the wind-hardened drifts in front of and beside the plow. This would make it considerably easier for the plow to make a passage through. Not only that but the wide, strong wings of the plow might be employed to better avail. This hadn't been possible before. The operator had had to depend on the nose of the plow to smash a way through.

The men worked the rest of the day and all through the night — each of them taking an hour or so off a couple of times to drop in at a nearby farmhouse to drink a cup of coffee and eat a much-needed sandwich. The women's organizations in both the Protestant and Roman Catholic churches heard about it and took turns taking coffee, doughnuts and sandwiches to the men. They were able to approach by car along the stretch of road cleared by the men and the snowplow.

About ten o'clock the next morning, with the sun shining, not a flake of snow falling or the stir of a wind, the operator of the snowplow turned off his motor. He was sitting outside the Porter farmhouse. The tired men gave a feeble little cheer. The Porter family, gathered on the front verandah, waved to them. And the ambulance, which had been following the snowplow for the last hour, to make sure it would be on hand when the plow got through, pulled up beside the front door. The driver and an attendant went inside with a stretcher and twenty minutes later old Mrs. Porter was in the ambulance and on her way to the nearest city hospital. The job was over.

It took over a week to get the rural roads back to something approaching normal. The first narrow track through the drifts was gradually widened until cars were able to pass each other without too much trouble. And gradually everything became more or less as it had been before the storm. Mrs. Porter stayed in the hospital for about a month. Then she was brought home with the advice to "take it nice and easy and you'll live to be a hundred."

Walter had been one of the men working overnight on clearing the road and he had his own reaction to it. "Holy Susie, them drifts was packed just like as if they was made of rock."

Charles, who was ordered not to wield a shovel for more than short periods at a stretch but tried to do what he could, had his own version, too. "One of the most neighbourly acts I've ever seen or heard of, Millie. That gang of men, so darned tired they were just about falling to sleep on their shovels by the end of the night, but still keeping on working. And this is one story that is sure going into my next column in the *News*."

Charles' story about the snowstorm and the rescue of old Mrs. Porter was in the *News* the following week. Not only that but there were pictures of the plow slugging against the snowdrifts. When Larry Dinsmore, the Managing Editor of the *News* heard about the plight of Mrs. Porter and the attempt to get her to a hospital he sensed that it was a human interest drama. He had sent up a photographer to take pictures. And, to Walter's astonishment, one of the pictures that appeared beside Charles' column the following week showed Walter shovelling like mad beside the snowplow.

24

"The Stuff that Andy Makes"

Ten days after the great snowfall Charles left on another story-gathering trip. He was headed for an area near Gravenhurst but on the way, only about forty miles north of Briarwood Farm, he had planned to call in and see a man named Carr; Larry Dinsmore at the *News* had told him that there might be a story there. When he came to the sideroad he was to turn west on, according to his directions, he saw a name on a mailbox: "L. P. Carr — west one mile." Accordingly Charles drove west the specified amount, saw an old house but without any further identification telling who lived there. He was just about to go in and inquire when a little, old, bent lady appeared at the other side of the car and opened the door.

"Who you lookin' for, Mister?"

"Oh, I'm looking for Mr. Carr."

"Oh, he lives right back there. You just passed it."

Charles was about to turn the car around when his informant held up her hand. "There's three Carrs, you know — the father, the son and grandson. There's Thomas and Matthew and Thomas, Jr. Say, there's one of them crossing the road now. I think they're drivin' the cattle into the other pasture today. No, they ain't, either, because they've decided to winter-feed them in the barn instead. Say, I bet I know what the trouble is. I bet they've decided to just leave them in the old pasture for the winter and let 'em rough it in the snow."

"I'd be able to see Thomas Carr, Sr. if I went over, you think?" Charles was finally able to interject.

"You might, I don't know which one it was that was crossin' the road there. My eyes ain't so good any more. It might've been Matthew or it might've been Thomas Carr, Jr."

Charles was about to try again to swing the car around when the old lady sidled up against the passenger window.

"Now that lane is pretty long, mind you, and when you turn in there you should take the driveway that leads around the left-hand side of the house. The driveway around the other side is smacked up tight from all that darned old snow we got. Or wait. No, it isn't, either. They had the man from the garage on the highway come in and plow it out. So now the driveway around the right-hand side of the house is really better than the drive around the left-hand side of the house."

Charles thanked her and nudged the transmission into "Drive".

"They've sure done wonders with that place since Matthew grew up." It was the voice back again and Charles was forced to put the car into "Park". "He was nothin' but a harum-scarum as a boy, you know. But I will give him credit, I certainly will. He cooled off and now he's a real hard worker. He went off to Toronto, you know, and got a job in a garage and he married this nurse and you know you might not believe it but she's a real nice girl, too, Matthew's wife is."

"Well, thank you. I'd better get going along now," countered Charles.

"Me and my husband we never got blessed with no children. But we got along all right because we never asked for very much. The Carrs over there they're fair to middlin' well off now, I expect, but they're real fine people in spite of that, I'll certainly say that for them."

"You know," Charles interjected quickly, "I think I'll just have to go. I'm getting behind my time."

"You know, when my husband — Fred is his name — when he got that disc slipped out in his back last winter young Thomas Jr., he was over here just about every day wantin' to know if there was somethin' they could do."

"I'd better go now. Thank you, Mrs. . . . ?"

"Mrs. Schamerhorn, I am. And that's quite all right. You go now. Say, there's one of them crossing the road back again to the other side. Now I wonder just what's goin' on there."

"Good-bye, Mrs. Schamerhorn and thank you."

"Oh, you're certainly welcome, I'm sure. Say, just a minute. I told you to take the drive-way around the right side of the house because it would be plowed out now. But come to think of it I remember now they're usin' that side as a parkin' place for their pickup truck in the winter time — so it'll be handy to get out, you know. I think, to be sure of it, you better just stop your car up there and walk in."

By this time Charles was so confused and behind in his driving schedule that he decided not to go in at all. If the Carrs were as long-winded as Mrs. Schamerhorn he might be there for hours. So he drove back to the highway and continued on towards Gravenhurst.

Five miles south of Gravenhurst, following his scribbled directions, he turned to the left along the narrow road leading towards the Severn River. Five miles in he turned right at a "Y" in the road and continued along until he came to a trail that led off to the right. He looked for the huge maple tree that was designated as marking the road and turned in. The trail became narrower and more hazardous as he went along and he finally found himself barely moving, in an effort to escape the rocks that threatened the bottom of the car. About a mile in he came to a rough, wooden, homemade gate made of saplings. He got out, undid the wire fastenings that held it shut and drove through. A hundred yards farther along he came to the first of seven or eight old shacks that were scattered around in a clearing. A few lean cows were fighting over a little hay that had been scattered on the snow. He drove past them and stopped at the first old shack. It was falling down in a number of different directions.

Charles waited for a moment, a little apprehensive about the whole setup. Then a little blonde girl came out of the house and stood on the verandah with her finger in her mouth. She was followed by a blonde boy a year or so older. Slowly, as if emerging in order of reverse seniority five more children appeared — each one about a year older than the previous one. They stood grouped on the verandah in various stages of undress, scratching their legs with their bare toes, even though it was about fifteen above zero. They had in their eyes the wild look of terrified little rabbits and as Walter approached the house they scurried for cover back through the open door.

Charles edged slowly up the two rickety steps onto the broken floor of the verandah. As he approached the door a man made his appearance. He had a black beard, black mass of uncombed hair and a colourless shirt with one sleeve ripped completely off at the shoulder stitching. He, too, was in his bare feet and stood there with his thumbs in his rope belt. He motioned Charles in with a twist of his head and mumbled that his wife was somewhere around.

"I keep her busy as hell," he said with a cunning smile, "so she won't have no time to get with another man."

"What doing?" asked Charles.

"What doin'? Hell! Puttin' down fruit, skinnin' rabbits, hoein' the garden and splittin' wood. And I keep her hair cropped right down short."

Charles soon found out how short that was as a woman made her appearance from a rough bedroom nearby. She just stood there, meekly, and said nothing. In fact no one said much for the next two or three minutes. The bearded man motioned for Charles to sit down and said he had to get some fishing tackle ready for fishing through the ice and he went outside. It took only a moment for Charles to appraise the kitchen. A cast iron stove stood at one side of it, two plain kitchen chairs were not far away from it, a rickety couch was under the window and a linoleum floor covering was spread over part of the room, with more holes than covering. A shotgun and a rifle hung over the couch. The wallpaper hung in tattered, tired-looking strips on the walls.

In the meantime the woman, still without speaking a word, had been making a cup of tea, the water for which was already boiling on the stove. She handed Charles a cup. He thanked her and got the merest murmur of acknowledgment back. Although she had a numb, immobile expression she had rather attractive blue eyes. Charles was curious to find out about her speech.

"This is quite a family you have here," he said, motioning to the seven youngsters who were strewn on the floor like cast-off dolls.

The woman looked at him blankly for a moment and Charles felt that she wasn't going to answer. Then, in a low, husky voice with a sort of confidential inflection she said, "Too many, ain't it."

Charles merely said he didn't know.

"He wants plenty, you know." The woman jabbed her finger towards the door.

"How long have you been married?" Charles asked.

The woman looked at him quizzically. "Married?" she said, as if amazed at the question. "I ain't married. I wouldn't marry him." Again she shot a glance towards the door. "He ain't dependable."

Charles wanted to laugh. It was a wonderful line. But he could see that the woman was completely serious. So he tried to keep his expression as sober-looking as possible.

"What does he work at?" Charles asked.

"Oh, fishin' and huntin'. He's good at blastin'. Anybody what wants any blastin' done always comes to Allistair Smith to do it. He's good at explosives."

"Have you lived here very long? How do you make out for food?"

"We been here ten years and we make out fair. We eat a lot of game. We keep it frozen. I got muskrat legs on simmerin' on the stove now. You want some?"

"No, thanks. I'm not hungry right now. Do you like living here away from people like this?"

"I got used to it. It's okay now. I better like it. I ain't goin' to have no better, as far as I can see. He don't like havin' a lot of things around — goddam possessions, he calls 'em. He just figures it's more things to keep fixin' and repairin'."

"What about marrying? Do the young people go outside, as I suppose you might call it, to get a husband or a wife?"

"Nah, what's the use of marryin'? No use tryin' to bring in women from the outside to marry. They wouldn't understand our way of livin' anyway. They wouldn't be in bed any longer than to get in a family way and they'd high-tail it out of here and back to where they came from."

At this juncture the man came back in and stood looking at Charles suspiciously for a moment, as if wondering if his visitor had been soliciting his wife. Charles decided it was time he left and after shaking hands, waving at the seven children and almost falling down the rickety steps he made his way back to the gate where he had left the car.

Driving out to the frozen highway and then on north to Gravenhurst he found himself muttering, "I don't believe it . . . I don't believe it . . . Holy Susie, I don't believe it." Charles decided, apparently, that he needed the entire afternoon to think it over. He checked in, after a light lunch at a restaurant in Gravenhurst, at a motel and rested for an hour. Then he walked for an hour around Gravenhurst, bought a mystery story magazine and a newspaper and went back to the motel. Here he dozed off, woke up, read some more and then had a delicious steak-and-kidney pie supper (his favourite) at the motel. He went to bed early still muttering, "Holy Susie, I don't believe it."

The next morning he decided he'd go on to another suggested location for a story. Since the tip he had been given about it the night before, when he was having a bottle of beer in the local pub before going to bed, made it sound rather similar to his experience of the former forenoon he didn't know whether to look forward to it or not. But he wanted to take back one more story for the *News*. But before leaving he went into an antique store in Gravenhurst where he had noticed something in the window when he was strolling around that he thought Millie might like. So he went in and asked the lady in charge if he might look at it. She took it from the window and remarked that it was beautiful. Charles had to agree. It was an old-fashioned coal-oil lamp with a bulging ruby-red globe. And it was the colour of the globe that fascinated Charles. It really was a thing of beauty, he decided. And he bought it without questioning the price, which was just as well, he decided later, as it was not inexpensive. Taking it back to the car at the motel he placed it up on the front seat beside him, shaped the motor rug so that the lamp couldn't possibly roll forward to the floor of the car if he braked quickly, and drove north.

An hour later he reached the spot where he had been told during the brief encounter with the man in the pub he should turn to the left along a little-used road for about a mile and he would likely find a gang of men erecting a barn. As Charles tried to negotiate the weed-grown track through a rough pasture he began to think that the majority of roads in the areas he had been through could be

termed "little-used" roads. Low-hanging branches scraped the top
of his station-wagon, weeds scuffed the bottom of the car and he had
to avoid driving over stones that threatened to damage the underside
of the car. Then he came out into a clearing much like the one he
had been in the day before.

Charles realized he must be in the right place when he saw a barn
in the course of construction — to the extent that the frame was up
on a fieldstone foundation and one end of the barn was partially
covered with siding. Then, as he brought the car to a stop, he started
looking around for the workers.

At first he didn't see a sign of life but when he turned his head
he saw a fire going over near the edge of the thick forest about 150
feet away. It was a huge fire and now that Charles knew it was there
he turned the window down so he could feel the heat of it. Although
he had almost decided to drive away, thinking it was too early in
the day for anyone to have started work, he now realized there must
be someone nearby so he got out of the car. Looking around at the
stumps which were all that remained of the trees that had been cut
to make room for the barn he began to see stumps that didn't quite
look like stumps. Each stump seemed to have an object growing up
out of it. And as he went closer and examined the nearest stump he
was amazed to discover that the object was a man. He walked over
beside the man-stump.

"Hello, there. Good morning," he said hesitantly but trying to
sound cheerful.

The man on the stump raised a tousled head of hair to reveal an
unshaven face, droopy mouth and bleary eyes. He tried to lift an
unwilling arm in an attempt at a greeting but it was too much. He
fell sideways off the stump and lay curled up on the snowy ground
as if dead. Charles was alarmed at first but as he bent over him he
became practically anaesthetized by the ascending fumes of alcohol. He staggered backward and almost into the arms of an approaching man.

"Had too much," the man said, chucklingly.

Charles tried to chuckle too. It seemed to be the best thing to do.
"I was told in Gravenhurst you were building a barn here and I
thought I'd like to see a barn-raising."

"Barn's raised. Look at it. The frame. All we got to do is close it
in. What you want to see a barn-raisin' for?"

Charles didn't think he should mention that he wanted to write
a column about it so he just said he'd always wanted to see one and
there weren't many barn-raisings around any more. He added that
he thought the man on the ground would be getting cold.

"Nah, he's got enough of the stuff that Andy makes to keep him
hot for quite a while."

"Yeah, but he's only got a shirt on and it's half off."

"He's all right. And seein' you're here how'd you like a slug of the stuff that Andy makes."

"Who's Andy?"

"Oh, he don't live too far away — back in the bush. Come on, I'll get you a shot or two."

Charles realized that if he was to get a story he should go along with the man and find out all he could. As they walked back towards the fire he became more and more bewildered as he saw two more men topple off stumps into the snow. It was the most macabre and unbelievable happening he had ever come across — even more so than the weird drama of the day before. And he decided he should see it through.

"You stay here by the fire, eh? I'll go back here and get it."

Charles watched the shiny leather coat of the man disappear into the edge of the forest, saw him kneel and retrieve something from under the branches of a low-branched spruce and come back with a labelled bottle.

"Don't pay no attention to this label. 'Johnny Walker Black Label', it says. Hell, the stuff that Andy makes is better'n Black Label anytime."

He gave the bottle to Charles to tip up. Then, when he saw him hesitate, he pulled a collapsible cup from his pocket, poured it half full and extended it towards Charles. "Bottoms up!"

Charles played for time. "For my first one I better just start out easy," he said as he raised the cup to his lips and sipped the contents. It choked him. He started coughing and spilled half the liquor. His eyes watered. The man began to laugh.

"I thought that'd give you a kick. Better'n the stuff you get in the liquor store, eh?" Charles nodded, wiping the tears from his eyes. At that moment the man turned to watch another man coming towards him and Charles took advantage of the situation to slosh out about half the remaining contents of the cup. He noticed that the man hadn't seen him. However, that didn't help much because when the man glanced into his cup and saw that it was nearly empty he decided that Charles must like it and he tipped up the bottle and poured it nearly full again, in spite of Charles' protestations.

"You're not much of a drinkin' man, eh?" he inquired, when he saw Charles sipping it.

"No, not any more. I have to watch it, you know." He gave the man a knowing wink.

"Startin' to get your guts, eh?"

Charles nodded and dumped some more whisky into the snow when he had a brief chance. "By the way, when was the barn-raising held?"

"Oh, be quite a while since we had that barn-raisin'. Be three years ago."

'Three years? And that's all the siding you've put on in three years?"

"It's hard to get these guys to work. They put on a few boards and get a little money to buy this stuff that Andy makes and it takes 'em a while to get back to work again."

Charles could believe that. Since it appeared that all the men except one had fallen off the stumps, it would be many years hence before the barn would be completed. "Are you going to build a house here, too?"

"Yeah, I aim to. But you gotta have a barn first. A barn is what a man makes his money from. Well, bottoms up. Come on, now. Keep drinkin' this time."

Charles had about a third of a cupful left and he managed to choke it down. It gagged him and he started to cough violently, to the great delight of the man. When he recovered he managed to say he had better get going — that his wife was expecting him home.

"Okay, bud, here's one for the road, eh?" He poured Charles' cup about a third full. "Bottoms up."

Charles decided that the fastest way to extricate himself from the situation and get out of the place was to finish it off and he did. Following another scene of choking he spluttered out a meaningless farewell, managed to get into his car and began the rough drive along the trail to the highway. Back at Gravenhurst he went into a restaurant and had wheat cakes and maple syrup, feeling that the syrup might make the stuff that Andy makes taste a little better and the wheat cakes might soak up a goodly quantity of the firewater. He did seem to feel steadier when he climbed back into the station-wagon but fell sideways a little as he prepared to start the car. His elbow came into contact with the red lamp but he managed to grasp it before it rolled off onto the floor of the car. With the idea of fixing it more safely in position he leaned it back against the seat at the outside corner and let the door of the car support it on the other side. He also packed the motor rug up against it. Then he started for Briarwood Farm.

On the way he decided that when he reached Briarwood he would try to sneak into the house with the lamp unknown to Millie, take off the unsightly paper bag in which it had so inadequately been packed and put it someplace he hadn't yet decided on — so that Millie would notice it quickly. When he pulled up in front of the drive-shed he saw that Millie was over by the creek talking to Walter. Neither of them had seen him.

Getting out of the car he walked around to the front passenger seat. Taking another look towards Millie he opened the door, keeping his eyes on Millie and Walter. Maybe that last look in Millie's direction was what caused it. The lamp, which he had leaned against the door, fell out. He tried to grab it but he wasn't in time. All he could remember afterwards was that he saw the lamp falling and lunged for it and then heard the shattering sound of the ruby-red globe on the gravel driveway. He looked down. The exquisitely moulded glass globe was shattered into a thousand pieces.

Charles leaned against the open door of the car, looking down at what was left of the lamp. The more strongly built base was still intact. And the wick-holder and wick were still in place. They looked plain and ordinary without the ruby-red globe above them. He felt sick in the stomach. And he couldn't help recalling that when he leaned the lamp against the car door before he started the trip home he was not quite himself. The liquor from the man in the clearing was still affecting him. He must have been careless. The more he thought about it the worse he felt. Then he began to wonder what he should do. Should he not show the lamp to Millie at all? Should he confess what had happened? Should he hide the lamp and try to find a red globe to fit it before giving it to Millie?

He decided to tell her the truth. And with this decision he gathered up what was left of the lamp from the gravel and trudged slowly up to the house, where he would wait for Millie to come in. As he went he heard Laddie barking a welcome from the sunroom. He was glad to be home.

25

Christmas Day—and Plans for a Wedding

One bright, crisp forenoon, a week before Christmas, with the sun scintillating on the big snowflakes of the night before, Charles and Walter brought home the Christmas tree. They cut it from a thick growth of spruce at one corner of the Brewster property. It was about six feet high and beautifully shaped to carry the varicoloured baubles, artificial snow and glittering gold entwined strings of decoration that would be spread over it.

Charles marched at the front carrying the tip and Walter held up the lower and heavier end. Since Walter couldn't see the terrain very well he stumbled about considerably and finally tripped on a snow-covered stone and went sprawling. Climbing to his feet and muttering words that Charles guessed at but couldn't quite understand he said he needed a rest.

"Anyway, I got somethin' to tell you, Mr. Brewster."

"I guess this is as good a place as any, Walter. You sound pretty serious about something."

"I was goin' to tell you and the missus at the same time but I figure I better tell you first."

"Okay, let's have it."

"Well, you know Sonny."

"Sonny Barton? Well, sure, Walter. You brought her to the corn roast — and you were supposed to bring her down to visit us but you never did."

"Guess I never got round to it. But anyway, I just wanted to tell you . . ."

Walter was obviously ill at ease. He kept looking down at the ground, squinting around at the landscape, squirting a gleaming amber arc of tobacco juice into the snow and registering complete discomfort.

"Walter, you might just as well come out with it. What about Sonny Barton?"

"It looks like we're goin' to get hitched."

"Well, let me be the first to congratulate you. She seems to me like a very fine person, Walter."

"Yeah, but . . . it seems funny . . . me makin' fun of women all along and sayin' how one tried to get me in bed once and I kicked her out and all that . . . now I up and figure to marry one."

"It's still being done, Walter."

"You figure I'm not too old, eh? I'm sixty. And Sonny is only fifty-one."

"So what? Walter, you've just fallen in love, that's all."

"Oh, I dunno about that. But you better not tell Sonny about them things I said about women. They don't sound too decent."

"Of course I won't tell her. That's only man-to-man talk anyway. When are you planning to get married?"

"Oh, won't be before the spring or summer I guess. She lives with her folks and she wants to see 'em through the winter before leavin' on account of they're pretty old and kind of feeble."

"Will they keep on living there alone?"

"Yeah, they aim to try to."

"Where are you and Sonny going to live?"

"We dunno yet."

As they carried the Christmas tree the rest of the way to the house Charles did a lot of quick thinking. The result of it was that he brought up the matter to Millie when they were alone down in the basement with the antiques later in the day.

"I've been thinking, Millie — about Walter and Sonny."

"So have I. I'll admit I'm surprised by their engagement but I have an idea it will work out all right. Sonny has a pretty good head on her shoulders. She sees in Walter a good, steady worker and an unsophisticated but honest man. And a man like that has a lot to be said for him."

"I didn't mean that. They don't know where they're going to live. And we need Walter right here. He's sort of a fixture around the place now. I was just wondering what it would cost to fix up the little cottage for them."

"Charles, I think you have the beginning of an idea. I wonder what it would cost. Probably plenty, these days."

"We could get an estimate. There are two small rooms there now. If they had a kitchen, bathroom and bedroom, in addition to the rooms there now I think they could make do. After all, there won't be any little Walters coming along. Eh, Mill?"

"I would hardly think so, Charles."

"Well, why don't we sound out Walter on it?"

"Good idea. At supper time."

Charles waited until Walter had finished the last forkful of his apple pie and well-aged cheese before he wiped his lips with his serviette and prepared to make his suggestion known.

"We've been thinking, Walter — about your engagement to Sonny and where you're going to live and all that."

"Yeah, I dunno yet. Maybe we'll get a place in the village. I s'pose I can do custom work around and the odd job here and there. It'll sure seem funny leavin' here, though. I been rattlin' around this place for quite a while now."

"Would you rather stay here, Walter?" said Millie, coming straight to the point.

Walter looked at her as if she had just asked a silly question. "You're tellin' me," he said flatly. "Either that or I'd like to buy a hundred feet off'n the corner of your orchard and put me up a little cottage for me and Sonny to live in."

Charles and Millie exchanged glances and Charles carried on from there. "Do you think the cottage where you are now could be enlarged to make a small house for two people?"

Walter began to catch on but he took his time answering and then perfunctorily. "Guess it could, yeah. No reason why not."

"It's only an idea, but we've been talking a bit about what it might cost to add a couple of rooms or whatever it needs for you and Sonny to live there — if you're interested I mean."

"Huh! Interested! Guess we couldn't help bein' interested. I can't see it worth your while to put all that money in it, though."

"We could get an estimate on it, Walter."

"Far's that goes," said Walter fumblingly, "I got some money from you buyin' my farm. Maybe I could go in with you. On top of that you could cut my wages in half. Or you could charge me rent. Somethin' like that."

Walter was now charged up and his ideas came thick and fast. It was then that Millie thought she should throw a new light on it. "Walter, what about Sonny, though? Hadn't you better consult her about it?"

"Oh, Sonny'd go for the idea of livin' here. She says your place is the nicest place around here."

"That's very nice of her but I think you should hear what she has to say. Then we can discuss it and see if it's practical to enlarge the cottage and what it would cost and so on."

"I'll sure see Sonny about it, Mrs. Brewster. I'll see her right away about it."

Walter lost no time in consulting with Sonny. Fifteen minutes later the truck went down the driveway and it was undoubtedly headed for 18th Avenue. Charles moved away from the table to an easy chair.

"I hope we're doing the right thing — if we do it, Mill."

"I think so, Charles. We know Walter's odd little idiosyncrasies and I think we both decided we liked Sonny."

"Well, I'd better get Sandy MacDonald from Crayfield up here to let him give us an estimate — as soon as we decide what we want in the way of an addition."

"We won't be able to do much at it until spring, though. They can't work through the cold weather, can they?"

"All depends on whether it's a mild winter. However, I don't think they've set a definite date for the wedding. They can always hold off till the beginning of the summer to move in."

"Well, it would be quite a thing. We start out, after selling to Mygrange, having a man doing odd jobs and looking after things and we end up with his wife as well — if we decide to go ahead with this. However, there won't be anything more decided on it during the next week or so, I wouldn't think. After all it's only a week until Christmas Day."

The week before Christmas was a busy one for Millie. She had her Christmas cake and carrot pudding ready of course, but there were many other preparations because the Brewsters were having six people up from the city — and they had decided that they would have Walter and Sonny with them — if Sonny felt she could leave her father and mother alone. They had also invited both their parents; Millie's sister, Dorothy, and her husband, Tom; and four nephews and nieces. Counting themselves that would make fourteen for dinner but Millie had methodically decided that the old rectangular oak table would accommodate four people on each side and one at each end. The four nieces and nephews could sit at a smaller table — and would probably enjoy being together, anyway.

As if to reward everyone for being good all through the year the weatherman sent down a soft, three-inch covering of gently-falling snow on Christmas eve — unaccompanied by any drifting winds like those of earlier that month. It seemed like a good beginning for a perfect Christmas Day.

Charles found Millie fussing around all forenoon, afraid that she was forgetting something, wondering if she had the proper presents under the Christmas tree — especially those for the young people — and fidgeting about timing the cooking of the turkey so it would be ready at 3 o'clock, the time set for the great feast.

"You're going to be a nervous wreck, Millie. Is there anything I can do?"

"Sure, Charles. Go over and sit in your tree-house for an hour or so."

Charles laughed. "I think I'll stay here but I'll keep out of the way. Golly, you've sure got a real home-grown country dinner here, eh?"

"Pretty well. Our own applesauce, our own potatoes, turnips, peas, beet pickle and rolls and the carrots for the carrot pudding. All we had to buy was the mince pie and the turkey. I know you preferred goose but it wouldn't have been big enough for fourteen people, Charles."

"Oh, that's all right, Mill. Hey, look at Laddie wagging his tail. I guess you know there's a Christmas dinner coming up, eh, boy?"

"I think Peter the Bantam does, too. He's been preening himself in each of your four shiny hub-caps for an hour."

"Yeah, he's quite a show-off. Oh, before I forget it, I understand the council is putting through the payment for our sheep in the next meeting right after New Year's. We apparently get between $35 and $50 per head, according to the value put on them."

"It's little enough, considering that the ewes had been bred and we won't have any little lambs for sale a month or so from now."

"Yes, I know. Well, we'll have to decide whether to start in with a fresh flock in the spring. The Canine Control officer has been working like crazy trying to locate the other black dog that was in on the kill but he hasn't been able to positively identify it."

"He's a very intelligent man, Howard Varley, and he works hard to do a good job. I wouldn't want his job, that's for sure. Now run along. Shoo!"

Charles departed, while Millie checked the temperature control on the oven once more, made sure there was a gay red, white and green serviette and a bright red Christmas cracker beside each plate. And Charles started fussing, too. He had already prepared the wood in the fireplace, ready to light a little later, with cedar kindling beneath and apple wood above it. Now he went out to the outdoor woodbox and brought in two more hardwood logs to have in readiness. Then he went up to the bathroom to shave and change his workaday clothes, as he called them, for his corduroy trousers, plaid shirt and green cardigan.

By shortly after twelve the guests started arriving. With each new arrival the beginning flutter of conversation grew more intense until it reached a hubbub that was overflowing with the excitement of the occasion. It was decided to open the presents as soon as everyone was there and had had time to exchange greetings. So shortly after one o'clock Charles announced in an imitation barker's voice that "Santa Claus has just arrived from his cold home at the North Pole and everyone is wanted around the Christmas tree."

The youngest niece was selected to reach under the tree and pick out the presents, one by one. These she handed to the youngest nephew, who read out the name of the recipient. Then everyone waited breathlessly while the present was being carefully unwrapped, followed by gasps, ejaculations and utterances of surprise. The unwrapping ceremony went on for nearly an hour, held up between each gift until the wrapper had been removed and the gift brought to view. But finally it was all over. Most of the gay Christmas wrappings were stuffed into a carton to be burned; but the more intact pieces were carefully folded, for possible use another Christmas time. Then there was an informal dispersal while the ladies helped with the last-minute chores which were the prelude to the dinner and the men sat around having a bit of fluid Christmas cheer. Then the call for dinner sounded and there was a general shift to the Brewsters' dining room.

For the next hour the conversation dwindled in volume to a great extent as the plenitude of Yuletide food shrank on each plate, down to the mince pie and on down to the point where only a few traces of Millie's carrot pudding were left on three or four of the plates. There was a great groaning following this and the rubbing and patting of stomachs and the reminder from someone that Christmas was "the day of the great too much". A tiny glass of wine was offered then for those who wished it. And suddenly the great dinner was over.

It was followed by a brief lethargic period when no one wanted to do anything that required much effort. Then the ladies decided there were many dishes, pots and pans to be washed; and the men drifted out to the west verandah where they stood around and speculated on many things — the high cost of living, the dastardly way the government was acting, the morals of the younger generation and the prospects of the weather for the rest of the winter.

Later came the departures of the people who had come from the city — the prolonged hand-shaking, the clinging of nieces and nephews to the necks of uncle and aunt, the "thanks ever so much", the charitable kissings on cheeks and the final, frantic waving of hands as the cars drove away. Only the Brewsters, Walter and Sonny were left.

"Well, it's nice to see them all again at Christmas time," commented Charles.

"They're sure a goin' concern," replied Walter.

"Sonny, did you enjoy it? I hope you did." Millie had been a little concerned about Sonny, who had been rather quiet most of the time.

"Oh yes, I did, Mrs. Brewster. I didn't say much because it was your family party but I sure enjoyed it. Walter did, too, didn't you, Walt?"

"Yeah, but you folks shouldn't have bothered gettin' Sonny and me a Christmas present."

"Oh, those towels were just sort of silly gifts, Sonny. I thought we'd start you off in setting up housekeeping — a towel for 'Him' and a towel for 'Her'."

"You're going to have me blushing," laughed Sonny. "And maybe now is a good time for me to tell you that I think it's wonderful for you to let us live here at the cottage, after it's enlarged, I mean — that is if it isn't going to cost too much. And I wanted to tell you that mother and dad have been holding some money for me that they'll be giving me — and I'd like to add that to the building cost. They never thought I'd be using it to get married, I'm quite sure but — well, here we are, Walter, at our age."

"Oh, age doesn't matter, Sonny," Millie assured her.

"Walter thinks it does — because he's sixty and I'm fifty-one. That isn't too great a difference, is it?"

"Of course not," Millie assured her. "We think you'll both be very happy."

And with that Walter drove Sonny back home and Charles and Millie had a post-mortem on the success of the day's events. They agreed it had been a very happy afternoon.

"The next thing is your birthday, Charles — on the 30th of the month."

"Yeah, a man has no right having a birthday so close to Christmas. I don't deserve to get anything. So you just take it easy, Mill. I got enough underwear and socks today to last me for two years."

"Oh, I have something else I think you'll like."

"Oh?" Charles' curiosity was whetted. "Give me a clue."

"I'll give you one clue only. I bought it last September at an auction sale I went to when you were away on one of your trips."

"Uhuh? Well, now. What could it be?"

"I don't think you'd guess if you tried for a week."

26

The Brewsters Speculate on the Future—and Charles Gets a Unique Birthday Present

As the old year drew to a close Charles realized that his first half-century was drawing to a close, too. He had never, except for momentary flashes, thought a great deal about it. Life had been good to him in many ways, unsatisfying in other ways. It had been no harder to take than for most of the men he had started working with as a young man. Although he had never made "big money" he had always had a job. He had been a good provider as far as a husband is concerned. But there were times when he was alone with his thoughts when he was acutely aware that certain dreams he had had when younger had passed him by. He had always yearned to write something "worthwhile" but the business grind had drained him of the energy and inspiration and he had finally settled down, as he knew many would-be creative people had, of doing his job as well as he could and trying to be as satisfied as possible.

But now that he was ready to turn the corner and start on the road along his second half-century he began to get restive in ways he couldn't entirely explain. During the days after Christmas and before his birthday on the 30th of December he thought about it a lot. Then, one day, while he was relaxing after writing his column in the tree-house—which was comfortably warmed by an electric heater—he suddenly realized that since he had good health there was no reason to allow himself to be depressed. He told himself that, with a little good luck, he might have another twenty-five or thirty years to try and do what he had originally wanted to do. He felt that the few poems he had written during the past few months held some promise and that he could improve in the months and years to come. And what was it an old monk had once said?—that oftentimes success is in the striving rather than in the attainment of success. With this homely philosophy as a catalyst he began to feel more positive and optimistic about life in general. Millie noticed the change in him, too, because her sixth sense had told her what had been stirring inside him lately. But she thought it best not to let him know that she had made any such deduction. It could easily embarrass him until he thought it through. Thus the day before his birthday, when they were out in the pig-pen, she spoke only about practical matters.

"You and Walter have done wonders already, Charles, at turning this old pig-pen into my future antiques shop."

"Mostly Walter, Millie. He's a pretty good carpenter. But the work will be slow this winter. We can only work on it on days when it isn't too cold. Of course this southern exposure helps. A good sun really gets this place quite warm during the day."

"I can just see this place, when it's done, divided into two rooms. One room for the refinished furniture and the other smaller room with stands and shelves for pottery and lamps and things like that. There's only one thing I'm worried about."

"What's that, Mill?"

"Overhauling this place and enlarging the cottage is going to cost us quite a lot of money. I know that Walter — and Sonny, too — will be helping to finance the cottage but still it is going to cost us quite a lot."

"This is known as a capital investment. If we ever sell the place — and perish the thought — it will be that much more valuable. Besides, even though we have to dip into our capital a bit think of the good we'll get out of it for the next twenty-five years — for the rest of our life, let's say. That's something that even money doesn't always buy."

"I feel that way, too. I'm glad you do, Charles."

"Well, if we make the cottage habitable for Walter and Sonny and get the old pig-pen fixed up so it will be attractive as the 'Briarwood Farm Antique Shop' for you, that should be the last capital expenditure of any great amount."

"And don't forget that my 'Briarwood Farm Antique Shop' will, hopefully, make some money to pay for the original investment."

"I'm expecting that it will, Millie. Well, a lot of things have happened this last year, eh? We've had our feeder cattle, had to get rid of our old cat, 'Tabby', lost our flock of sheep, I've acquired a treehouse, written my column for a few months now, you've gotten into the antique business, we've had Walter get engaged, seen it starting to build up into a subdivision not far away from us — with houses to come on our land not far in the future. That's a lot of change, both good and bad, for one year. Now, with my birthday tomorrow, I start on my second half-century, eh?"

"And you seem just as healthy as the day I married you umpteen years ago."

"Oh, I dunno. I've got this pot, you know, although I've taken off about ten pounds this last year. And I find myself slowing down from the way I used to be. I take longer to do things."

"Don't we all? Don't they say we start to decline after we're about twenty or twenty-five or some such thing?"

"Huh, we start to die the minute we're born of course. But let's not get morbid about this. I've got a lot of kicks in me yet."

"By the way, I'd better just make sure that you're going to be available for tomorrow."

"Be available? Of course I'll be available. Is the Queen coming to bring me a personal birthday greeting?"

"No, but someone else is coming. And if you spent from now until then trying to guess who it is I don't think you would get anywhere."

Charles did spend quite a lot of time trying to think who it might be but decided it could be any one of a dozen people so he gave it up. He awoke about six-thirty, climbed out of bed at seven, had scrambled eggs and toast for breakfast and then went for a walk with Laddie down along the creek. The snow had a heavy crust over it and this made for easier walking than it was when he had had to struggle through snow to his knees, which was tiring. So he walked along at a lively pace — which proved to be his undoing when he came down to where the willows grew along the river.

The crusted surface of the snow was slippery in places and it was at one of these places that it happened. His feet slipped, one leg skidded sideways, the other leg shot straight out in front of him and before he could say "ouch" he was sitting on the hard snow, his blue eyes blinking and his dignity hurting. Then he realized that something in addition to his dignity was hurting and he reached around and rubbed the spot on his posterior that had taken the brunt of the fall. To make it worse Laddie was standing a few feet away looking at him. His mouth was open as he panted and he seemed to be laughing at him.

"Holy Susie," he said quietly, using the expression he had picked up from Walter. "And all you do is sit there on your haunches grinning at me." There was a mock roughness in his tone which brought Laddie over. Standing beside him he licked Charles' cheek. "Okay, boy, that's better, eh? Well, I better try to rise to the occasion, I guess."

Slowly he adjusted his legs so he could clamber to a stand-up position, where he proceeded to rub his posterior but that didn't seem to help much so he set off for the house, promising himself a walk later that day when his buttocks felt more normal. On the way home he heard Laddie barking excitedly behind him and turned to see him treeing a squirrel. He had never heard him bark with such animation. Apparently Laddie's days of rejection and abjection were over. He was a free dog. From now on the world was his to enjoy to the utmost.

Charles still had some difficulty at lunchtime when his posterior came into contact with the seat of his chair. He winced and then gave a silly embarrassed little laugh as he saw Millie and Walter smiling.

"Your rump still hurtin' you, Mr. Brewster?"

"Oh, just a bit, Walter, just a bit, you know. Gosh, I didn't think the snow would have that heavy a crust on it. I just barely dented it when I went down."

"Little thawin' and freezin' does that."

"It's just as well you didn't land on your back," Millie commented. "You might have been hurt much worse."

"That wasn't too good a birthday present, eh? But how about the birthday present I got, Mr. Brewster?"

"Let's see now — which one, Walter?"

"That letter in the mailbox — seein' my birthday was on April Fools' Day."

"Oh yes . . . yes . . . I remember, now."

"That letter signed by somebody named Bunny. And you know what I started thinkin' where that letter might've come from?"

"No, I don't."

"Well, when I started cogitatin' I began thinkin' it might've been one of your April Fool jokes on me."

"You did, Walter?"

"I never said nothin' before but it's all right sayin' it now because I know doggoned well it was you wrote that letter."

"All right, Walter. I might just as well own up to it right now. I did write the letter. And Millie gave me heck for it, too. She said it wasn't a very nice thing to do."

"Mr. Brewster, I owe you a lot for writin' that letter. At the time I didn't think it was very funny but it sure turned out all right. I wouldn't have met Sonny if you hadn't written that letter."

Millie heaved a sigh of relief. "Walter, am I ever glad to hear you say that. I've been worried about that letter ever since April Fools' Day when Charles put it in the box."

"Well, sir, it's funny how things happen sometimes, eh? I wouldn't have been gettin' myself married this comin' summer if you hadn't written that letter. Yes sir, that was the best thing you ever done for Walter Purdy."

And on that note of good cheer the Brewsters and Walter finished eating the steak and kidney pie that Millie had made especially for Charles' birthday.

At precisely two o'clock the knocker on the verandah side-door clanked and Millie opened it to welcome in Hector Patterson. Watching from the chesterfield Charles saw an elderly man with a likeable smile and walked over to meet him.

"Charles, this is Hector Patterson — my busband Charles."

They shook hands and Charles led him over to a chair in front of the cheerful fire. Then he noticed that he was carrying a bundle done up in newspapers which he deposited beside his chair. There was a metallic jangling sound as he set the bundle down and it made Charles curious as to what Mr. Patterson had brought with him. Charles observed him as he let himself down slowly into the chair. He seemed to be in his early or middle eighties, medium height and with a heavy torso. His hair was gray and plentiful, carefully parted on the side. He obviously wore his "Sunday-go-to-meeting" clothes, as Walter always termed them and instead of low shoes he wore the old-fashioned boots and they had been carefully shined. A brown shirt and brown tie and dark-blue suit completed his dress. When he was adjusted in the chair he folded his hands across his stomach, intertwined his fingers and nodded towards the fire.

"Great old fireplace that. One of the best in these parts. That old crane has had a lot of pork and beans stretched on its old neck."

"I guess it has, Mr. Patterson. I hear your house is pretty old, too, although I've never been over to see it. You're on the third concession."

"Oh, yes . . . yes, on the third. That's right. It's not as old as this house by quite a bit, though — not as old, I say."

"Oh, it isn't, eh?"

"I was telling your wife about it that day she was over at the sale."

"Oh?" Charles glanced at Millie, who had adopted a poker face.

"Yes, I was telling her about it. I won't be around much longer to see it anyway so it doesn't matter much I guess. Well, I brought these down, Mrs. Brewster, like you and me planned."

Charles looked at Millie and this time she was smiling. "All right, Charles, I guess the time has come for me to confess."

"Yes, I guess it has. What's going on between you two?"

"Well, as you likely remember Mr. Patterson had a sale last September. You were away on a trip at the time and Mr. Patterson let me know the day before the sale that a certain something was to be sold the next day that he thought we might be interested in. So I went over to see this certain something and then went back the next day and bought it. Right, Mr. Patterson?"

"Pardon? Oh, yes . . . yes . . . you did. You bought them both."

"I think it's time," announced Charles, "that I saw this certain something or these certain somethings, eh?"

"Mr. Patterson, will you take the newspaper off and show my husband?"

"Yes, I will . . . sure . . . be glad to." And with that he proceeded to slowly extract the contents from the roll of newspapers. Charles watched with a curious frown knitted on his forehead. Then he saw emerge from the wrappings two objects which Mr. Patterson lifted, with some difficulty, around the front of his chair and deposited on the floor in front of where Charles was sitting. Charles leaned over and studied them for a moment.

"Hewing axes?" he queried, looking towards Mr. Patterson. And Mr. Patterson nodded.

Charles picked up the larger one and passed the other over to Millie to examine, who had a further comment to make about them. "They're very special hewing axes, Charles. These are the axes that squared the timbers we have in our main barn, which was built over a hundred years ago. Isn't that right, Mr. Patterson?"

"Yes, that's right. They're the ones all right . . . over a hundred years ago."

"And Mr. Patterson's father . . . no, his grandfather, I mean, lived here then and built our barn and he used those axes to square the round timbers."

"Well, I'll be darned, I was never quite sure how old the barn was. I know it isn't as old as the house."

"I'm not quite sure, Mr. Brewster, right down to the last year. I would say about one hundred and ten years. You see, I was born in this house. My father died in 1956. And my grandfather, John Patterson, lived in this house until 1899 and when he moved he took these hewing axes with him. He is the one who built your barns. He took both that scoring axe and the hewing axe with him and they've been in the family since then."

"Can you tell me a little about the shape of them, Mr. Patterson?" asked Charles. He handed the axes over to the old man.

"Well, there isn't much to tell, I suppose. The most important part is that in this larger axe the hewing blade is twelve inches wide. And it weighs five pounds, which is a very great weight for an axe. The other axe is smaller. Now, you'll see in this hewing axe the off-set helve or handle is bent outward. And that's so the knuckles of the workman's hand would clear the log as he swung the axe back and forth while he squared the timber."

"Yes, I see that. It's very cleverly done. You see, Millie?"

"Yes, and I was looking at the way that hardwood shines — especially at the spots where the workmen's hands held it. And you've polished the blades up a little I see, too, Mr. Patterson."

"Oh, I rubbed them over a little. There were a few specks of rust here and there."

"Well, we're awfully proud to have them. I'm glad you let me know they were going to be sold at the sale."

"Oh, I just thought you might prize them. I'm afraid you had to pay more for them than I figured, though, especially for the big axe."

"Oh, that's all right. They're one of a kind. Now I'm going to get you a cup of tea and then drive you home."

"Well, thank you. I could enjoy a cup of tea. Then, my nephew is coming to drive me back, a little later. But the tea would be fine."

An hour later the Brewsters made their farewells to old Mr. Patterson and then took the two axes down to the barn.

"Just to think, eh, Millie? These axes were responsible for squaring those huge timbers. Look at that one — thirty-six feet long. And those other beams — the same length to go across the width of the barn. And the other shorter timbers."

"I imagine the twelve-inch width of the axe blade would fit right into those marks on the timber. Try it, Charles."

Charles lifted the axe above his head to the bottom of the lowest timber.

"You're right. It fits exactly. This old axe blade bit right into that very mark we see right there, over a hundred years ago. It's a little weird, when you try to carry yourself back and imagine it, eh?"

"I can almost see John Patterson back a hundred and ten years ago or whatever it was, swinging this axe against the side of the log. And he left his autograph for us, you know that."

"His autograph? John Patterson's autograph?"

"On the window on the west side — looking out over the verandah."

"Yes, of course, of course. Good Heavens, yes. I just didn't connect the two. He scratched it on the glass pane with a ring or some such thing."

"Yes. John Patterson, Mapleville. It's a pity he didn't write down the actual month and the year."

"He left that as a mystery for us to think about."

"We have another visible reminder of the past right behind the barn — about fifty feet from where we stand — that hollow depression scooped in the side of the hill."

"Yes, where they took the blue clay to make the original bricks for the house."

"And it must have been awfully good clay, Charles. Our house still stands. And the colours in the brick are getting more beautiful every year."

"Well, I guess you and I will be satisfied to get old together along with the old house, eh?"

"I can't think of a better companion to have as we get older — the house, with its old bricks, this old barn with its hand-hewn beams, these old hewing axes with all their memories of the past. The thoughts we think as we get older should be good thoughts. I think they might do a lot to keep us younger, eh Mill?"

In answer Millie took Charles' arm and they walked slowly down the ramp away from the barn towards the old farmhouse. And their thoughts as they went were good thoughts.